kiss me, judas

will christopher baer

Lawson

Lawson Library
A division of MacAdam/Cage Publishing
155 Sansome Street, Suite 550
San Francisco, CA 94104
www.macadamcage.com
Copyright © 2004
ALL RIGHTS RESERVED.

Library of Congress Cataloging-in-Publication Data

Baer, Will Christopher.
    Kiss me, Judas / by Will Christopher Baer.
    p. cm.
    ISBN 1-931561-80-X (hardcover : alk. paper)
    1. Kidneys—Transplantation—Fiction. 2. Ex-mental patients—Fiction.
3. Ex-police officers—Fiction. 4. Loss (psychology)—Fiction. 5. Denver
(Colo.)—Fiction. 6. Drug traffic—Fiction. 7. Prostitutes—Fiction.
8. Widowers—Fiction. I. Title.
    PS3552.A3323K57 2004
    813'.54—dc22

                                                            2004014846

Paperback edition: June, 2006
ISBN 1-59692-186-2

Manufactured in the United States of America.
10 9 8 7 6 5 4 3 2 1

Book and cover design by Dorothy Carico Smith.

kiss me, judas

will christopher baer

for Elias McCulloch Baer

obscurely through my brain
like shadows dim
sweep awful thoughts, rapid and
thick. I feel
faint, like one mingled in entwining love;
yet 'tis not pleasure.

—Prometheus Unbound, *Percy Bysshe Shelley*

one.

I must be dead for there is nothing but blue snow and the furious silence of a gunshot. Two birds crash blindly against the glass surface of a lake. I'm cold, religiously cold. The birds burst from the water, their wings like silver. One has a fish twisting in its grip. The other dives again and now I hold my breath. Now the snow has stopped and the sky is endless and white and I'm so cold I must have left my body.

I drift down an elevator shaft to the hotel lobby. I see myself walking across a gold carpet. Time is slowed to a crawl and I'm looking through a filter but it's me. The familiar skull shaved to stubble and the eyes like shadows. The gray skin pulled tight on my face and my hands flashing white as if cut from paper. I wear a black suit and tie and a dirty white shirt. The clothes hang loose, as if borrowed. The truth is I am losing weight. I look like I'm dying of cancer. I stop and turn a slow circle. I think I'm looking for the bar. The prick of nausea. Someone else is watching me. A woman in a red dress. She sits in a leather armchair, long legs crossed and yellow. She has long black hair streaked with blond. Her lips part slightly and I can see her teeth. I pass behind a marble column and disappear. I slip inside myself again and I can hear the sound of a piano.

I sit at the bar and order vodka.

Vodka how? the man says.

I don't know. With a lemon and some ice.

He brings me a glass. I sip it and feel better. The woman in red sits down beside me. She is younger than I thought. It's been too long since I sat so close to a woman and my first impulse is to move away. I loosen my tie and look at her. She has a scar at the edge of her mouth and disturbing eyes. She doesn't seem to blink. Her body is like a knife. A dull black stone, shaped like a teardrop, dangles from a string of silver in the cold hollow of flesh above her collarbone.

Are you a tourist? she says.

I'm not even sure what city this is.

Denver.

I'm a salesman.

That's funny. You look like a cop.

I've just been released from a mental hospital.

Perfect, she says.

I finish my drink and push it aside. She dips two fingers into the glass and I see her nails are painted blue. She fishes out the twist of lemon and eats the pulp. I turn my head slightly and her face is two inches from mine. She takes a deep breath and exhales slowly. I breathe her dead air.

You must be a terrible salesman, she says.

I am.

Do you want to buy me a drink?

I'm not dead. Terribly cold but my eyes are open. I'm staring directly into a white overhead light and when I close my eyes I still see it, as if the white is burned into my brain. I try to take shallow breaths. I'm in a bathtub. I'm naked and the tub seems to be filled with glass. I don't think I'm bleeding. I'm fine, really. The glass is smooth and somehow comforting. There's a strange tickle down my left side, below the ribs. I want to scratch it but I can't move my arms.

She says her name is Jude.

What are you drinking?

Silly question. Tequila sunrise, she says.

Why is it silly?

Look around. It's island night.

I swivel on my stool. The waitresses are barefoot and wear plastic flowers in their hair. They serve multicolored drinks that sport happy little umbrellas like hats. On the dance floor are belly dancers cut from cardboard. Surf music drones in the distance.

The dancers, I say.

What about them?

They're not real.

She laughs. You are clever.

The bartender brings us a glowing pitcher of tequila sunrises and two tall glasses. I drink cautiously from mine. It tastes like children's vitamins. Jude drinks hers with a straw.

I used to be a dancer, she says. I was thirteen and I wanted to be famous.

How sad.

Don't you want to be famous?

No.

She gazes at me, her mouth crooked.

There's something wrong with you, she says.

I stare down at my limp body. Wet black hairs against the white skin of my torso. The genitals shrunken as those of a corpse. The scar of a bullet on my left thigh like the mouth of an unborn twin. My knees blue with cold. What I thought was glass is in fact ice, and it has a familiar smell. The trapped air of a hospital, a morgue. Disinfectant or formaldehyde. The ice is red but I don't see a wound.

The tequila is gone and by now I have one hand well up Jude's dress. She has swimmer's muscles and goose bumps along her thigh and she is so sweet and lovely I might weep.

Do you want to go upstairs?

Oh, yes. I pat my pockets but can't find my key.

Room 411, she says. A key dangles between her blue nails.

That's my key.

Of course it is.

I try to fondle her in the elevator but she isn't having it.

This is going to cost you two hundred, she says.

The elevator stops at the second floor but no one gets on.

Do you have two hundred?

I'm sure I do.

The elevator rises, groaning. She stares at the floor.

What's wrong with you? she says.

My reflection in the mirrored doors is shadowy, grotesque. I must look like a corpse to her.

Why don't you want to be famous?

I'm terrified of crowds.

In the room she drops her purse on the bed. It's square and black, oddly like a doctor's bag. It looks heavy. Jude pulls her dress over her head. There is a strange tattoo between her shoulder blades: a third eye, staring at me. I fumble through my wallet and come up with a wad of bills I can't bear to count and a decayed-looking condom. She takes the cash and puts it in her shoe. I try to tear open the condom and she takes it away.

Don't you worry about disease?

I never worry, she says.

A stranger's blood can kill you.

It's okay, she says. I'm sure your blood is clean.

She puts her arms around me and finds the gun clipped to my belt. She holds it up with a smile and I shrug. She already has my money. She tosses the gun aside and says, you don't need it. I push her to the floor and she surprises me with a tender kiss on the mouth.

I'm awake. Shivering so badly I have to lock my teeth to keep from biting off my tongue. The ice has melted and the water feels oily, like mucus. There's a complimentary bathrobe hanging from a hook behind the door, less than three feet away. It looks warm and soft and I can't move. I can't move. I don't think I can sleep anymore. I have been asleep in the ice for a day, for two days. In my left hand is a piece of paper. Black ink in round girlish script.

If you want to live call 911.

There's a telephone between the tub and the toilet. I keep reading the note over and over and finally reach for the phone. It takes at least five minutes for me to dial.

Emergency operator.

I need some help.

Please describe your situation.

I'm in a bathtub.

Are you injured, sir?

I was with a woman, a prostitute. Now I'm in a bathtub full of ice and I might be dreaming.

Are you injured?

I'm cold. And there's blood coming from somewhere.

I'm sending an ambulance right away. You are at the Hotel Peacock, is that correct?

Room 411.

Can you determine the source of the blood? It will help the paramedics.

It's coming from my left side.

Try to reach it. You may have been shot.

I can feel thin pieces of metal, a half inch apart. Like staples.

Did you say staples, sir?

I'm pretty sure.

Remain calm, sir. Help is coming.

What did she do? What the fuck did she do?

Silence.

Remain calm, sir.

Please tell me. I've got staples in me.

The paramedics wear black rubber coats. They touch me so delicately, as if I'm a bomb. They strap an oxygen mask over my face and give me a shot. I wake up as they load me into a helicopter, the blades beating furiously. I hear someone whisper in a low sexless voice. *Don't worry, you really only need one kidney.* I'm sure it is Jude's voice. We lift off and for a moment the city lights glow like an overturned Christmas tree and I feel fine.

two.

I sleep forever. I drag up bits and pieces of memory and slowly recon-
struct a bad dream. She must have put some kind of horse tranquilizer in my tequila because I was never really unconscious. I was brain
dead and paralyzed but my eyes and ears were functioning. The flash
of a scalpel. Gloved fingers against my skin. She said she was sorry
and rolled me over. Funny that she wore latex gloves to cut me open
and ten minutes earlier I was inside her without a condom. It's a wonder I could even point my dick in the right direction but I have a feeling the sex was not bad.

   I remember two things: Jude talks to herself when she's nervous
and she kissed my eyelids before she left. I think she fell for me.

A part of me still sleeps beside her, twitching and bloody in a cooler
meant for soft drinks. I see her driving a stolen car with the windows
down and country music on the radio. She sings softly to herself and
I'm sure she has a lovely voice. She's taking my kidney to Las Vegas.
She's going to trade it to the devil for a record contract. I will find her.
I will come to her dressing room with champagne and chocolates and
I will kill her.

This isn't a dream. I'm alive and this is a hospital room like any other. I'm hooked up to an IV rig and a pale liquid drips into me. There's a tube up my nose. It's a rude feeling and I want to remove it. I flex my hands. They aren't restrained and I tell myself it's not that kind of hospital. I wonder if the tube is keeping me alive and then I pull it out. There's a little blood but no immediate change in my condition. I try to sit up and the pain is so bad I think I pass out for a while. My belly is made of fire and I could use a morphine button. I have to pee badly and I'm aware that my dick is very sore. It feels like she fucked me to pieces. I tell myself it's not funny. She ruined me. I must have heard the nurses talking while I was out because I know that my left kidney is gone and that it was crude but professional work. Or else I would be dead. I realize there's another tube extending from my dick and I gratefully empty my bladder. I'm wearing a sexy little gown and I hope my clothes are here somewhere. It's really time to go.

I sleep some more. There's a police guard outside my door. He's a big boy, a chunk of meat in blue. He stands with his legs wide apart, like a tree. I can't see his face and the back of his neck is less than comforting. I'm not sure if he's meant to keep people out or keep me in.

The next time I wake up I disconnect the catheter. It's not so easy and it makes a terrible mess. Then I manage to stand up without screaming out loud. I want to wait a few minutes before I jerk the needle from my arm. The IV must be doing me some good. I drag it to the little bathroom and pee weakly into the toilet. I don't want to but I take a peek in the mirror. I suppose I could look worse. I seem to be growing a beard. I tell myself it's a disguise. The front of my gown is smeared with blood and snot and other uncertain fluids. There's a small closet and I'm surprised to find my clothes inside. Everything is there. My shoes and my pitifully small suitcase. A plastic bag containing my personal items: keys and wallet with no money, pocketknife and wristwatch, silver cigarette lighter that my dead wife gave me but no cigarettes, hotel room key number 411, a broken silver chain with a black stone shaped like a tear. Jude might have left it for me; something of hers in exchange for something of mine. But the chain is broken and it must have happened while we were fucking. She just didn't notice. The cops must have found it and thought it was mine. I look at it closely and it appears to be a locket, but I'm too stupid to open it. I slip it into my pocket and suddenly feel sick. I've lost my gun.

The date on my watch is December 21, the first day of winter. It certainly feels like winter. I'm naked and cold and nearly dead and it hurts to laugh. I was out for a day and a half and I wonder if they call that a coma. I wasn't planning anything special for Christmas. Maybe a nicer hotel room. A bottle of spiced rum and an expensive whore. That's out of the question, of course. But the last place I want to be is the hospital. I pull the IV, trembling slightly. I don't care for needles. I get dressed slowly, hoping no one comes in. I turn in the mirror to look at my wound. I have frantic black stitches halfway around my belly and back, like ants marching. I assume they yanked the staples and poked around in there, then sewed me up. The surrounding flesh is raw and puckered and I feel as if my head will float away.

Slow hiss as the door swings open and I have plainclothes cops in my room. One of them is Detective Moon from the 9th. I'm glad to see that he hasn't changed; he wears the same gray corduroy jacket and the same wide blue tie with a single yellow fish. He wears white pants that are too short for him and I can see his socks. He is short and

heavy and wears glasses that make his eyes forever vague. I invest-
igated Moon once, in connection with a case of prostitutes being
executed by cops. His partner was a suspect, but Moon never was. He
was curiously agreeable about the inquiry, as if he were bored and
lonely and a little scandal might brighten his day. The other guy is a
stranger. He has a massive fever blister on his upper lip and a white
bandage over his right eye. His face is bruised and puffy as a toad. His
face is wrecked. He has oily brown hair, hanging over his eyes and ears
like a helmet. I had a haircut like that when I was six.

Detective Moon sits down on my bed. He looks miserable.
    Hello.
    Moon doesn't quite look at me. The Blister stands with his back
to the door and his arms crossed and I can tell he's going to be difficult. He wears white gloves and he wants to do all the talking.
    It hurts to smile, doesn't it?
    He doesn't seem to breathe. How do you mean?
    Your face is a disaster, I say.
    The Blister examines his tie and flicks a gloved finger at nothing,
at an invisible soup stain, at the lost wing of a fly.
    I glance at Moon. Do you still bite your fingernails?
    He blinks and coughs. Sometimes, yeah.
    I toss my shoe at him. See what you can do with that knot.
    The Blister clears his throat.
    Can I help you? I say.
    Your name is Phineas Poe, is that correct?
    Yes, it is.
    What are you doing in Denver?
    Passing through.
    What did I tell you? says Moon. He doesn't like strangers.

The Blister licks his lip. You were a cop in this town for six years.

Oh, well.

There's a fat file on you.

I'm sure.

A special agent in the Internal Affairs Division.

Moon is whistling softly as he works on the knot.

I stare at the Blister. And you hate IAD. What's new?

You were assigned to investigate Internal Affairs from within.

The rat among rats. I was never even sure where my orders came from.

You must have had some problems with trust.

I must have.

The Blister puts a cigarette in his mouth and smiles.

Have you got another one of those?

No. I don't.

I'm sorry about your face, I say.

How did you lose your shield? says the Blister.

Moon growls. Is this shit really necessary?

I shrug. It's okay, Moon. Tell him.

Moon shrugs. Nervous breakdown, he says.

The Blister laughs, looking at me. I read the incident reports. You lost it on the firing range and started shooting at imaginary people. You took an ounce of crystal meth from an informant and later spooned it into your coffee. You locked yourself in the cage with a female prisoner and allowed her to urinate on you.

It's an uncommon sensation. Try it sometime.

I don't suppose your kidney was removed by imaginary people?

Fuck you. Take your wrecked face and go home.

The Blister steps close to me. His eyes are slitted and he looks dangerous.

Moon, I say. I don't like your friend.

Then who did this to you? says the Blister.

I don't know.

Wasn't there an accident involving your wife? says the Blister.

I open my eyes wide. My face feels blank, a piece of ice.

A hunting accident, I think it was.

Okay, says Moon. Shut the fuck up.

The Blister forces a smile. Well. Let's save that for later.

I sit on the floor for a long time after they leave. I hear myself whistling and it occurs to me that I never did see the Blister's badge. He might not have been a cop. He had poor Moon squirming under his thumb like a bug, though. He could have been a fed, an assassin, a bill collector. It doesn't matter, really. I'm sure I will see him again. Jude is my problem. I put my shoe on and look out the window. It's snowing, small hard flakes swirling in the dark. I don't want the cops involved. I have nothing to hide. I just don't like cops.

I wonder how long a kidney will keep on ice. Human tissue surely goes bad in a hurry. If I were receiving a foreign kidney I would want it to be fresh.

I poke my head out of the room cautiously. I have a vague idea that I might ask the police guard for the correct time. Engage him in some friendly banter. Invite him into my room to watch Letterman do stupid pet tricks. Smoke cigarettes and argue about hockey and which nurse has the best pair of legs. Lull him to sleep with a song. Then disarm him and leave him hogtied in my tiny bathroom. Something like that. But he's gone and I'm not sure he was ever there.

*

I'm gathering myself to leave and a single word chimes in my head: *antibiotics.* My poor torso is surely alive with infection. I decide to improvise. I leave my things in the room and wander down the hall. Two doors down I get lucky. A woman lies unconscious and alone. She's a burn victim, on heavy life support. There's a med cart beside her bed. Ordinarily I would grab condoms and sterile gloves and other novelty items, but I ignore this shit and look for the drugs. I find a tray of ampoules marked penicillin. Pills would be better but what can you do. I take a handful and start looking for needles. The thought makes me ill. I'm going to fucking faint every time I have to shoot up.

I turn to go and the woman stirs. Is that you, Joey?

I hesitate. Her face is heavily bandaged and she can't see.

It's me, I whisper.

Did you feed my Groucho? He likes his milk warm.

Of course, I say.

On rainy days I give him the canned salmon.

Don't worry about a thing.

I'm so afraid, Joey. Will you pray for me?

She extends a veined hand the color of stone. I have nothing to lose.

I crouch beside her bed and stumble through the only prayer I know: *now I lay me down to sleep and pray the Lord my soul to keep.* It's appropriate, I think. And still I feel worthless. I want to comfort her, to chase her fears into the snow. But sympathy is buried in me, like a stone in the belly of a goat. And the goat is the rare animal that will eat garbage. I hold her hand until she falls asleep, then steal fifty dollars from her purse.

three.

The weight of my suitcase pulls me slightly off-balance and stretches my damaged skin. If I put it down I will have to bend over again. I ride down the elevator grinning like a jackal. The emergency room is so silent it makes me nervous. Two morose students in green scrubs sip coffee and stare at the clock. I get the feeling they're waiting for a truckload of bodies. One of them is looking at me, staring at me. She has dark, crooked eyes and red hair. Her skin is like milk.

Can I help you, sir?

I hope so. Would you call a cab for me? I was just discharged.

Gladly, sir.

Please don't call me sir. It depresses me.

She smiles, a shadow. She picks up the phone as I sit gingerly on a bench.

A few minutes later she taps me on the shoulder. I'm sorry, she says. The cabs are swamped because of the snow. It's going to be at least an hour.

Oh, I say. I'm in no hurry.

Are you all right?

My forehead is sweating ropes and I feel shattered. I'm fine, I say.

You don't look well.

I just want to go home.

She presses her lips together for a moment and when she pulls them apart they look frozen and pale as a scar and then the blood rushes back into them. She fingers her stethoscope like a rosary. She stands on one foot as if it helps her think.

My shift is almost over, she says. I could give you a ride.

Do you know karate?

No, she says. Why do you ask?

I might be a strangler.

Oh, yeah. You look pretty feeble. What happened to you?

My kidney was stolen by a prostitute.

She laughs, nervous. No, really.

I have an irregular heartbeat and sometimes it just stops.

Well. Then you had better come with me.

What's your name?

She holds out her hand, the fingernails unpainted.

I'm Rose White, she says.

She carries my suitcase for me. The parking lot is slippery and I take small birdlike steps. The snow stings my face and it feels good. Rose jingles her keys and points at a little black Mustang.

This is me, she says.

She unlocks the passenger door and her car alarm begins to whoop.

Did you steal this car?

Rose doesn't laugh. She whispers to herself, oh you motherfucker. She fumbles with the keys for a long angry moment and the alarm finally stops. She smiles and puts my suitcase in the backseat. My head throbs.

*

The car hums quietly over the fresh snow. She hasn't asked me where I'm going. I can't breathe and I crack my window. She lights a cigarette and mutters an apology. I want one but don't ask. I don't like this at all. She's either a cop or a freak. The Blister knew I would run. He pulled the fat uniform from my door because he was too easy. He threw me a knuckleball: a nurse with eyes like a virgin. Or else she's a freak. She looks like a schoolteacher but she's really a pervert. She has a fetish for nearly dead strangers. She takes them home and euthanizes them on red satin sheets. I remember a piece of soft porn I saw years ago. A sweet young girl with thick glasses and a nervous stutter and a body like a centerfold. Her father rapes her when she's sixteen. He visits her bed every morning and one day dies of a heart attack upon entering her. The girl goes slowly insane. She leaves the corpse in her bed and begins to bring home men she finds sleeping in alleyways. She kills them in her father's bed. She waits until they roll away from her and begin to snore, then stabs an ice pick deep into their ears. She believes she is retrieving her virginity.

I'm curious. Why did you bother with me?
    I don't know what you mean?
    Do you know me?
    Rose glances at me then away. Her cigarette glows bright.
    No, she says. You haven't even told me your name.
    And no one assigned you to watch me?
    She blows smoke. I don't like this conversation.
    Are you really a doctor?
    I'm a medical student.
    I thought cigarettes would kill you.
    They do, she says. But it takes a long time. What's your problem?
    I want to know if I can trust you. Why did you offer me a ride?

She stops the car suddenly and we slide onto the sidewalk.

Because you have a sweet face. You look like someone broke your heart.

Then this isn't a sex thing.

She laughs at that. I'm not sure I like you.

The engine dies and we sit in cold silence.

My name is Phineas.

It's nice to meet you, Phineas. Do you want to walk home in the snow?

No, I don't. I would be dead by morning.

She restarts the Mustang and revs the engine. Then stop talking crazy.

Are you hungry?

Rose smiles. Yes. In fact, I'm starving.

Let me buy you breakfast.

The diner is busy with people caught in the snow. The floors are slick and waitresses move in slow motion. Rose eats an omelet with bright yellow cheese. I look at her closely now. Her hair isn't naturally red. She takes small bites. I have a Belgian waffle under a mound of whipped cream. My blood races with sugar and I remember that I haven't eaten solid food in days. I ask Rose if she's ever been involved in an organ transplant.

She flinches. Why?

I'm just curious.

Not really, she says. I was on duty once when a donor died on the table. I held the sponge and bucket while the doctors harvested his liver.

Interesting. What happens next?

What do you mean? Rose reaches across the table and dips her fingers in my whipped cream. There is a birthmark in the shape of an hourglass on the back of her hand.

She licks the finger quickly and smiles and briefly I adore her.

I mean do you toss it in the freezer until someone needs it?

Someone always needs it, she says. The organ is transported immediately.

It's packed in ice, though.

Of course. But it has to be sterile ice.

I guess regular ice from the foodmart is no good.

She laughs. Ice from the foodmart is crawling with bacteria. The organ would be contaminated.

And where do you find sterile ice?

Why do you want to know? Her eyes are slanted and dark.

Oh, you never know when someone is going to die in your kitchen with a perfectly good heart.

No, she says softly. You never know.

Rose drops me off at the Hotel Peacock. The snow has stopped.

I'm sorry.

What for?

For not trusting you. I was rude.

It's okay, she says. You have to be careful.

You remind me of someone, I say.

Who?

Never mind.

She laughs. Who?

My wife, I say.

Is that a good thing?

I lean over and give her a gentle kiss on the side of the mouth. Her skin is warm and I'm tempted to ask her up to my room. But I doubt she would be interested. I've seen myself in the mirror. I'm a fucking wreck. And I'm far too weak and distracted. I can see her in a small apartment with a cat; she watches television with the sound off and eats ice cream. She takes a bath before bed and masturbates.

But she surprises me. Why don't you come home with me, she says.

No. I don't think so.

Are you sure it's safe here?

I'm not sure of anything.

Rose gives me a phone number and says, please call me.

Thank you, I say.

She drives away, headlights swinging across the snow.

Her hair is slightly askew. Like an ill-fitting wig. Maybe that's why she reminded me of my wife, my dead wife. The hair sends echoes through my body.

I still have my room key and I try to cruise through the lobby as if I live there. I don't have a care in the world and no one pays any attention to me. I share the elevator with a little old man who loudly chews his lips. The door to my room is bright with yellow tape. *Police Line Do Not Cross.* I reach for my knife to cut the tape and I see that it has already been cut. A nearly invisible slit, fine as an eyelash. Maybe one of the cops forgot something. Maybe Jude came back for me.

four.

The room is unfamiliar. I might have been born in this room and I might never have been here before. It doesn't even look like a hotel room and I realize this is because it hasn't been cleaned. The sheets are ripped and dangling from the mattress. There's a pillow on the floor and I pick it up. It smells and I turn it over. It's been burned. The smell is scorched foam. Nothing else looks touched. I never slept in this room. I didn't unpack and I didn't use the toilet. I had twisting, violent sex with a woman and I had unexpected surgery. I get down on my hands and knees and crawl the floor like a dog. I find a spot on the rug that could be semen. I think of Rose, her arms white with whipped cream. I have a partial erection and I move my hips, trying to remember Jude.

Skin raw and painful. She had a perfect ass, curved like an egg. No rubber between us and I didn't want to bleed. She could be a carrier, or I could be. Her third eye staring at me, watching me.

I can't find a drop of blood in the room. It doesn't seem possible and I feel a peculiar ache like loneliness. My blood is missing. I have lost some blood and I want to see the stains. I want to touch, to be sure that it's mine. I crawl into the bathroom and soon my head clears. I sit on the toilet staring at the claw feet of the tub. Jude was in this room. I glance at the mirror, half expecting to see her there.

Blue and white tiles and the mirror gray with steam. Lightbulb hanging. Shadows of arms and legs stretching, melting into torsos. Naked on a sheet of plastic. Gloved fingers elegant and fierce. Mechanical birds. Smell of disinfectant and blood. The sound of television and someone vomiting. Dark reflection in a window. A fat man with sideburns, a cast on his arm. The glow of a cigarette and the toilet flushing. Jude's lips touching my eyes soft as butterfly shadows. Her breath was tequila and smoke.

A bathroom is the perfect place to torture someone. Hard shiny surfaces and mirrors and running water. Forced intimacy and screams falling hollow, trapped in a claustrophobic box. It will be months or years before I relax in a bathroom. I limp to the bed and realize I'm holding my belly. The pain is visual, an endless white space. I can go inside it and disappear and I wonder if it was a good idea to leave the hospital. I lie back on the bed and try not to think. I'm afraid to dream and I'm afraid not to. Sleep is effortless, merciful.

Pale morning half awake. Tangled sheets between my legs. Noise of garbage trucks and a woman screaming far away fuck you fuck you. My face is wet. I'm crying and I can't stop. My nose is bleeding. Jude is in the room. I can smell her perfume. She's in the next bed pretending to be asleep. The next bed is a lifeboat drifting on a dead calm sea. Blank blue eyes and a naked yellow sun. Two people in the boat, a man and a woman. The man is drunk or catatonic and something is wrong with the woman. The top of her head is blown off and she has a gun in her hand.

I search the room again and my missing gun is nowhere. Some idiot cop put it in his pocket. It wasn't evidence. He picked it up and muttered, say hello to my new unregistered weapon. He filed the serial numbers down that very night. I tell myself bad dreams are good for you. My clothes stink. I need to bathe but I can't face the bathroom. I open my little suitcase and stare at the contents briefly before closing it. Socks and underwear and a slightly less stinking shirt. I must have other clothes somewhere. Then I remember the car. My car is parked in a garage two blocks from here.

Let's just get our shit together, I say.

I straighten my tie and tuck in my shirt and generally pull myself together. Outside the room I start feeling better. The hallway is painted a soothing mint green and the carpet is geometric green and white. A room service tray has been left outside the next room. I pour myself a cup of coffee and stroll to the elevator.

The lobby is a wasp's nest. Too many people and voices and I feel a panic attack coming. The sun is very bright through high windows and the floor is wet with mud and melted snow. I keep hearing a distant tinkling noise like glass touching glass. The noise is coming from me.

May I help you, sir?

What?

I slap at my pockets to find the noise. I pull out a fistful of glass vials. The penicillin.

Of course.

Sir?

For the infection, I say.

The man staring at me wears a bow tie and a name tag. He must work here. His face is cocked sideways, waiting. I pull back and realize that I have instinctively drifted to the front desk. My heart is like a hammer. He presses his lips together and rolls his blue eyes at me.

I have a sudden and arousing urge to claw those eyes out and I can't help smiling.

Do I have any messages? The name is Poe.

One moment.

I turn to face the lobby and take deep breaths. A cluster of tourists waiting for taxis and staring grimly at their luggage. A man and a woman groping each other on a sofa. Two salesmen with visible hangovers. One blond woman in black jeans and a leather coat reading a newspaper. Detective Moon sitting in a sunken blue armchair with a glum face. He sips orange juice through a straw and his cheeks are bright red. I force a mad grin but I don't see the Blister anywhere.

Here you are, sir.

The desk clerk is brandishing a bright yellow envelope with my name on it. The handwriting is familiar and I recoil slightly. If you want to live call 911.

Excuse me, sir?

Nothing, thank you.

I take the envelope without looking at it and turn to face Detective Moon. He doesn't smile and I remember something. He was one of the few cops who sent flowers after Lucy died. I hold out my hand and his grip is like a vise.

It's good to see you, Moon.

Wish I could say the same. He touches his upper lip, which is freshly shaved and dotted with sweat.

I glance around. Where is your shadow?

That motherfucker, he says. He's not my partner.

I'm glad. He was a nasty one.

You look terrible, says Moon. If you don't mind. Like a junkie with no friends.

Thanks.

You want to talk outside, maybe?

Yes, I say. Outside is better.

Let's grab a bite, then. He is clearly tempted to take me by the sleeve but stops himself. I walk with him into bright and awful sunlight. There is a café next door and I follow him, a few steps behind.

Moon orders coffee and a Texas omelet. I force another smile and say I will have the same. Moon stirs his coffee for a long time and doesn't say anything. I wonder if I'm still dreaming and I stare at the fish on his tie as if it will transport me to another place.

How long have you been out of Fort Logan? he says.

Only a few days.

And you checked into the Peacock right away. What was your state of mind?

How do you mean?

Were you cured or rehabilitated or anything? Did they noodle with your brain or was it all jigsaws and watercolors and quiet time?

They diagnosed me with borderline personality. I'm paranoid and antisocial and I have an unusual indifference to violence. They said I don't believe the rest of the world is real and consequently I don't trust anyone and I don't mind hurting people and what else is new? I used to be a cop. That shit is normal. It's perfectly normal.

Moon licks his lips and looks around for the waitress.

They put me on drugs, I say. Lithium and synthetic dopamine

inhibitors and god knows what. Some kind of sensory deprivator. But my hands shook all the time and I had insomnia. The drugs made my skin itch and fucked up my vision. I had to stop taking them.

He nods and loosens his tie.

Listen, he says. I came by the hospital this morning and was told that you released yourself. The doctors didn't think that was such a good idea.

No, it wasn't. I think I'm dying here.

Moon smiles. I wanted to apologize about last night.

And who was the fucker, exactly?

Lee Harvey Oswald, says Moon. He might as well be. He claims to be with Internal Affairs, right. He comes in the station yesterday and flashes a badge and a pocketful of attitude and nobody says boo. They don't want any static with IAD and plus, they don't like you anyway.

Imagine that. Do you have any aspirin?

Our food arrives and Moon shovels in a mouthful of steaming eggs with green peppers and bits of meat. He swallows and wipes oil from his chin.

Yeah, he says. Imagine.

Moon is a violent eater. I watch him destroy his food for a while.

Anyway, says Moon. The guy doesn't smell right. He's a fucking spook. But he's somebody, and he's slick enough to fool a roomful of cops.

Did he fool you?

He made me nervous, says Moon.

The waitress appears from nowhere, her pink dress stained and cut low in the front. The edge of white lace peeks out, brownish from grease and smoke. It does nothing for my appetite. She bends to fill my coffee cup and I look away.

I talked to the bartender who was working that night, says Moon. He said you were with a girl that looked like a whore but wasn't. There was something military about her. Like she could kill you as easy as blowing her nose.

I shrug and poke at my eggs.

He put her at five foot seven and one hundred twenty-five pounds. White girl with maybe a touch of Asian blood. Black hair with blond streaks and wearing a red dress that didn't hide much.

I barely looked at her, I say.

Did you get a name or anything?

I shake my head. She put something in my drink. I don't remember anything.

You took her upstairs and woke up in the bathtub missing a vital organ.

It was painful. It was like being born.

She didn't say anything that might help us trace her.

No, she didn't. She didn't tell me anything. I gave her two hundred dollars for a half hour and she took my kidney for fun.

Moon pushes his plate away. Well. She's probably in London or Tokyo by now and she won't be back. Organ smuggling is good money, I'm sure.

I have to go. I have to get out of here.

Wait, he says. Let's go for a ride.

I don't trust you. I'm sorry.

Come on, he says. Five minutes.

I'm not going anywhere with you, Moon.

Phineas.

I need some air and I back away from the table. The idea that Jude has left the country is like a thousand pounds of freshly turned earth on my chest.

I'm sorry, Moon. I will call you if I need anything but I doubt it. And thanks. Thanks for breakfast.

Salt and gravel and black snow. The sidewalk is flooded by a puddle deep enough to drown a horse. Moon didn't say a word about my gun. A crosswalk and the sign says walk, don't walk. It beeps for blind people. I stand against a brick wall and shiver. He could be saving the gun for later. Or maybe my new friend the Blister has it. The light changes again and again, still beeping. My feet are wet and numb. I watch the flow of people until I feel serene.

five.

I find the parking garage without difficulty. The kid in the booth is reading a comic book. He asks for my claim ticket. I don't panic. I'm sure it's in my wallet and it is. The kid rings me up and says I'm looking at fifty dollars even. Fabulous. I slap a credit card on the counter and I have no idea if it's still good. I whistle as he runs it through. The card is good. The kid slides me the keys and tells me to have a nice day.

The car still surprises me. It's a silver Volkswagen Bug, a convertible. I don't remember buying it. It seems I picked it up at some point during the lost time. The hours and days I spent underwater. I lost my job and my apartment in early July. The last thing I remember is beating a cab driver half to death during a hailstorm. Then six weeks of consciousness disappeared. And in September I checked myself into the hospital at Fort Logan. I had this car and some clothes and maybe four hundred dollars.

The Bug is not bad. The body and interior are nicely restored and the engine purrs like a fat cat. The only flaw is the passenger seat; it's cut or torn and messily patched with duct tape. I climb into the backseat to change clothes. It's high time I stopped dressing like a cop. I strip down and stop to examine my shirt. I'm leaking a lot of blood and I try not to freak out. I tell myself to get dressed and go see Crumb. If anyone can fix this for me, he can. I dump out a duffel bag looking for clean socks. I find my lucky knife, the tanto. It's a Japanese fighting knife; the blade is four inches of Damascus steel with a slanted, almost blunt tip. The handle is hammered white chrome. The tanto slides into a wrist sheath that I can wear under my shirt or coat. It's almost undetectable; I once wore it with a tuxedo. I find one unregistered handgun, a Smith & Wesson I took off a dead pimp. It's a sexy little gun, a killer's gun. It's a lightweight alloy .38 with an enclosed hammer and a hollow grip. I wear it in an ankle holster and I feel better as soon as I put it on.

My registered weapon was a Browning 9mm; it was surrendered with my badge soon after the accident. They were going to use it against me but I stole it from a rookie cop who was half asleep, working the evidence room on a graveyard shift. And it's almost funny. I always dreaded the day I might lose my gun, or have it taken from me. The very idea made me feel green. I always thought I would rather chew off my foot than lose my gun. And now I've lost it twice. It doesn't feel quite as bad as the new yawning hole in my belly, but I do want that fucking gun.

I don't want to but I get out the penicillin. I break the protective seal on one vial, then unwrap a hypo. The needle thin and bright. I draw out ten cc's and look at my arm. Muscle or vein. I can't decide. I roll the back window down. The muscle seems safer. I do it quickly and promptly throw up.

A man walks past my car twirling an umbrella. He gives me a funny look and I don't blame him. I'm still sitting in the backseat. I'm bleeding and naked except for the ankle holster and my shorts. I'm clutching a needle and there's puke down the side of my car. I dig through my clothes for something inconspicuous that won't show blood. I find jeans and a black T-shirt. I try to wiggle into the jeans without ripping open my side. I put on steel-toed shoes and leave them unlaced. And my leather coat is so stained I don't think a little blood will make any difference.

I open the envelope. It's scented and my head whirls. The dark smell of musk, of earth. I think of animals in cages, pressed close against each other. The note is from Jude: *when I'm depressed I go bowling.*

I roll out of the garage and a long white Lincoln sits across the street, dark windows rolled halfway down. The Blister drinks coffee from a Thermos, steam swirling merrily. I can hear music coming from his radio. He stares right at me, then looks away. After a moment, I see the white car in my rearview mirror, bobbing along like a cheerful little cloud.

A red light and I find myself staring at the passenger seat. The duct tape doesn't make sense and I peel it back. The leather is slit open as if by a razor. I reach inside and pull out a brown envelope full of cash. It's at least three thousand dollars. I'm dumb with nausea and glee. I must have stashed the money in a paranoid funk. I'm pleased by my own cleverness but I shudder to think what else I'm going to find. I take out a thousand and stuff the rest back into the seat.

I'm sure Crumb will tell me I'm a dead man.

*

The Witch's Teat is a little sex shop downtown. Next door is a coffee-house that features questionable poetry readings. It's always dark in the Teat and the music is so loud I feel sick. Drums and horns and venomous distortion. The air itself throbs. A girl sits behind a glass display case of S&M gear. She is perhaps eighteen and bored to death, flipping the pages of a magazine. She wears a black rubber bra and her eyebrows are shaved off. Her shoulders and cheekbones are marked with ornamental scars and burns. I tell her I need to see Crumb and she shrugs; she wiggles her tongue at me and goes back to the magazine. Her tongue is dyed black and my stomach twitches.

I lean close to her. The magazine is opened to a spread featuring genital piercing.

Do that again, I say.

The tongue darts out, black as ink. I try to grab it, to snatch it from the air like a housefly. The tip of her tongue slips from my fingers, warm and velvety.

She grins at me. I'm Eve.

Lovely, I say. Where is Crumb?

She points at a sheer blue curtain, like a veil.

Through the blue and the terrible horns grow louder. Crumb sits on a stool before a wall of mirrors. He holds a scissors in one hand and a small mirror in the other. He wears a bath towel around his waist. He's cutting his hair, badly. It looks like a dog got hold of his head and it makes me a little nervous. Crumb ignores me for a moment, then puts down the scissors. He flicks off the music and examines his hair.

What the fuck was that?

Sun Ra, he says. Intergalactic death blues.

A poor choice, I think.

He laughs. Whatever do you mean?

Look in the mirror.

I am looking in the mirror. I'm a handsome bastard.

I'm sure you are. But your hair is mangled.

Crumb smiles and puts aside the mirror. He motions for me to sit down. I sink onto a very soft purple sofa and think I might like to close my eyes and die there. Crumb removes the towel and reaches for a pair of pants. It's so nice to see you, Phineas. I'm afraid you don't look well.

Is there anything to drink?

Tea or gin? he says.

Both, I think.

Crumb disappears to boil water. He comes back with a pint of gin. He sits down next to me on the sofa. I take small, careful sips from the bottle and tell him what happened. The kettle begins to whine.

I think I had better have a look at you, he says.

Crumb isn't really a doctor. He does cheap abortions and gunshot wounds and even dental work for the mad and desperate. Crumb reads a lot. He has a closet full of old surgical textbooks and a lot of stolen equipment. And he doesn't try to fake it. If you come to him with a ruptured bowel or a crushed spine he gives you a cup of tea and sends you to the hospital.

A half hour passes. I lay naked and ashamed on Crumb's table, my clothes crumpled and damp beside me. The shame is curious. I didn't do this to myself. And it could have happened to anyone. Jude was an efficient predator, a cat. I was a mouse with a bad leg.

What's the story?

You are nearly dead. In fact, I'm surprised you are walking.

Crumb holds a hypo to the light, tapping it for bubbles. I stare at the bubbles until I think I can hear them. But that's impossible. The noise is my heartbeat.

I can hear my heart, I say. If I can hear it I must be fine.

Crumb sighs. Are you listening? he says. The external wound itself is not so bad and there's no sign of infection thus far. How much of the penicillin did you take?

Ten cc's, I say. Straight into the muscle.

It should be enough, I think. If you're still alive in ten days you might take another dose. For good measure. As for immediate concerns, your white cell count is very low. You are dehydrated and you have a fever of 102 degrees. You have some bleeding inside. I can't say what else without opening you up.

But I feel strong. Almost high.

Adrenaline and loss of blood, he says. Invigorating but alas, temporary.

He comes toward me, the hypo pointed like a hideous eleventh finger. I look away.

Roll over, please.

The needle stings and I feel warm. A detailed map of Denver dissolves in my head. I'm looking for bowling alleys.

What should I do?

Be very careful, says Crumb. Do not fight or fuck anyone. Those stitches could easily tear.

My face feels strange. I think I must be smiling. Every muscle in my body is like a piece of nylon rope. What kind of shot was that? I speak slowly. The words pass my lips dense and textured as meat.

A mild speedball. Morphine for the pain. A touch of methamphetamine to give you energy. Do you have any money?

Money, I say. Oh, yeah. What do I owe you?

No, he says. This visit was free. But I suggest you pick up whatever drugs you can find on the street. When that shot wears off you will realize how much pain you are in.

I start to get dressed but Crumb's face bothers me. He has the expression of someone who wishes the rain would stop.

My wife had leukemia. Her own blood cells were attacking her. When she was twenty-six a doctor told her she would be lucky to live another year. She had one failed bone marrow transplant; she had a seemingly endless course of chemical therapy. Her fine black hair dropped out, it fell away like dust. She began to collect wigs. She had a grim drawer of phony hair. Glittering blond and impossible red and gunmetal blue. She didn't want anything that looked like her own short black hair. She rarely let me see her bare skull. She had a few stubborn and lingering strands, gray wisps. She hated them, she said. When she was very weak, she would ask me to bathe her. Heavy silence would fall between us as I washed her failing flesh. She wouldn't let me touch her head. I would turn away as she raised her skinny arms to pour water over herself. Whenever I stared into her wide black eyes I saw a terrified girl who would never grow old, and for a moment I could feel how it was to be dying. It was heartbreaking and I rarely felt closer to her.

Lucy's dead now and the doctors were wrong; she lived to be twenty-nine.

Eve glides through the blue curtain. She gives me a cool stare. Her lipstick is silver and I wonder if her pubic hair is shaved to match her eyebrows.

Crumb, she says. You have a phone call.

Thank you, dear.

Crumb reaches for a portable phone and begins to murmur. Eve stands with her pelvis thrust forward. She wears a leather miniskirt slung low across her hips. I'm sure she doesn't wear underpants. And I doubt she would blink if I asked about her pubic hair.

Eve, I say. If you were to go bowling, where would you go?

That's easy, she says. The Inferno.

Her belly is smooth and the skin transparent and I'm aware that I'm high as a kite.

Well. Are you in the mood?

Am I in the mood?

To go bowling?

She grins. Always.

I can't help smiling.

Give me five minutes, she says. And she disappears through the curtain.

Crumb puts down the phone. I believe she fancies you.

Does she have a driver's license?

Crumb frowns and pours more gin. I'm sure I said that sex in your condition would likely kill you. And definitely so with one such as Eve.

Oh no, I say. I think I need her to drive.

Five minutes or five hours later and I haven't moved. Eve leans close and blows on my face. The scars beneath her eyes are like fallen petals. The effect is lovely. As if she's been crying and she's too proud to dry the tears. I notice that she has painted on slim blue eyebrows. There's no sign of Crumb.

Hello, I say. I can't feel my legs.

Let me help you, she says.

She pulls me up and now I'm light as a feather. I take a few steps.

My muscles are fluid and distant. Eve has changed into boots and jeans and a long leather coat. She still wears the black bra and I crouch down to examine her belly. It appears normal.

Come on, she says.

She leads me outside. I'm surprised by the dark and I take deep breaths. The air is cold and thick in my lungs. I spread my arms like wings and close my eyes and I hear a thousand televisions.

Where is your car? says Eve.

I don't know. It's silver. A silver Bug.

six

Eve drives. I sit in the passenger seat and whisper.

Every time I close my eyes I'm dreaming. I am in the woods. My reflection is a knife blade. Throat and chest scratched and bloody, burned by the sun. The face blackened, hollow. Lips cracked and white with salt. I move in widening circles, away from the lake. I can still hear the water. She floats. Her face is gone. When the sun rises again I press the knife into my arm to make the ninth cut.

An endless red light. Eve smiles at me. I turn my face to the window. There is a long white car stopped alongside us. The driver stares at me. His face is familiar and I realize it's the cop from the hospital. The man with the blister on his mouth. I get out of the car and stand there clutching my stomach.

Open the fucking window.

I fall against the white car and slap at the roof. The window glides down with a soft electric hum.

What's the trouble, young fellow?

I thrust my face into the car spitting like a cat.

Piece of shit, I say. Follow me and find yourself dead in the morning.

I beg your pardon, the man says. An elderly man in a camel hair coat. He wears glasses and has a fine white mustache. A black silk scarf is tucked around his neck. In the passenger seat is a woman wrapped in fur and heavy perfume. The old man is pointing a small antique gun at me; I think it's a Derringer, of all things.

I'm very sorry.

The light is green and I get back in the Bug. Eve is smoking a cigarette. I look over my shoulder and the white car is nowhere to be seen. Eve doesn't say a word. It has to be the drugs. I chew on my finger to convince myself I'm awake.

What are we looking for? she says.

I'm distracted, trying to find something on the radio that doesn't make my skin throb. Eve hits the left turn signal. I look up and see the word *Inferno* blinking in red neon. What?

She slides the car in between a cruiser on jacked-up wheels and a hump of gray snow. The engine dies abruptly. I notice that my fingers are stiff and brittle from the cold.

Listen, she says. I like you. You have a nice face and in another lifetime I might find you mildly attractive. But Crumb says you're dying and you're obviously too pitiful to swing a bowling ball and you don't think this is a date, do you?

Oh, boy.

And you're old, she says. You're ancient. It would be like having my stepfather grope me.

I'm thirty-three.

She smiles and lights another cigarette. Are you cold?

Why do you ask?

Because your lips are blue.

I'm fine, I say. Let me have a drag.

She leans over and holds the cigarette to my mouth. Her lipstick tastes like licorice. I blow smoke and try to smile. The facial muscles are still a bit vague from the morphine. Eve is patient.

I want to know what we're looking for, she says.

A woman. Her name is Jude. White or possibly Asian and approximately twenty-five years old. A little taller than you and a nice body. Black hair with blond streaks. Tattoo of an eye between her shoulder blades. Last seen wearing a red dress. She has something of mine.

Eve laughs. And you want my help?

Of course. And by the way. In another lifetime I would gladly drink your bathwater. But Crumb advised me not to touch you, which reminds me. How old are you?

Today is my birthday. I'm nineteen and I pee in my bathwater.

My god.

Let's go. This is gonna be fun.

Did you say it was your birthday?

Yeah, she says. Why?

I have a superstition. If someone tells me it's his birthday, I give him something on the spot. A present from my pocket, whatever is there. I have given away some nice things: knives and watches and expensive cigars. On a few occasions I have had nothing in my pocket but loose change and chewing gum and I offered it as humbly as I could. I reach into my pocket and pull out Jude's necklace, the black teardrop. I give it to Eve and she is so surprised and pleased that she kisses me.

Inside the Inferno. A schizophrenic coupling of honky-tonk and gothic. Sawdust on the floor. Mirrors cracked and gleaming on every wall. Antique farm equipment and weapons hang from the ceiling. Hammers and sickles, a massive yoke and harness, crossbows and axes and bayonets. Christmas lights swing from the rafters. The bar is a long slab of unfinished oak and the bartender wears a monk's robe. The waitresses are dressed as prostitutes and schoolgirls and French maids. Eve leads me to a dark table. I'm surprised to see actual bowling lanes; on several of them people are even bowling. A schoolgirl comes to take our order. She wears knee socks and an obscenely short skirt.

Eve asks for beer and a whiskey shot.

Two, I say. And bring me a glass of milk.

The girl blinks and scratches her thigh. We don't have milk.

You must have water.

She rolls her eyes. It's a dollar if you want ice.

I tell her I don't care but she's already walking away. I like this place, I say.

Eve isn't listening. She puts her arm around my neck and leans close. Her tongue flicks the edge of my ear. Someone's watching you, she says.

Where?

It's too easy if I tell you, she says.

I let my eyes relax and wander. I've been a civilian too long. My senses are dull. But this is obvious. At the end of the bar is a knot of bikers. One of them has a big belly and white muscle shirt that's too small. It clings to him like it's pasted to his skin. Leather riding chaps and army boots. His left arm is in a cast smeared with oil and Magic Markers. He has matted blond hair and sideburns like the ears of a lazy hound. He is staring at me like I'm a sandwich and I've seen him before.

Fat man with the broken arm.

Gotcha, says Eve.

The schoolgirl returns with our drinks. She brings two beers and two shots and a glass of tepid water.

Enjoy, she says. Eve gives her ten dollars and tells her to keep it. I drink some of the water and wash it down with beer.

I'll be back in a minute, I say.

I get up and walk straight for the fat man. He blinks rapidly and his face turns faintly red. He is surprisingly handsome, in a brutish way. I come close enough to shake his hand, to feel his pulse.

Don't I know you? I say.

Then I veer off and head for the bathroom. I can see him in three different mirrors, splintered and turning to follow me. I step inside the bathroom and turn off the lights. Someone grunts and curses in a stall.

Very sorry, I say.

I lift my leg and palm the Smith & Wesson. I take a long shallow breath. The air is sour, like artificial fruit. It smells like violence. I take another breath and ignore my rattling heart. The bathroom door swings open and the fat man pauses, confused. The doorway a halo around him. I grab him by the throat and pull him inside, then switch on the light. I jam the gun into his left eye.

Oh fuck me, he says. You're the guy.

That's right. Who are you?

I'm nobody.

Did you hold me down, I say. Did you actually touch my kidney? Did you put your fucking fingers inside me?

I don't know you.

But you do. You were in that bathroom the other night, at the Peacock.

I don't know you, he says. I don't want to know you.

And you watched her cut me open.

His face falls. It was terrible, he says. I puked my guts.

I don't say anything. I hold the gun like it's a feather.

He eyes me carefully. Are you even supposed to be walking around?

I'm fine, thank you. I'm a new man.

He laughs and I jab him with the gun.

Who are you?

He squirms. My name is Winston but my friends call me Pooh. Like Winnie-the-Pooh.

I poke him with the gun once more and he whimpers. This pleases me, but I shrug as if I'm bored and I might put a bullet in him for laughs. It was very nice meeting you, I say.

Hold your horses. This isn't the way it goes.

Did she send you to scare me, Winston? Because you aren't very scary.

I'm stoned, he says. When I'm stoned I get soft.

The skin is turning white around his eye. I pull the gun back but leave it in his face. Then I notice the sheen of tears on his cheeks.

What the fuck. Are you crying?

This isn't the way it goes. You weren't supposed to fuck her, he says. She slips you the little orange pill and you go to sleep and she cuts you open. You don't fuck her. You don't fuck my girlfriend.

She's your girlfriend, huh. Your sweetheart.

Yeah, that's right.

Come on. Are you gonna marry her and move out to the suburbs? Fill her belly with little Winstons and hope she doesn't burn the pot roast?

His face turns red.

Be realistic, Winston. How long have you known her?

A week, he says. Five days. But I'm the only one who fucks her.

And I should be the one holding a gun, okay. I got a gun.

I frisk him quickly and find a snub-nose .32 in his waistband, the barrel clammy with his sweat. In his pocket I find a film canister. I pop it open with my thumb and there are a dozen small blue capsules inside.

Muscle relaxers, he says. Blue moons. For my busted arm and some good shit, too. Ease the pain and make you happy as a cat sucking himself. I could get you some at low cost.

That's nice, I say. Where is Jude?

One hundred dollars. For a hundred I can get you twenty of 'em.

I give him my warmest smile. Winston, I say. Don't be so fucking greedy.

He grins, sheepish. Okay. For you I could do thirty for a hundred.

It's getting hot in here, I say.

I might need the hundred up front, of course.

Of course.

I smile and he swings his cast at me like a chunk of firewood. I duck under it, stupid and shocked. I didn't think he had it in him. But he narrowly misses smashing the cast to bits, his exposed fingers thumping into the side of the white sink behind me. He grunts in pain and shoves the fingers in his mouth.

Oh, fuck me.

I pull him close and hug him like a brother. He smells faintly of Jude. I fill my lungs with that smell. I stroke the back of his neck and take a fistful of his hair. I don't pull it, not yet. His face is crumpled.

I'm sorry, he says. I'm so fucking sorry.

Take it easy, I say.

What about a load of smack, he says. I can get you a ton of the pure white shit. It's straight out of Turkey or someplace. It's the best shit. It's going to the top, with a fucking bullet.

That sounds too good to be true.

Believe it, he says. This shit is the truth.

Winston, I say. I'm not a buyer. I'm the guy you're looking for. Jude sent you to find me. To tell me something or do something to me. Remember.

Pooh sniffs. She didn't send me to do anything. I come here all the damn time. The beer is cheap and I like to throw darts. I meet lots of chicks here.

I'm sure. But where is she?

Well, he says. I don't exactly know. But I do have a rendezvous with her tomorrow.

A rendezvous.

He shrugs. Business and pleasure. Has to do with the smack.

Listen, Pooh. I'm tired of this and I have to pee and I'm going to shoot you in the eye if you don't tell me the time and place.

Tomorrow morning at the train station. Eleven o'clock. Jude likes to sleep late.

I drop his pills in my pocket. Why don't you stay home tomorrow? Watch cartoons and forget about Jude. I want to talk to her alone.

He frowns and I can almost see his brain scrambling.

Or else I could just shoot you.

Pooh smiles. I think I will stay home tomorrow, after all.

Do you like surprises?

Oh, I love a good surprise.

Then don't tell her I'm coming.

Okay.

My legs are feeling watery and I suddenly want Pooh to go away. I give him twenty dollars and tell him to go have a beer.

Hey, he says. Don't tell her I cried.

Don't worry. I'll tell her you scared me half to death.

Pooh scratches himself. Can I have my gun back? It's not even loaded.

Are you ticklish? I say.

He hesitates as if it's a trick question. No, he says.

Close your eyes, then. Think good thoughts.

I press the .32 to his soft belly and pull the trigger. He flinches.

When I come out of the bathroom Eve is arguing with another woman. I sit down and sip my whiskey. It tastes like burnt wood. The woman is long and skinny and bald. She turns to glare at me.

Is there a problem? I say.

She flicks her finger at me. Eve is with me, she says.

I look at Eve and she shrugs. This is Georgia.

My heart is still banging too fast after the encounter with Pooh. The stitches have begun to itch, far away and maddening. My hands are cold and damp and I hold one out to Georgia.

I don't think so, she says.

Delighted, I say.

Eve sits between us, her eyes closed. She looks so young. I retract my hand like a piece of machinery. Eve stands up and I see the blood rush into her face.

Let's go, she says. Do you want to go?

I'm finished here.

Georgia leans forward and gives me a curved shard of glass from a mirror, thin as my finger. I glance at it and see only my eyes. I'll see you later, she says.

In the parking lot Eve rubs snow on her face.

It stops me from crying, she says.

I take a breath and the frozen air stings my throat like nettles. I'm a bit dizzy.

Are there any motels nearby?

No, she says. You're coming home with me.

Home, I say.

She takes my hand.

It's not far. Georgia lives with me.

I lift her small, cold hand and hold it to my lips. I want to tell her how tired I am.

It's okay, she says. You can sleep on the couch. It's velvet.

seven.

The water is warm, the temperature of blood. I swim through it, laboring. My limbs so heavy and strange. Lift my head to breathe and I can see the boat. Adrift, barely moving. A woman's arm dangling over one side. Her fingertips gliding at the surface of the water like the legs of a spider, leaving no trace. The sun is high in a cloudless sky. Her skin is fair and will burn easily. I close my eyes and swim. I hear terrible echoes. When I open my eyes I am alongside the boat, near enough to kiss the woman's hand. I pull myself up to look at her. She wears a short blond wig that seems to crouch on her head like a yellow, flightless bird. She is naked, as if she fell asleep sunbathing. She has small, delicate feet. Her face is a giant black hole that moves and shifts in the light. Tiny particles detach themselves from the hole and drift away to land on her thigh and I comprehend that this is a mass of flies. My handgun is in the floor of the boat. I pull it overboard and let its weight drag me under. I'm sinking fast and the water is much colder below. There is almost no light and I'm swallowing water, breathing it as I push the gun into soft black mud. I want to leave it but I can't. There will be no fingerprints but mine and I don't care. I push myself to the surface and choke in the open air. I swim away from the boat and regain consciousness on a cold floor beside a velvet couch.

There is a dark face leaning over mine. The breath is hot and sickly sweet.

Get on your fucking feet, she says.

Georgia, I say.

She flicks on a lamp and thrusts her arm at me. A dog bit me, she says.

I blink in the yellow light. Her lips are raw; she's chewing them.

My arm, she says. Look at my arm.

She has smooth skin, the color of chocolate. There is a small, crescent scar on her biceps and the mark of a recent needle. The flesh is otherwise undamaged.

Don't you see it? she says. She's breathing rapidly. Her eyes are like sunspots.

There's nothing there, I say. Close your eyes and it will go away.

It's still bleeding, she says. There's blood everywhere.

What kind of dog was it?

Her face goes blank. There is a sharp pain in my foot. She's squeezing it like a lump of dough.

A black dog. Or yellow, I think.

I pull my foot away from her and begin putting on my shoes.

Do you want something to drink? I say. A glass of water?

She hisses at me. Water is poison.

I shake my head. Water is good.

It's rabies. I could have rabies, she says.

Oh, yeah. You might be right.

The basement, she says. You should lock me in the basement. If it's rabies you will have to shoot me in the morning, shoot me dead.

I fish out the blue muscle relaxers I took from Pooh. There are only ten of them.

Open your mouth, Georgia.

And her mouth pops open. As if she's ten and I'm her uncle who always has gum. I place one pill on her tongue and push her mouth closed. I slip another one into her hand and she makes a fist.

This should make you feel better, I say. If not, take the other one.

And I lead her down the hall to the closet. There's no basement, I say.

She kneels obediently on some dirty sheets and blankets.

I'm going to go out for a while, I tell her.

Her face contorts and I'm afraid she will start screaming.

Don't worry, I say. If it's rabies, I promise I will shoot you in the morning.

Georgia smiles, rocking back and forth. I leave the door cracked. In one of the bedrooms I find Eve. She is curled into a ball in the middle of her bed, shivering. Her blankets are on the floor and I pull them over her. I sit on the edge of her bed and watch her sleep. I bend close enough to smell her breath. It is sweet, like toothpaste. It would be nice to have a daughter.

My wife and I tried to make a baby. When things were good between us, when she wasn't dying. She wanted one so badly, and we tried. Every night for months. I thought this was fine at first. All the sex I wanted and we did it in every room of the house. The idea was that the bathroom might be luckier than the kitchen and so on. We tried different positions that might improve the sperm's ascent. I fucked her underwater and upside down. We used leather and dogs and vegetables and ice and cellophane and handcuffs to make it interesting. I fucked her fully clothed in the rain. Her face was ever a grim mask. She couldn't enjoy it, she said. Because she had to concentrate. I fucked her until I had nothing left, until my penis shrank at the thought of her. None of it mattered because I was sterile and when the doctors told us so, her face became a death mask.

Then outside. The snow has stopped. My watch says it is four. The sun will be up soon and I start to walk. I limp slightly, to the left. This eases the pain in my side but I have to be careful not to fall off the sidewalk. I buy cigarettes at the glowing foodmart. Six hours until I meet Jude and I have no idea what I will do to her. I'm wide awake and almost happy but on the edge of weeping. As if I'm thinking of a lover and I can't wait to see her. It's pitiful and I bite my lip to clear my head. The wind is picking up and I duck into a phone booth to smoke a cigarette. I need someone to talk to and I decide to call Crumb. But I don't know his number. I don't know anyone's number. I call my old number and get a recording that says disconnected, try again. I dig through my wallet and find two scraps of paper. One is the original note from Jude. If you want to live call 911. It's wrinkled and the ink is a little smeared. The handwriting is curved and sharp, girlish but bright with intent. She has strong fingers. I can almost see her. I can smell her cold yellow skin. The other bit of paper is from Rose White. Her name and phone number. Her handwriting is softer, dreamier than Jude's. I pick up the phone and drop a quarter.

Hello, she says. She is suspicious but awake.

Rose, I say. It's Phineas.

Oh. Good morning.

I'm sorry. Did I wake you?

No, I'm glad you called. Are you okay?

I don't know. I need to tell you something.

What is it?

My wife is dead.

Oh, I'm so sorry.

It happened six months ago. I just wanted you to know.

Where are you?

I'm nowhere. A phone booth.

I think you should be in bed. You're not well.

It wasn't my fault.

What?

My wife. It was an accident.

Do you want me to come get you?

The thing is, I taught her how to handle a gun. She knew.

Phineas, listen to me. Where are you?

I don't know what to do.

What do you want to do?

I have to meet Jude at the train station.

Who is she?

She stole something from me and I have to get it back.

Okay. What time are you meeting her?

At eleven o'clock. She took my kidney.

Of course. Your kidney.

Do you know the story of the goose and the golden eggs?

She sighs. I hope you're not the goose.

I'm the fucking egg.

Phineas, she says. Let me come get you.

My wife was a good shot. She could take the head off a bottle.

Tell me about her.

Jude? She's a hell of a woman. Mean as a snake but nice to look at, god love her.

Your wife, tell me about your wife.

My wife. Her name was Lucy and she was a teacher. Ninth-grade math.

What did she look like?

She had short black hair, cut like an elf from a fairy tale. When I first met her I was sure she had pointed ears. Her eyes were dark and a little slanted.

What about her body? Was she smaller than me?

Lucy was soft. She had a nice round ass and strong legs. A little bit of a tummy.

And did she dress like an elf?

She wore sharp little designer suits. Like a short gray flannel skirt with matching jacket. High-heel shoes and she loved white stockings. She was a sweetheart but she had a dirty mind. Because she was dying and she wanted a little excitement. She didn't wear underpants sometimes and she said the boys in her class could sense it and they got pretty hot and couldn't tell you five plus six.

She sounds like fun. Did she like to dance?

I don't want to talk about her anymore. She's dead and sometimes I'm glad.

You don't mean that. You don't.

She was always dying. And then she was dead.

Phineas, you're scaring me. Tell me where you are.

Why do you want to know?

Because I can take care of you. I'm a nurse.

I'm weak. I need to be strong when I see Jude.

Let me help you.

No. I need to do this alone.

What are you going to do?

I'm going to take her to a hotel room.

I don't want to know. I really don't.

I'm going to drug her and fuck her senseless.

Phineas. That's enough.

Then I'm going to kill her.

The phone is chirping in my hand and the sky is turning pink. It's morning and I'm stiff with cold. My left hand is a claw, frozen to the phone. On the back of my hand is a note to myself. Blue ink and my uneven handwriting. *Rose 1013 Alpine 2 P.M.* There's a burnt stub of cigarette in my other hand. Rose must have hung up on me and I fell asleep or blacked out. Either way I'm still standing. And it looks like Rose and I have a date. Maybe she wants to go to a matinee. Two o'clock. I can take care of Jude by then, I'm sure. I'm hungry and I drop the phone. There's a diner down the street.

I must look bad. The waitress asks if I have any money before she will give me a menu. I show her twenty dollars and still she is slow with the coffee. I'm the only customer. I stare at the eggs on my plate. I asked for them sunny side up because it sounded cheerful and now they won't stop jiggling. I chew a piece of bacon for a long time, grinding it into tasteless paste.

This was a bad idea.

Excuse me? The waitress sucks the end of her pencil and stares at me.

The food, I say. Sometimes I hate to eat.

What's wrong with it?

I would rather be a machine. Or else just take a pill and be done.

Listen, mister. If you don't like it you can take your funny ideas someplace else.

You don't understand. This place is the same as any other. It's the need to consume food every day in order to sustain the flesh. It depresses me.

I'm sorry you got problems. But mostly I don't care.

I gouge the eggs with my fork and the yolk is bright and putrid.

Is there more coffee?

But she doesn't look up. I drop a few crumpled dollars on my plate and go.

eight.

A long white Lincoln idles in an alleyway. The windows are tinted but I know who it is. I walk to the driver's side and stand there until the black glass slides down.

Are you feeling better? says the Blister. He still wears the white leather gloves.

Oh, I'm a peach.

The engine growls. The Blister is nervously tapping the accelerator. My breath swirls away from me thick as smoke. The Blister wears a black fur coat and a red silk tie. The coat hangs open and I see he's got a small cannon in his shoulder holster.

I had a funny idea, I say.

What's that? says the Blister. The gloves squeal and pop as he grips the wheel.

The idea is that you aren't a cop. I never saw your badge.

That's a scream, says the Blister.

But I really don't mind you following me. It's comforting.

The Blister shrugs and his big gun is pressed gently into my testicles. I never saw him move. He leans out the window, as if he wants directions. I'm not a cop, he says. I'm a bunny rabbit. Now get in the car.

He kicks open the passenger door and I stroll around to get in. I suppose I could run. But I'm so feeble it would be embarrassing. He could smoke two cigarettes and daydream awhile, then go have a bite and still drop me from fifty yards with that gun.

I fasten my seat belt and the Blister rests the barrel of his gun on my shoulder.

Get used to that feeling, he says.

Where are we going?

The Blister smiles through me. A vein in his neck throbs visibly. The silence is crushing. The car gleams as if new. The seats are a soft, pale leather that must have come from baby calves. The dash is oiled mahogany. The car feels computerized, climate-controlled.

I love the car, I say. Very glamorous.

Isn't it fantastic. I just drove it off the lot the other day.

Oh, yeah. It's a fucking beauty.

I hope so, he says. It cost a small fortune.

Too bad, though. It smells like a dead boy's asshole.

He glares at me. Be careful with your tongue.

Do you have a name? Or a serial number?

Silence.

The gun at my ear twitches and I realize he's trembling. His face is dreamy, unfocused. I'm crazy, of course. But I think he's got a little erection and there is a brief unwanted rush of blood in my own genitals, because there is nothing so arousing as fear and submission and the threat of violence. And he could easily blow my head off when we hit a patch of ice.

My mouth is very dry. Do you mind if I smoke a cigarette?

If you like, says the Blister. You are not a prisoner, Mr. Poe.

This isn't the way to make friends.

If I meant to kill you I would have done so. If you were a prisoner, you would be riding in the trunk with a broken collarbone.

The collarbone?

Very painful. It leaves you extremely docile.

What about the gun in my ear?

Oh, well. A gun is only a tool.

Why don't you stop driving in circles and tell me what you want?

The Blister sighs and pulls over. He kills the engine. Now, he says. I will get to the point. In less than an hour you are meeting a woman named Jude at the train station. I will be watching you.

I smoke and try to appear undaunted.

The Blister taps the wheel with a gloved finger. I don't want to kill you. I want to help you. And perhaps you can help me.

Thanks. But I don't like you.

Don't be clever. That's the last thing you want to be.

This isn't happening.

I'm afraid it is. The minute you took Jude up to your room you entered into a world of shit.

Unlucky in love, I say.

The Blister smiles. Jude works for me, he says. Rather, she once did.

Okay. Who is she and why does she want my kidney?

It doesn't matter who she is, he says. She can be whoever you want her to be. And she doesn't want your kidney.

Oh, well. Someone must want it.

Indeed.

I stare at him, growing irritated. Who?

The Blister smiles like a generous king. I might want it, he says.

You hired her to steal my kidney.

He shrugs. My dear brother is dying.

And she gave you those bruises. She fucked you up. What did you do to her?

I'm a gentleman, he says.

Let me guess. You didn't want to pay her and she decided to keep my poor kidney.

It is no longer your kidney, says the Blister. It is mine. Or my brother's to be exact. Unfortunately, Jude has failed to deliver it.

My knife is out of the wrist sheath, fast and silent as a cat's heart. I slash upward and think, if I cut his lips off he might stop talking like such a wanker. The Blister brings the barrel of his gun down on my wrist and I drop the knife; my fingers are numb and I hope the wrist isn't broken. I hope I don't cry like a baby when the feeling returns to my hand. The Blister picks up the fallen knife, holding it by the blade with two fingers. He gives it back to me without a word.

Listen very carefully, he says. If you try that again, I will cut off your thumb.

I apologize. I tell him I'm a little sensitive about my body parts.

A natural reaction, he says.

Okay, I say. Tell me what you want.

I want you to kill her and return the kidney to me. I will pay you one hundred thousand dollars.

Your little scenario is flawed.

Why do you say that?

Because I already have a plan. I'm going to kill Jude this afternoon for fun. And then eat my own putrid kidney for dinner. This will bring me strength and good fortune.

The Blister laughs. You won't kill her. Not yet.

Oh, really. Why not?

Because I can see it in your eyes. You can't wait to touch her, to fuck her again.

She fucked me, I say.

Whatever you say. But when you get tired of her, you will kill her for me.

I blow smoke and try to connect the dots between Pooh and Jude and the Blister. I try to open my window but the button doesn't work. The Blister has a master switch on his side and I'm sure it pleases him to control everyone's window. He seems like a control freak, a little Hitler with equally bad hair. I turn my head and the gun is at my Adam's apple. The Blister's face is blank as the gray sun. He's suddenly a thousand miles away and his left hand is busily squeezing and poking at a pimple on his chin. He's eager to pop it but he needs both hands. He needs to take off those stupid gloves.

Aren't you neglecting something? I say.

He blinks at me.

What about the heroin?

The Blister turns a delicious shade of pink. Heroin?

Heroin, I say.

The Blister waves a hand and stutters. It's nothing. Jude is simply killing two birds with one stone.

I laugh. Am I a bird or a stone?

If you must know, she is using you as a mule. When she removed your kidney she also made a deposit. There is a large amount of raw heroin in your lower intestine. Today she will pretend to be surprised and angry to see you; she may even threaten to kill you. Then she will allow you to gain the upper hand; she will reluctantly invite you to become her partner. You will travel to El Paso with her and cross the border. Then she will sell you to her buyer, as if you were a package, or a dog. The buyer will remove the heroin by whatever method he chooses.

You just made that up, I say.

I did not, he says.

Come on. Are you trying to tell me she is letting me walk around town with a balloon full of smack in my belly, unaware? What if I accidentally shit it out in some public toilet?

When was your last bowel movement?

I don't really know. Maybe three days ago. Before I met her.

Precisely, he says. She has no doubt made alterations to your digestive system. Staples in your stomach perhaps, for the very purpose of protecting her merchandise. And I'm sure she drugged you. I assume you have no appetite? Food repulses you, am I right?

I just had breakfast, I say. Bacon and eggs. Fucking delicious, too.

Whatever you say; the heroin is irrelevant to me. My only interest is eliminating Jude and recovering the kidney.

I look at the Blister, amused. A large quantity of heroin is never irrelevant.

His gloved fingers clench and relax as if they are stiff with cold. He starts the car.

I could use something to drink, the Blister says. Where shall we go?

There's a drive-through burger place down the street.

The Blister drives pitifully slow, as if he's not used to driving on snow. He's staring at the road like he's afraid it might disappear. I rub my belly, reluctant to believe that there is anything inside but empty space and disconnected wiring. Blood and white noise.

Let's make it two hundred thousand, I say.

One hundred. Not a penny more.

Easy money. Like falling out of bed.

A piece of advice, says the Blister. Don't take her too lightly. Jude is a very dangerous girl. She has tasted your blood and she enjoys it.

Likewise, you wouldn't want to disappoint me.

I'm sorry. But you just aren't as dreadful as you mean to be. I think you might want to shave your head and grow a little goatee. And you could use a foreign accent, maybe French.

Imagine, says the Blister. Imagine waking up with no vocal cords and your eyes like jelly, your hands and feet cut off and soaked in acid, your teeth removed and crushed to powder.

I try to smile, to savor this moment.

At the drive-up window the Blister orders for both of us. A diet soda for himself and coffee for me. I reach for my wallet but the Blister waves it away. He parks the car and leaves it running. I light a cigarette and offer him one. He takes it and smiles. Thank you.

For a few silent minutes we blow smoke at each other, like best friends.

The Blister glances at his watch and when I finish my coffee, he presses a button that unlocks my door.

Good-bye, he says. I will find you when Jude is dead.

Excuse me. I haven't agreed to anything. And I think a little money up front would be a nice gesture.

The Blister smiles through white and yellow teeth. He pulls a slim leather wallet from his breast pocket and counts out five thousand dollars.

The rest upon completion, he says.

What is this. A little cigarette money?

Don't be rude, he says. Take the money and go.

Who the fuck are you?

This time he doesn't smile. I wait for him to whip out that big foolish gun.

I'm afraid it's time for you to go, he says.

It's snowing, I say. The least you could do is give me a ride.

Don't be foolish. Jude will be watching.

Tell me again: why should I do this?

The money. Do it for the money. Then you can buy your wife a new dress.

My wife is dead.

Of course she is.

What do you know about it? I say. I'm disgusted by the sound of my voice.

He shrugs. I might know who killed her. Or who didn't.

I look at my hands; there is no blood on them. I tell the Blister I will think about it.

nine.

It's a long walk to the train station.

Five minutes until eleven. The station is old and cavernous. It echoes like a cathedral. I stand in the center and let people stream past me. The panic of faces and thoughts colliding. Slow breaths and a half smile. I am a fool. I told Jude I was afraid of crowds and she will use it against me. I turn a slow circle but I don't see her anywhere. I close my eyes and sniff the air. I try to feel her. I was sure that she would arrive early and take the high ground. But she's expecting Pooh and she isn't worried. She might still be sleeping, white sheets wrinkled around her yellow skin. Her fists clenched, her eyelids fluttering. She might be dreaming of me.

Twenty minutes later I'm sitting on a wooden bench. I'm watching two kids argue over a video game. Jude sits down beside me. She's chewing her lip, angry. But her eyes glow.

You should never have come here, she says.

It's twenty-nine degrees outside and snowing. Jude is wearing a short white ski jacket. A black dress that stops halfway down her thighs and cowboy boots the color of wine. Her knees are pale and cold. She has her hands buried in her pockets. She looks everywhere but at me.

Are you insane? I say.

She crosses her legs. I have very warm blood.

I might want to kill you.

And I might say the same thing.

But you're glad to see me.

Hardly.

My senses are jangled and the pain is becoming unbearable. I remove Pooh's film canister from my pocket. I rattle the pills around, trying to think. Jude watches me, amused. One pill could leave me too goofy to function and I would rather she didn't know I was high.

She grins. Did you like Pooh?

Her hair is slightly frozen, as if she just washed it. Her eyes are impossibly green and I wonder if she's wearing colored lenses. She unzips the jacket a few inches to show her tender throat. She's wearing lipstick and suddenly I want to crush my mouth against hers. I want to suck her blood.

Pooh is a sad tomato, I say. He's in love with you.

Of course he is.

He must have a massive dick.

I'm sure he does. Like a horse. But I wouldn't know.

Oh, really. Pooh tells me a different story.

And who do you believe?

I don't believe anyone.

She laughs. Pooh is terrified of me. His penis would run and hide if I uncrossed my legs.

Then what use is he?

He carried eleven bags of ice up four flights of stairs to keep you alive. He never even complained.

That shuts me up. I pop one blue muscle relaxer into my mouth and roll it between my teeth. I bite it in two before it dissolves. I swallow half and spit the other into the palm of my hand.

Let's pretend to be friends, I say.

Close friends, she says.

I hold the bitten pill out to Jude and she bends to take it with her lips.

Where is my kidney? I say.

It's hot in here, don't you think?

Did you know I used to be a cop? I could make you disappear.

Disappear, she says. I love that word.

She crosses and uncrosses her legs. A muscle like rope along her inner thigh.

Let's go somewhere less public, she says.

Why not, I say. But I sit like a statue, a stone frog crouching in someone's garden.

Don't be afraid, she says.

The urge to kill her returns and I feel warm, as if the sun has slipped from behind a cloud.

Why would I be afraid?

I've already wounded you, she says.

Terribly.

But I can't hurt you anymore, she says.

No, I say.

She stands and I can hear every whisper and rustle of her clothes. I can almost see her body through the nylon and leather. I can nearly see the organs beneath her skin, clustered and purple. Busily pumping and thrusting, keeping her alive. For a moment I wonder if my kidney is in there, knitting itself to her flesh. I tell myself I want to kill her, to punish her. I want my kidney back. But such thoughts only float away, foreign and weightless. I feel myself dissolve. She dangles a gloved hand and I take it.

Jude and I stand on the street corner waiting for the light to change. I still hold her hand. I'm afraid she will run away. The wind is bitter and I want to shield her from it. I have this ridiculous idea that I can protect her, that she needs me to. Three nights ago she took me apart like a dog eating stolen meat. She tore into me.

Across from the train station is a nameless motel.

It's ugly, she says. But it does have room service.

I step out into the street, her hand still in mine. She flinches and I look around me. Pooh is standing behind a streetlamp; his face is hidden but his arms and shoulders and half his belly are clearly visible. His dirty white cast is bright against the dark mist in the air. I'm weirdly embarrassed by his incompetence. Jude growls and reaches into her purse. She comes out with a square black hairbrush, gripping it with the bristles turned down. She pulls away from me and takes several steps toward the streetlamp, holding the brush out like a gun. Pooh's arms begin to flail and I am reminded of a children's puppet show. Then he turns and runs down the sidewalk. Jude turns back to me, smiling and I shrug, as if she has just chased away a cowardly mugger.

The parking lot is black with snow.

Jude leads me up a flight of stairs to room 212. The door is heavy and swings shut slowly. Jude sits down on the bed and takes off her cowboy boots, dropping them to the floor. She reaches for the remote control and flicks on the television. She finds a soap opera and turns down the volume. I still stand by the door. The gun is in my ankle holster. I could have it in my hand. I could shoot her between the eyes and go. I could kill her with my knife. I could sit down beside her and offer to rub her feet and when she smiles I could grab her by the hair and pull her head back and cut her throat. I could keep the Blister's insulting money and take Eve to Disney World.

Jude glances at me. Why don't you sit down?

I bend to one knee and remove the Smith & Wesson. Jude watches me, unconcerned. I place the gun on top of the television, then put my knife down beside it.

Jude smiles. In my left boot, she says. I have a stinger, like a wasp.

I pick up the boot. The leather is slick and smells new. There is a sheath sewn into the inner wall of the boot and I pull out what appears to be a sharpened dentist's surgical tool, much like a stiletto with a hooked tip. It's a nasty little thing. The silver grip is slightly curved and wrapped in leather cord. I fold my hand around the grip and slash at the air and I like the feel of it.

Did you use this to rip me open?

She laughs. Of course not. It's not meant for such delicate work.

I put the stinger down. What else do you have? I say.

Jude unzips the ski jacket. Her dress is cut low across the neck and her collarbones are sharply defined. The flash of a black satin strap. I roll my eyes away and try to concentrate. She pulls a small silver automatic from the inside pocket of her coat. She tosses the gun at me, a Beretta .25 with a skeleton grip.

It suits you, I say.

Jude shrugs. I always wanted to fuck James Bond.

Dreams are all we have. But I'm looking for another gun, a nine millimeter.

I don't have a nine, she says. I don't care for big loud guns.

But I did have one. The night I met you. And now I can't seem to find it.

She lounges back against the pillows, her legs like scissors. The black dress is like tissue and I'm dying to touch her. I'm sorry, she says. But I didn't take it. Maybe the cops have it, or the bellboy. Even Pooh could have it. He was in the room and he has very sticky fingers.

Detective Moon has it in his desk drawer and he hasn't decided what to do with it. I should close my eyes and walk out of here. I should go down to the station and walk in like I'm coming home. I hope you boys are thirsty because I got money to burn and by the way, Moon: where's my fucking gun? But he might just laugh at me and say whatever do you mean? I take off my coat and drop it to the floor.

Tell me about yourself, I say.

I'm an only child.

Only children tend to be spoiled.

They are selfish, she says. They never had to share their mother's breast.

The shadows in her room are short and malformed, squatting in the corners like sullen trolls.

Are your legs cold?

Very, she says.

I touch her knee with the tip of a finger. Slowly trace a line down to her ankle. There's a fine black stubble, barely visible but rough as stone.

Let me rub your feet, I say.

She uncocks the left leg and drops her foot in my lap. I look at it without touching. A small pale foot, with a high arch. A crooked purple vein. The heel is callused. The toes are well shaped, evenly spaced.

The nails painted blue as a clear sky. I begin to stroke and fondle her foot as if I'm petting a kitten.

I'm curious, she says. What's so special about that gun?

Silence.

I used to be a cop.

She stares up at the ceiling, bored. That cloud looks like a lizard, she says.

I could easily break her ankle. I could twist her fucking foot off.

So you used to be a cop. So what?

A cop doesn't like to lose his gun. It makes him nervous, I say.

Is that the only reason?

I whisper for her to shut up and bend to kiss her, to bite her.

Jude reaches for the phone. She says she's starving.

She orders blueberry pancakes and coffee for two. I look down at my hands, clasped around her foot. They are strange to me, unfamiliar. I look at the television instead. Two actors are kissing vigorously on a phony riverfront as white smoke swirls around them.

Jude lights two cigarettes and gives me one.

For ten minutes we smoke and watch the silent soap opera. Jude tries to explain the intricacies of each character's sexual history but I'm not really listening.

They have money and posh cars but they're still a lot of inbreds, she says.

A gentle knock at the door. I go to answer it and a boy in a red suit stands there with a tray of food. I sign the slip and give him five dollars. Jude tells me to hang the DO NOT DISTURB card. I ignore her and set the tray down on the bed. Jude moves to crouch like a wolf over the food. She uncovers the steaming pancakes. They are stained by the burst blueberries and the smell is heavy and sweet. Jude smears them with butter and eats them without syrup. She pours coffee and hands me a cup.

Look in the bathroom, she says. There's a bottle of brandy in the sink.

For the first time I look closely at the room. It is clean and neat; housekeeping must have come recently. Still, there are no random possessions laying about. There are no clothes hanging in the closet. A compact black garment bag dangles from a hook. I would dearly love to poke through it but it is zippered shut and tight as a drum. I have a feeling Jude is ever ready to walk out the door. Even in the bathroom there is little sign of her presence. No clumps of tissue, no toothbrush and feminine gear. A half bottle of brandy in the sink. A green rubber icebox on the floor. I unscrew the brandy and take a short swallow. The hairs in my nose shrink as if on fire. The icebox is padlocked.

Jude has disposed of her pancakes and is freshening her lipstick. I give her the brandy and sit down to smoke a cigarette. You should eat, she says. The pancakes are getting cold.

I'm not hungry.

It's a shame. They're delicious.

I blow smoke and watch it swirl toward her.

Why didn't you meet me last night?

What do you mean, dear?

You left me a note. When I'm depressed I go bowling…

Oh, she says. I suppose I changed my mind. And you found me anyway.

Strains of early afternoon light. Pooh's blue moon gives everything a fine glassy sheen. The room is thick with electric heat and it's difficult to breathe. The soap opera has given way to thumb-sucking midget versions of Bugs Bunny and friends. The sound is muted but I keep thinking I can hear their helium voices. Above the television is a large round mirror and a watercolor of a duck. I sit in a chair beside the bed. On the nightstand there is a phone book and a *TV Guide* and the Gideons' Bible. The chair has no arms and I don't know what to do with my hands. My pants are unbuttoned and Jude kneels before me with my dick in her mouth. Her teeth are small and sharp and it's like her mouth is full of powdered glass. She may have drawn blood and I can't separate the pleasure from pain. I don't want her to stop. Jude lifts her head before I come. She breathes and smiles. The lipstick is gone and her lips are pale. She climbs into the chair and I'm inside her and I remember Crumb telling me to be careful, that sex could kill me.

The brandy is gone. Jude lies with her head in my lap. We share a cigarette back and forth. She is naked and has thrown the sheets off the bed. I am memorizing her body and I really don't need to. She is already as familiar to me as a recurring dream. Her eyes are wide apart and shaped like lemons; the lids are hooded and I remember my mother telling me those were mongoloid eyes, the devil's eyes. She has fine white teeth, slightly crooked and sharp. Her skin is a pale creamy yellow. She has small breasts with nipples the color of wet leather. Her belly and thighs are long, muscular. Her pubic hair is shaved like the narrow wing of a baby crow.

Phineas, she says.
    What?
    You saw the icebox.
    Yes. Didn't you want me to?
    I suppose.

It has my kidney in it.

She doesn't say anything. I stroke her throat and she passes me the cigarette.

It's strange, I say. At first it was like my wallet was gone and I wanted it back. And now I don't feel anything. It's just used flesh. It's garbage.

It's not garbage. It's worth a lot of money.

Who is the buyer?

A land developer in El Paso named Gore. One of his children has a bone disease or something.

What if the kidney isn't compatible?

Don't worry. I took tissue samples and had DNA tests done. Mr. Gore wasn't the only prospect. It could have easily gone to a baseball player or a politician in Canada.

Jude is never completely still. She twists a piece of string between her fingers and her foot bounces up and down. Her whole body seems to vibrate. I watch her face closely and her eyes never fade. She doesn't scratch her nose or twist her lip or change colors. I'm sure she's lying and then I'm not sure.

I have two tickets to El Paso, she says. A cozy little sleeper car.

I don't want to but I smile. What are you saying?

I'm willing to give you half.

Only half.

I've done all the legwork, she says.

Why give me any of it?

I need a partner. Someone to watch my back. And I kept thinking of you.

That's nice. How much are we talking about?

A lot, she says.

When I was ten years old, I thought fifty dollars was a lot of money.

I think it's impolite to discuss money.

There's nothing polite about any of this.

She sighs. It's quite cheap, really. Two hundred and fifty thousand.

I slide out from under her and begin to get dressed. Two hundred and fifty thousand. It seems ridiculous. The kidney is a small lump of fatty tissue that processes waste and sends it along to the bladder in liquid form. The kidney makes urine all day. Then again, someone might have a daughter whose life depends on a used kidney and how much is that worth? I am very sore and my brain is like a dead balloon. I am hoping that sex with Jude will eventually make me stronger. For now, she will have to help me put my boots on. I stop and smile at our weapons lined up in a neat row. I take my gun and stroll into the bathroom. I pick up the icebox and I'm almost disappointed. It should be heavier, somehow. I come out of the bathroom, my gun pointed lazily at Jude. She is still naked. She doesn't blink and she doesn't pull a gun from her ear like a coin.

I'm taking this with me, I say.

What will you do with it?

I feel like screaming.

I don't know. I might put it back where it belongs. I might fry it up with some purple onions and have it for lunch. I might just sell it myself.

You could never find a buyer. Not in a thousand days.

When does the train leave?

Tomorrow at nine thirty-five A.M.

Give me my fucking ticket.

Are you going to kill me?

I thought so, earlier. Or I wanted to think so.

Jude rolls onto her stomach. The eye tattoo black beneath her strewn hair. I adore her strong sleek ass. She reaches for the white ski jacket and pulls out a blue and white ticket, flashing it like a trump card.

ten.

The average drug mule swallows a dozen or more fat, skin-tight latex packets shaped like bullets and filled with heroin or coke. He or she has perhaps thirty-six hours to make delivery; otherwise the digestive system breaks down the latex, dissolving it. The drug is released into the bloodstream, and the host is dead within minutes. I have long passed thirty-six hours and I'm still breathing.

I could care less about heroin that may not exist. But Jude has her teeth deep in my heart.

Everyone is throwing money at me today and I'm feeling like a car wreck. I decide to live a little and take a taxi. It's ten after two. I'm late for Rose but I think she'll understand. I haven't been myself.

The driver is a young guy, slouched down in his seat. I tell him the address. He grunts, chews his gum. I'm lucky and he doesn't want to talk. The radio is tuned to an oldies station. A little Johnny Mathis and then the Temptations. I stare out the window at faces in passing cars.

*

A green Volvo station wagon pulls alongside the cab. There is a woman at the wheel, perhaps forty with severe hair. Her lipstick is a ferocious red that is smeared along her jaw and in the back window I see naked faces pressed against the glass, dirty and emaciated. Lost children, tortured and pleading for help. The faces dissolve and waver and become ordinary children, five and seven. The woman is their mother and there is something wrong with me.

I bounce around in my seat, manic and juiced. My skin doesn't feel right. It feels rubbery and stretched, as if two people are sharing it. Soon it will come apart. I'm stupidly high, of course. Jude could have slipped me something. Or Pooh might have lied. Perhaps those little blue pills were not muscle relaxers at all, and I remember poor Georgia. I hope she has come down from Pluto and is no longer rabid as I would hate to shoot her. I hope she suffered no ill effects from the pills I gave her. She was already on a bad cocktail of some kind; heroin and ecstasy perhaps, with a dash of crystal for kicks. Sudden death is always an eyelash away and I hope she didn't perish in that closet. Eve might find her while innocently looking for toilet paper.

What will I tell Eve, I wonder. What will I tell Rose. That I decided not to kill Jude. In fact, I massaged her feet and had breakfast with her. I take out my pocketknife and begin to trim my nails. I let her suck me like she was stealing gasoline and then I fucked her as if there was no tomorrow. The knife slips back and forth across my fingertips and white slivers fall to my chest. She has me wrapped around her little toe and I like it. I cut my thumbnail too short and soon it starts to bleed.

Is this it?

The cab has stopped at a haunted little bungalow with dark red shutters and a black tile roof with a weather vane. A curved hardwood front door, like a Hobbit hole. There's a gargoyle birdbath in the front yard, and a FOR SALE sign.

Is this it?

How do I know, man? It's the address you said—1013 Alpine.

It's way the hell across town.

Yeah. And you owe me thirteen dollars.

I stare at the house. I was half asleep when I spoke to Rose. I could have written down the wrong address. There's a scrap of paper tacked to the door, white and twisting in the wind. It might be a note.

I think I've been here before.

That's great, man. Do you want out or what?

I pass the kid some money and tell him to keep it. I get out and watch him drive away. I'm immediately very cold and I can tell by looking at the house that no one's home.

The note is unsigned, addressed to no one. *If I'm not here at three please wait.* I press my face to the cold windows. Dark rooms with minimalist décor. Wooden furniture and thick red carpets. No sign of life. I sit on the stoop to smoke. The wind is picking up and I waste a dozen matches before I get a light. It's quarter to three. How long do I want to wait? It's cold enough to die out here and I need to see Eve before I leave town. I want to have a shower and pack a few things and ask her to keep the Bug for me. And I should really see Crumb. Perhaps he can reinstall my kidney for a small fee. At the very least, he can give me a cup of tea and a little sympathy.

A car pulls up at the curb, a red Subaru wagon. A woman gets out and it's not Rose. She wears a long gray overcoat and rubber boots. A bright blue scarf and gold earrings. She holds a leather briefcase in one gloved hand. She's obviously a real estate agent.

Hello. Her voice is practiced, friendly. Are you my three o'clock?

I nod and smile and apologize for being early. She eyes the green icebox and I shrug. Some people carry briefcases, some don't.

That's fine. What about your wife?

She's not going to make it. I'm all alone.

Super, she says. Are you ready to see the house?

Please. I'm nearly frozen.

I offer my hand as she approaches the steps. She smiles and produces a massive ring of keys. The door swings open and heat rushes out. There's a damp smell of cats.

After you, I say.

Do you have children?

No…I don't.

There's a lovely little bedroom upstairs. Perfect for a baby's room.

I drift through the front room and look for details, photographs. There is almost nothing. Not a book or candlestick or ceramic ashtray. Behind me the woman is reciting square feet and water pressure and morning light and nearby schools. I tell her I was hoping to meet the owner.

I'm afraid Miss Hunt is not well. She's quite old, you know.

I try to mirror her expression of polite but uninterested pity.

It's hard to be old, I say. What is she like, Miss Hunt?

Actually, I have never met her. A lawyer arranged for the sale.

But she has a daughter, then?

A daughter, no. I don't think she was ever married.

I stare at her, nodding. Is there a telephone I can use?

She shows me the phone and hovers nearby as I dial the number

Rose gave me. She watches me with nervous brown eyes. Three times I get a busy signal. I give up and call for another cab.

eleven.

The second cab driver is fat and cheerful. He wants to talk about foot-ball but I'm not in the mood. I tell him I don't like football and he turns around to glare at me, as if I'm a pervert. Eventually we arrive at the address I gave him and he gets a good look at the Witch's Teat. He nods and mutters to himself, eager to get me out of his cab. I give him a big tip anyway.

Crumb is watching the store and he doesn't look too happy about it. He grunts when I walk in. He holds a sleek leather riding crop in one hand.

I'm killing flies, he says.

Where is little Eve?

She never came in. He swats at a fat winter fly and misses.

Maybe she's not feeling well.

I don't care, he says. She knows I don't like to work the counter. The customers are a lot of freaks.

Do you ever get any customers in here?

Well. It's a little slow today. But sometimes it gets crazy around Valentine's Day.

I'm sure. I stare at a grotesque display of vibrators shaped like rodents.

What can I do for you? he says.

I lift the green icebox like a trophy, like the head of a deer.

Crumb shudders. Is that what I think it is?

Have you had your lunch?

I'm not hungry.

Excellent. This will be easier on an empty stomach.

Phineas, he says. I helped a woman give birth once. It was a difficult procedure and she very nearly died. But she didn't. I kept her alive and she delivered a healthy baby girl. Six and a half pounds. The woman was so grateful that she asked me to help her eat the placenta. I was ill for days and I could never eat meat again.

I laugh helplessly. I'm sorry.

What is so fucking funny.

I'm not going to eat it. And if I were, I wouldn't share it with you.

Oh, I see. Phineas was making a little joke.

Not a very good one, it seems. I didn't even know you were a vegetarian.

Crumb sniffs. What do you want, then?

I want you to cut me open and put this little jewel back where it belongs.

Crumb locks the front door without a word. He hangs a sign in the window that says he has gone fishing. He grins faintly and tells me the sign was stolen from a barbershop. I follow him into the back and he motions for me to sit down. He bustles about as before, boiling water for tea and tinkering with the radio until he finds a moody Bach fugue. I sit on the purple sofa and flip through a magazine that is five years old.

Crumb finally sits down.

This is not a good idea, he says.

Why not?

When was the kidney removed?

Three days ago. Maybe four.

Then it is surely worthless.

I stare at him, insulted.

He sighs. I never went to medical school, remember. I don't know everything about transplant technology. But I don't think human tissue can survive outside the body much longer than a day.

But there's a chance, I say.

It's very doubtful.

Then let's open it and have a look.

Do you have the key?

No. But we could probably pry it open.

If the kidney is still viable, then forcibly opening the icebox would probably fuck it up. I would need all sorts of fancy equipment and two or three extra hands to do the operation. And I would have to do a little reading on the subject first.

Well. That's just fucking great.

Listen, he says. You have had something terrible done to you. It's like being mugged, or raped. You have been violently invaded and you aren't thinking straight.

Fuck you. Don't you think I know that?

Crumb closes his eyes. Where the hell is Eve? he says.

I light a cigarette and immediately put it out. I wish she were here.

What do you expect from me, Phineas?

The kettle has been whistling tunelessly for several minutes now. I just want some tea, okay.

*

Crumb serves the tea with a tray of stale English cookies. I chew on a cookie and Crumb smokes his pipe. Steam twists from our cups and the Bach fugue gives way to an unknown cello piece that is frantic as razors against glass. I do have another problem, I say.

What's this?

I may be carrying around a bag of heroin in my belly.

Are you serious?

I don't know. The information is unreliable.

My, my. That would be diabolical. To steal your kidney and leave such a package in its place. I'm not sure it makes a lot of sense, though. What if you had died, for instance? The heroin would be largely unretrievable.

No shit. The plan is so full of holes you could swim through it. But then who would hassle a wounded ex-cop at the border?

Interesting. What do you want to do about it?

I don't want to choke down a handful of laxatives and spend the day on your toilet. Especially if someone is only fucking with me.

I have an idea, he says. But don't laugh.

Crumb is making a lot of noise. It sounds like he's kicking a cardboard box to death. I can hear him wheezing and cursing and for once I wonder how old he is. Finally he drags a grocery cart with jammed wheels from his closet. The cart contains a machine that looks like the vile offspring of an old black-and-white television and a microwave. A variety of wires and dusty cords extend from its guts. It reminds me of a broken stereo I used to have. It was such a piece of shit that no one would steal it if I left it on my front porch.

What the hell is that?

Your ignorance betrays you, boy. This is a slightly used but perfectly functional ultrasound machine. I stole it many years ago from a hospital supply company.

Oh, boy.

Take off your shirt, he says.

Again I stretch out on Crumb's table and wonder how many strangers have lain bleeding here. Crumb plugs in the machine and adjusts the small humming screen so that I can see it. He smears cold, odorless jelly over my skin that looks innocently like spermicide, like a friendly lubricant.

That goo is the same shit the paramedics use before they shock your dead heart, isn't it?

Your heart is fine, he says.

And when they electrocute you. They smear that same jelly on your skull.

Crumb whispers for me to hush. He shows me a round black paddle that is wired to the machine and looks a lot like a Ping-Pong paddle.

This sends sound waves into your abdominal cavity, he says. The waves bounce around in there and the machine uses the information to construct an image. Submarines and bats navigate by the same basic principle.

Fantastic.

Crumb rubs the paddle over my belly like a magic wand. I watch the screen but it remains black. My belly is a bottomless pit. A small child could crawl in there and take a nap.

You're a quack, I say. A hopeless fucking quack.

He grunts and fiddles with the machinery, and finally a grainy image appears on the screen. Random black and white shapes, endlessly shifting. I could be staring through the dark leaves of a tree against the gray sky before a storm. I remember watching television in the middle of the night when I was a kid; the broadcast would abruptly end at four in the morning and I was left staring at a window of blinding snow, at a thousand insects killing each other.

Have you ever seen anyone make sausage? I say. They take all the nasty leftover bits of a cow or pig and grind them up until they look exactly like this.

Shut up.

Weather patterns, I say.

That large chaotic mass is your large intestine, he says. Nothing unusual.

Thanks. What about that gray area?

What gray area?

Lurking off the coast of California, I say.

Oh, that could be anything. Scar tissue or undigested cabbage.

I don't like cabbage.

And he mutters dryly, it could be a bomb.

Jesus, I say. Why can't you just lie to me like a normal doctor? Tell me it's my appendix. Tell me it's an undescended testicle or something.

Crumb has a wicked laugh. The bomb could be wired to your heart. If your heart stops, the bomb loses an electrical charge and good-bye, Phineas.

Oh, you motherfucker. Doesn't my heart stop whenever I sneeze?

Sorry, he says. I was up late last night, watching a bad spy movie.

Last night was a hundred years ago. I dreamt of Lucy last night.

I've only actually used this machine once, says Crumb. And I mistakenly told a woman she was carrying twin girls. For all I know, you have a bag of shit in there the size of my head. Or you might well be pregnant with a litter of puppies.

I feel so much better.

Latex would have surely dissolved by now, he says.

Of course. But drug smugglers are pretty imaginative these days. They may have come up with indestructible baggies made of bullet-proof Kevlar.

Well, he says. Then I suppose you can't be fucked.

twelve.

It's a short walk to Eve's place. The snow has stopped but the wind is still vicious. My shirt sticks against my skin where Crumb rubbed that foul jelly. I wiped most of it off but a fine sheen remains. I decide not to worry about the heroin. I will pretend it's another imaginary tumor. I often dream that I have a brain tumor, and in the dream, I take strange comfort in the idea that I know how I will die but not when.

But I may as well go with Jude to El Paso. I'm pitifully drawn to her, like a moth. I remember when I was seventeen; I always went running back to the girls who tore my heart out. The kidney is apparently worthless, but I can still kill Jude if I want to. But I will kill her for my own reasons. The Blister can rot.

My car still sits where Eve left it, a friendly pink parking ticket fluttering on the windshield. I climb in and start shoving things into the duffel bag. A box of ammunition, razor and toothbrush, most of my clothes. I count my money and decide to leave some of it with Eve. I might die before I spend it all.

*

Her apartment is dark and quiet, as if no one's home. I'm wondering if I can break in through a window but I try the door anyway. It's unlocked. The air smells faintly of lemons and smoke. I step inside and flick on a light. The apartment has been torn apart; clothes and papers are strewn everywhere, like garbage ripped apart by dogs. Silverware and books and toiletries lay scattered. Someone came looking for me, for something I have. Perhaps the kidney in my icebox is not so worthless. It might have been the Blister, but this isn't quite his style. He wouldn't have left a trace. The person who did this was furious, manic.

I take off my shoes and slip through the kitchen. I hold my weapon like a bird's egg. I hear my grandfather's voice: *Hold it tight, now. But don't try to crush it. Pretend she's a bird's egg.* And I told Lucy the same thing when I taught her to use my gun. First I circle through the living room to be sure. Nothing has changed and I move down the hall in silence. Stop and poke the door of the linen closet with my foot; it creaks open. Empty and I keep moving. The bathroom. Toilet and sink and clothes hamper. A window too small for an adult to pass. Push back the shower curtain and Georgia is there, naked and shivering. She is unharmed, but she looks at me with terrible eyes. Her pupils have swallowed her eyes. She looks like a tortured dog. She spits at me and I want to throttle her, to hold her head underwater until she comes out of it. But I know she's already tipped over the edge.

Eve's room, she says finally.

Walk down the hall, don't run. Remain calm and be sure no one is behind me. Push open the door to Eve's room and enter at a crouch. The gun is an extension of my arm. Eve is facedown on her bed, naked. Her wrists are bound with tape and tethered to the bed frame.

Her ankles are thrown wide apart and tied to either bedpost. She isn't moving and I smell blood. I cut the cords from her hands and feet, roll her over and there is so much tape around her face and skull I'm not sure she's breathing. Even her eyes are masked. I ease the tape away from her mouth and she gasps for air. I tell myself she's alive, she's alive. She doesn't make a sound and I hug her to me with my left arm, my back to the wall. The gun in my right hand trembles ever so slightly.

Where is he? I say.

She points at the window, the fire escape. I want to hold her but I need to examine her. I tell her I'm sorry and lay her gently down. There are bruises on her thighs and breasts and I've seen their kind before. The sheets are bloody. I know she hasn't been shot or cut but I have to check her anyway. Georgia is in the doorway, weeping.

Eve is alive, I say. She needs you.

Georgia creeps into the room as if she's moving through water. She stops crying and holds Eve to her chest like a mother with a child. There's a phone beside the bed and I call 911 for an ambulance. I bend to kiss Eve and she pulls away from me. I touch Georgia's cheek.

Listen to me, I say. You will have to talk to the police. Your attacker was unknown to you. He left the scene and you freed yourselves. I wasn't here. I was never here.

When I hear the sirens I too climb out the window. I close my eyes and listen for voices. I try to become someone else. I think of Pooh, his heavy, clumsy body. His stinking flesh and his giant hands. Pooh saw me with Eve; he followed us home. I pick up a chunk of broken cement and whirl around in a circle and finally let it go at my own car. The windshield becomes a spider's web but doesn't break and I have something to remind me of this.

The stitches in my side are screaming.

I drive with one hand. The other hand is torn between smoking a cigarette and clutching my wound to keep my guts from spilling out. The pain begins to ease and I let myself have a cigarette. I glance at my watch. I have nowhere to be until the train leaves tomorrow morning. I can take care of Pooh at my leisure. I'm not worried about finding him. He's a creature of habit. He will be thirsty. I don't believe he really has the stomach for this kind of thing and his knees will be rubber before long. And he will go somewhere familiar, somewhere comfortable. He will go to the Inferno and I will get there before he finishes his first beer. And then we will see. I have revenge to spare today; suffering that was meant for Jude will not be wasted. I will give it to him.

Late afternoon and the Inferno is empty and cold. It smells of dead fish and beer. Sick yellow sunshine filters through unwashed skylights. Two waitresses sit at the bar, bored and smoking cigarettes. They wear ill-fitting dominatrix gear: gleaming leather and vinyl and too much exposed flesh. Their faces are blank and humorless. A bartender dressed as a hunchback stands half in shadows. He is drinking a glass of milk. I circle through the bathroom and back to the bar. I don't see any sign of Pooh. I realize I'm walking like a cop. I become a junkie and force myself to walk as if I have stomach cramps. It isn't hard at all. I chew my thumb and stare at the floor. The bartender gazes at me like I'm a bug he can't be bothered to kill.

You seen Pooh, I say.

Don't think so, partner.

I need to find him. I need to find him in the worst way.

The bartender adjusts his hump and is silent. One of the women takes out black lipstick and a small mirror. She examines her face. The other one gives me a thin smile. Her eyes are blue and gentle.

You must be Christopher Robin.

I laugh like a chicken.

What's the matter with you?

I'm sick. Can't you see I'm sick.

The bartender sighs. I already mopped. I don't need any junkie regurgitating his lunch in here so why don't you get the fuck out?

There is a long silence. I scratch myself and cough. I stare mournfully at those soft blue eyes. Then turn and limp outside. I crouch down like a beggar and begin picking up wet cigarette butts.

After a minute she comes outside. I know what it's like, she says.

I'm dying here, I say.

I know, she says. And you need to get a fix. Everybody looks right through you.

It's like I'm a leper and my nose is fallin' off. How could you not notice that?

My knees buckle and I'm sinking but she catches me. Her touch is tender. She digs through her handbag and comes up with a slightly mashed chocolate bar.

Eat this. The sugar will make you feel better.

I'm afraid I'm going to laugh. I cover my face and moan as if I'm sobbing.

You're a nice person, I say.

I can tell you where Pooh lives.

The sun drifts behind a cloud and I look at her with my eyes open. She is dressed like a vampire, a cyberpunk whore. Her face is painted white. Her hair is an impossible black, almost blue. It must be synthetic. Her breasts are fake, round and plump as grapefruits. Her lips are bloated with fat taken from her ass. But her eyes are like pools of new rain. I eat the chocolate bar gratefully. I let her hold my hand and soon I am almost sorry for deceiving her.

thirteen.

My wife used to say I was a terrible liar, that it was the only time I smiled. But she was wrong; I smiled when I was telling the truth.

On a winter morning one year ago I told her, without smiling, that she wasn't dead. She was sitting on the kitchen floor, crying. And she kept saying that she was dead. She wasn't supposed to live this long and I could hear the boy still breathing in our bedroom. I caught them together and it was embarrassing. They were fully dressed watching television and their thighs were barely touching. I wanted to be furious but I wasn't.

I don't remember when she started bringing home the high school boys, but I had been aware of it for months and pretended not to be. The house was wired for sound and video. Hidden cameras in every room. I didn't intend to watch her. I had been having blackouts and long episodes of sleeplessness and I didn't trust my memory. I wanted to watch myself. I wanted to know what I was doing when I disappeared, and I found myself watching Lucy instead. She brought home boys who barely had pubic hair. She let them see her naked, the odd glimpse as she came out of the shower, the flash of a breast where her robe fell open. They hung around for the possibility of more. Lucy helped them with their homework, she combed their hair and let them watch TV in bed with her. She asked them about girls and cars and baseball. She asked them what were they afraid of, what they dreamed of, and she pretended they were her children.

I could not give her any children but sometimes I could watch myself fuck her in the middle of the night, when I was unconscious and dreaming of my former self. Her shrunken body crushed under mine, her bald head glowing like an egg.

I told her I didn't care about the boys. Lucy borrowed youth and time and strength from them, things she couldn't get from me. I told her I had problems of my own and I wanted her to be happy. I told her she wasn't dead; the doctors were wrong and she had years to live. I told her I loved her and I didn't smile, because I wanted her to believe me.

The boy in the bedroom had asthma and later I would sit in the dark and listen to his terrible wheezing on my headphones.

Pooh lives in a basement apartment. The windows are covered from within by greased wax paper. I can already imagine the smell. The door is easily forced open. There is one room plus a closet with toilet and sink. Television and mattress and refrigerator and strewn clothes. The carpet foul and stained. I squat in the center of the room and breathe his air. I gather saliva in my mouth and spit. In the refrigerator is a box of aged jelly doughnuts. I poke through his clothes and find only pennies and bits of tobacco and strands of hair. In a metal crate beside his bed are comic books. A small collection, perhaps a hundred. They are well cared for. Each is in a plastic sheath to protect it from dust and moisture and bugs. I pull out a *Spider-Man* from twenty years ago and light a cigarette.

Spider-Man is tangling with Doctor Octopus and getting the shit pounded out of him. He keeps the wisecracks coming and manages to slap a glowing spider tracer on Doc Oc's leg before he gets away. Then the cops give him a hard time and he goes to see MaryJane and she's pissed because he is two hours late and I'm thinking: She never sleeps with you anyway so why bother? Then he drags himself home and has soup and sandwiches with his feeble Aunt May before he has to go hunt down the Octopus.

Pooh followed me and Eve home from the Inferno the other night. He was stupid with drink and he wanted to do something to me. He fell asleep and when he woke up he was sober and there was bile in his mouth. He went inside. He told himself he was going to kill me but I doubt that. He just wanted to scare me, to squeeze me for some money but I was gone. Instead he found two girls naked and cuddling on the couch and he just went crazy. Pooh would certainly hate lesbians. They would offend his moral sensibilities. He screamed at them and waved the gun around and said he would cut out their tongues. Then he tied them up and preached hellfire and motherhood and how they hadn't been fucked by the right fellow. He was going to leave but one of them said something to him. He took the little one and her smart mouth back to the bedroom and stripped her down and gave her a piece of Pooh.

I gave her a piece of Pooh.

*

The washed gray light before dawn. My head rests on Pooh's pillow and I am clutching his ratty blue blanket in one hand. My clothes smell like Pooh. For a moment I think I am Pooh. I have a grim and throbbing erection and I'm sick to realize I dreamed of raping Eve. My watch says it is six A.M. and I must have slept over fifteen hours. I was underwater, unconscious. I wasn't myself. I'm confused at first because I feel good. I feel rested. I go to Pooh's little bathroom and piss in his toilet. I drink from his faucet and eat some of his toothpaste.

The *Spider-Man* comic still lays open on the bed. I glance at it once more before I leave. The pages are slightly faded and the corners are worn soft and I imagine Pooh has read this a thousand times. He washes his hands every time and is careful not to crease the pages.

I have to get out of here before I lose the taste for killing him.

I step out Pooh's front door and there is Detective Moon. He is sitting on the top step with two cups of coffee. He looks tired and cold and slightly ill. His breath is white.

I was waiting for you to come out, he says. I thought it would be less complicated than trying to explain why you're asleep in a drug dealer's bed.

Is one of those coffees for me?

No, he says. I like to have two on a day like this. But I'm willing to share.

I sit down beside him and light a cigarette, glancing at my watch. The train leaves in a little over three hours and I'm going to be on it.

I don't normally work rape cases, he says. They make my stomach hurt. But your description came up when the uniforms questioned the neighbors. A little old lady, somebody's granny. She said you climbed out the window and looked exactly like a rapist. He laughs. What does a rapist look like?

He looks like a beggar, I say. A lawyer, a thief. He looks like somebody's brother. He has a sister, a mother. He has a granny that loves him.

This particular granny watches a lot of TV. And she was hot to come in and work with a sketch artist. In about eighteen hours your happy face will land on a lot of desks.

I never wanted to be famous.

Your name is already dogshit at the station.

Listen to me, Moon. This isn't connected to that other thing. Eve is a friend of mine. I'm just trying to find the guy who did this. Once a cop, you know.

But you aren't a cop, are you? And you're looking like a bad guy.

I'm not a bad guy. I'm not.

Let's take a ride, Phineas.

I take the coffee from him and gulp half of it. It's cold and too sweet and I dump it into ashen snow, splattering Moon's feet. If he has my gun, why doesn't he just say so? I can't let him arrest me. I'm in no condition to fight, but I'm not going downtown. I will rip open my wrists with my teeth before he puts me in a cage. I don't think Moon will shoot me but you never know. I shake my head. Moon openly stares at the green icebox I hold on my lap, and I realize it's like a deformity, a third leg. Some people stare at it and others pretend it's not there.

Have you found what you were looking for? he says.

Maybe.

There's an unverified story going around, he says. Five days ago a beautiful woman with dark hair walked into an emergency room in

Colorado Springs. She wore a long white coat and she was carrying a Styrofoam ice chest. She handed the ice chest to a nurse and walked away. She disappeared. The ice chest contained a viable human kidney. It was used to save the life of a little girl in Phoenix. Some people are calling the woman an angel.

That is a terrible story. It's fucking nonsense. And it has nothing to do with me.

Moon looks to the east, at the colorless sky.

Every day, he says. The sun has to eat its way through clouds and smoke and poison.

Spare me, I say.

I danced with your wife once, he says. At the Christmas party last year. She told me you were in the bathroom and I danced with her. She said you were sick.

I close my eyes. She wore a little white dress. As smooth and tight as new skin.

Moon licks his lips and looks embarrassed. She told me her underpants were green velvet. This made me nervous and I offered to go see if you were okay. I thought you must have passed out in the toilet. She said you weren't sick from drinking. She said you were sitting in the last stall with your gun in your mouth. She said you were losing your mind and every day you put the gun in your mouth and thought about it.

She was drunk, I say. The doctors said she wasn't supposed to drink but she did.

She was dancing real close to me, says Moon. She was smiling and all I could think about were those little green panties and how it would be to slide them down around her ankles and I started to panic. I wasn't like that. I went out in the parking lot and smoked a joint with some guys from the arson squad and they said they were going to the Black Heart to shoot pool and did I want to come. I was glad to go and an hour later I was lining up the two ball in the side pocket and it hit me. That maybe you were in that bathroom about to eat your own gun and I didn't do anything about it. I didn't try to save you from yourself or even go see if you needed saving because I was too busy trying to visualize your wife's panties.

Moon looks at me. His face is miserable. A lot of guys wanted to fuck my wife. She was a terribly sexy woman. She could have fucked them, all of them. I wouldn't have blamed her. But she never did. She waited for me to touch her again. I was too busy disappearing; I woke up next to her one morning and asked her who she was. I am tempted to put my arms around Moon and tell him not to worry, but I don't. I want to know if he has my gun. I scoop up a handful of snow and pack it into a hard gray ball of ice.

I remember those panties. They smelled like eucalyptus.

She didn't want me, he says. She was dying and she wanted you to love her.

I did love her. I loved her.

The next day I waited for my phone to ring, he says. For the voice that would tell me some poor bastard from Internal Affairs had blown his brains out and isn't it a damn shame, ho ho ho.

Do you have my gun?

What fucking gun?

My registered weapon, a Browning nine millimeter. The gun that may or may not have killed Lucy. It disappeared from evidence, remember?

Is this some kind of confession?

This is a conversation. Let me put it this way. The gun disappeared from evidence and came into my possession. I had it, and now I don't have it.

I don't have your gun, Phineas.

I still have the ball of ice in my left hand. I give it to Moon and tell him to let it melt, to forget he saw me here. He doesn't say anything and I know that he will let me disappear for now. But he will search Pooh's apartment after I'm gone and he will question Eve. If he finds anything that points to me then he will forget about Lucy's green panties. He will come after me without pity.

fourteen.

I ease the little Bug into the parking lot of Jude's motel. There's a red pickup truck parked crazily, sideways. It's jacked up on fat tires with mudflaps that read: *Jesus was a U.S. Marine.* I don't like the look of this but maybe it's nothing. I'm breathing hard and the pain in my side has resumed its high-pitched whine. Moon made me nervous and my body is not well. I sit on the hood of my car to rest for a while and I find myself staring at the red truck. It's a beauty. The phallic but nervously whiplike antenna for a police scanner and the requisite gun rack above the back windshield. A small animal skull hangs from the rearview mirror. The hood is painted to resemble the American flag, with Playboy bunnies in place of stars. I can't wait to meet the owner. Then I notice the custom hood ornament: it's Winnie-the-Pooh flashing a killer smile.

He's with Jude. I don't know why I didn't think of it sooner. Of course he would run to her. I climb the stairs to room 212. Air escapes my chest as if I've been punched. I sit down on the frozen steps. I don't want to do this. I'm too tired. The taste of metal is gone from my mouth. When I saw Eve I wanted to kill him carefully. I wanted to use the tanto, to take him apart very slowly. Now I want to be done with him. I want him to walk out of room 212 with his hat in his hands and a big satisfied grin on his face. Then he will turn and see me, the gun in my hand. He will never hear the shot. And he will drop softly, like a scarecrow. The stuffing will come out of him and dogs will rise out of the snow to tear at his shoes. I feel unclean and I realize how badly I need a shave and a bath. I want to soak in painfully hot water and wrap myself in one of those thin white motel towels and lie down next to a woman. I want her to stroke my hair and whisper nonsense into my ear.

None of this happens. I sit there until I'm stiff with cold. I wonder what he's doing in there. I can't imagine Jude bothering to sleep with him. He's so clumsy and foul. Of course, she slept with me and I'm hardly a prize. I smoke two cigarettes and watch the end of the sunrise. The sky turns the color of mucus streaked with dirt. Finally I knock on the door of room 212 and Jude throws it open. She is dressed for travel; her hair is sleek and pulled back. A white silk shirt buttoned to the throat with a big French collar. Dark red lipstick but no jewelry. Black pants that cling to her hips and thighs and flare at the ankles. She's barefoot.

Are you ready? she says.

I'm looking for Pooh.

He's in the bathroom.

Her voice is flat and cold. As if she's annoyed that I look like shit and I still haven't kissed her. I hand her the icebox and smile. A gift, I say. She steps aside and I slip past her. I pull my gun and try the bathroom door. It's locked and I glance at Jude. He likes his privacy, she says.

I poke the door. Pooh. Let's go, boy. The bell tolls.

There's no answer.

When did he get here?

I don't know. Midnight, I suppose.

He's not really in there, is he?

Kick it down if you don't believe me.

She lights a cigarette, smiling. I lean against the door and look at her.

This isn't a movie, I say. Doors are not so easy to kick down.

Jude rolls her eyes and sucks at her cigarette.

I talked to the cops, I say.

Oh, really.

They don't seem to have my gun.

She smiles. That's strange.

Someone has that fucking gun.

Who are you going to believe?

The door is compressed sawdust. I stab my knife in and wiggle it until the doorknob pops. Pooh is wedged naked between the wall and the toilet. His hair is wet. His skin is pale and turning blue. He sits in a small puddle of blood. There's a wide gash on his left thigh; the femoral artery has been cut.

There's not much blood, I say.

I did it in the shower.

Why did you move him?

She drops her cigarette in the toilet. I had to wash my hair.

I sit on the edge of the tub. Pooh has a simple, placid face. The backs of his thighs and buttocks are purple with the puddle wealth of his blood. Tomorrow he will be an unclaimed corpse at the coroner's office, soon to be cut apart by bored and restless medical students.

And why did you do it?

Oh. We had a fight about money, about you.

Well, I say. I was going to kill him myself.

Why did you want to? she says.

I think he hurt someone, a friend of mine. He raped her.

She nods and her eyes slide away from mine.

I know, she says. He told me about it. He said it wasn't really rape because he didn't come.

She sits down next to me and kisses my ear, my throat.

What is her name?

Eve, I say. She's nineteen.

I'm very sorry. I know what it's like.

Merry Christmas, I say.

She isn't wearing a bra and I can't help running my hand up her shirt. I love the feel of silk. She pulls away from me and goes to the mirror. She wets her fingers and smoothes her hair. Her lipstick is smeared. She takes a tissue and wipes the rest of it away. The color has disappeared from her face. She looks sick.

My toothbrush is in my purse, she says. Will you get it?

I don't like to dig through a woman's purse. It doesn't feel right. I think of the old woman in the hospital. She was dying and thought I was her son and I stole from her. And I think of my wife. She kept secrets in her purse. Jude's is soft black leather and no bigger than my head. Still there seem to be a hundred things inside. I dump it out and find a plastic tube that holds a travel toothbrush and paste. I find a small black device, shaped like a stereo remote control. It's a stun gun, very powerful and certainly illegal. I have no choice but to confiscate it. There is also a small silver key on a ring, the kind of key that fits a padlock. I glance at the lock on the icebox and I'm surprised. The icebox contains valuable merchandise and the key would be so much safer around her neck. I believe she trusts me. How touching. I put the key in my pocket and replace everything else from her purse.

I give her the toothbrush and watch as she smears it with blue gel. She leans against the sink with her face bent forward. She brushes her teeth slowly, methodically. I look at Pooh.

What should we do with him?

She spits. Did you want to take a shower?

A bath, really.

She looks at her watch. It will have to be fast. Then we move him back into the tub and lock the door. The room is registered in his name. It might pass for suicide.

The cast is on his left arm. The cut on his left thigh is at such an angle that it could have been self-inflicted. I uncurl the fingers of his right hand. There are no defensive wounds, no signs of a struggle at all. She said she killed him in the shower, and the curtain isn't even pulled down. She would have had to spread his thighs apart and push the knife in at a difficult angle, then pull the blade up and away.

Was he asleep when you did this?

No, she says. But his eyes were closed.

Jude rinses her toothbrush. I am still kneeling behind her. She turns and stands over me and I stare up at her. The black pants fit her like a glove. My mouth is two inches from the curve of her crotch.

It was like this, I say. Wasn't it? He was in the shower and you asked if you could join him. Oh, you dirty girl. The knife behind your back. You knelt in his bathwater and took his dick in your mouth and brought the knife up when he closed his eyes.

His dick was in my hand, she says. If you must know. I wanted to cut the fucking thing off. But that would hardly pass as suicide.

And the blood came down like rain. That's why you had to wash your hair.

It was terrible. And it was glorious, too.

You're much braver than me.

She smiles, embarrassed. I take her hands and pull her down on me. We kneel before Pooh's body and grin at each other like two kids with a secret.

I fill the tub with hot water and begin to undress. Jude tells me to turn around so she can inspect my wound. The dressing Crumb gave it is filthy but holding fast. Her touch is cool and efficient.

It looks okay, she says. I want to clean it, though.

Are you a doctor?

Not exactly. I had paramedical training in the army.

Please tell me you have some painkillers.

She goes to get her medical bag and I sit naked on the toilet beside Pooh. There's a mirror on the opposite wall and I decide I look nearly as bad as he does. Jude comes back wearing surgical gloves. She gives me a shot of liquid Valium and I don't look at the needle. I think of the last time she drugged me, and I think of Prometheus. He pissed the gods off and they chained him to a rock; a bird came and ate his liver and the liver grew back while he slept. The bird returned every day, to eat his liver again and again.

I trust you, I say. I don't know why.

There is a sudden fist of warmth at the base of my spine.

Jude smiles and wipes down the wound with a damp, sterile cloth. She smears on a clear jelly that stinks of iodine and then gives me a fresh dressing.

I hate to tell you this, she says.

Am I dying?

She laughs. No, you aren't dying. But I can't let you take a bath.

The wound shouldn't get wet. These stitches are made of a soluble plastic. In ten days you can take a bath and let them dissolve.

Jude, please. I haven't had a bath in days. You must have noticed I'm getting ripe.

I like the way you smell. She grins at me. You can take a shower if you're very careful.

Oh, no. A shower is no good. Anyway I would slip on the soap and crack my skull. I just want to smell like I'm not dying.

She pulls me to my feet. If you were still in the hospital, you would be getting a sponge bath every day. From a pretty little nurse, if you were lucky.

I'm anything but lucky.

Jude spreads a few towels on the floor. She fills an ice bucket with liquid soap and warm water from the bath. I stand on the towels, naked and feeling a little foolish. I'm not crippled, I say.

She ignores me. The only sound is humming lights, the drip of water. Jude takes a washcloth and soaks it in the ice bucket. She washes my feet first, and slowly works her way up my body. Every few minutes she stops to wring out the washcloth. In the mirror she is thin and beautiful and serious. She is a priestess, preparing a corpse for burial. I think I love her and I tell myself it's the Valium. She washes my face, the blunt stubble on top of my head. When she's finished I feel a thousand times better.

Together we move Pooh to the bathtub. We both wear gloves. He's heavy, and he's not stiff yet. It's like moving a drunk. The hot water makes the blood run from his leg and the bath turns a dull shade of brown. It still doesn't look right. There's not enough blood. After a minute I pull the plug. The bloody water drains away and Pooh lies there, bloated and pale as a fish. I turn the shower on and the water hammers down. It seems insulting but more realistic. Jude puts the knife in his hand.

It's his knife, she says.

She wipes down every surface in the room. I carry her bags outside. The moon is orange and still visible. It shares the sky with a glaring sun. The sound of the shower is disturbing my Valium haze. I'm not sure why, but I leave the green icebox on the bed. It might be a show of good faith to let Jude carry it for a while.

I smoke a cigarette and after a minute Jude comes out with the icebox. She is wearing the wine-colored boots and for a second I think she's stepped in blood. The door swings shut and is locked. I want to look at the room again, to be sure we didn't forget anything. But the keys are inside. Jude left them on the bed, with Pooh's wallet. She has a dark look in her eyes.

What are you staring at? she says.

Nothing. I think it might be a nice day.

She glances at the sky. The moon is orange, she says. It's a bad sign.

I smile. Why?

The blood of a stranger will be spilled.

It's pollution, I say. It's atmospheric weirdness. The sky is toxic and it doesn't mean anything.

I'm sorry, she says. I think I'm getting my period.

I stare at her dumbly.

This isn't going to work, she says. The suicide angle.

No, I say. It doesn't matter now.

Let's go, she says. We have a train to catch.

*

I follow her across the street. She walks with one arm protecting her belly. The green icebox swings at her side and for a moment I see a small child walking on the beach with a pail full of sand.

fifteen.

The Blister was lying. Or I have decided he was. He wants me to kill
Jude, and he fed me the heroin story to give me the trembles. I don't
believe him. I don't believe him. Heroin is cheap and plentiful in
South America. No one smuggles smack from the north. It would
make as much sense to sneak a box of snow into Canada. It's funny
though. The balloon or glove or whatever it is could dissolve at any
time and fill my bloodstream with heroin, killing me like an internal
supernova. And the idea electrifies me. It calms me at the same time.
I felt this way once before, stepping out onto a dark highway and staring into the lights of oncoming traffic.

Jude sits on a bench, one arm dangling protectively over the green
icebox. She crosses her legs and asks me twice if I have any gum. Her
voice has taken on a menstrual edge. I'm distracted and I tell her I'm
going to the men's room. She says she needs gum and magazines and
tampons. She's examining her nails. I think I'm going to scream, she
says. Her face is blank. Maybe she didn't say anything. The voice came
from inside me. I can hear the blood in my ears and my fingers tingle
and for a second I think I'm going to hit her.

Don't scream, I say.

She doesn't even look up. Is something wrong?

I'm going to the men's room.

Fine, she says. Don't be long.

I pass a wall of telephones and I think of Eve. I should call her but I'm not in the mood. I would have to call the hospital and listen to static and soft jazz and a weather report as I was placed on hold. I would be transferred to her room and I would have to speak to her mother or sister or someone else before they let me speak to her. I would have to be a normal person, a friend. I would have to pretend I didn't find her naked and bloody in her own bed.

The men's room is silent. One guy stands at a urinal, his eyes cast up at the ceiling. Another bends over a sink, one side of his face white with foam. The other side is shiny and pink and he is holding his thumb against a bleeding cut. There is hair on the floor around him, a straight razor in his hand. He's disposing of a beard. Our eyes meet and I know he is on the run from someone. I shrug and close my eyes. He lifts the razor to his face. I push open the door to each stall but there's no one else. I'm sure the Blister is here somewhere, watching me. I don't care. But I would love to say hello and see that cocksure smile fade from his mouth. I would ask him why he's so afraid of little Jude. I go into the last stall and force myself to vomit. It's not hard, really. I close my eyes and think of Pooh. Dead bodies never fail. My nostrils burn but I feel better. There's a streak of blood in the toilet but I hardly notice it. I flush it away and go to wash my hands.

I stand beside the shaving man. He is bleeding in several places now and doesn't seem to mind. The blade scrapes his face in long, urgent strokes. I hold my hands under a stream of cold water until they are numb. I stare into my own face. The eyes pale and gray, like dirty ice. The sockets are sunken and black. The shaving man has one brown eye, the other a fierce blue. His lips are thick and meaty and his nose is crooked. My own beard is getting thick, blond with traces of red. The shaving man is wearing a white shirt and a blue down vest. I am wearing the black T-shirt and jeans I put on two days ago, the filthy leather jacket. The man has finished shaving, his face bright and sore. His eyes find mine in the mirror.

Are you looking at me, brother?

I'm sorry. I'm looking at myself.

He wipes his mouth. Don't take me wrong. But you look like shit, brother.

He is wearing a faded green baseball cap with the word *Crash* across the front. It looks like a lucky hat. He takes it off and a mass of dark hair falls to his shoulders. He reaches into a brown paper bag for scissors and a bottle of peroxide. My hands are starting to hurt from the cold and I turn off the water. I wipe my fingers dry against my chest. The man is cutting his hair in fistfuls.

I like that ring, he says. That gold ring.

He means my wedding ring. I never took it off after Lucy died and I don't know why. I don't think it will come off; it feels grafted there, melded to my flesh. But I'm wrong. It slides over my knuckle as if my hands are oiled. I have lost so much weight. I lift it to the light and turn it before my eyes. It is so smooth, almost unmarked. Gold is a soft metal; it should be cut and scarred by five years of marriage.

I could use it, he says. For my new identity.

Who are you?

I don't know, brother. How do you like the name Henry?

You could do worse.

That's what I'm thinking. And Henry sounds like a guy that's married.

I give him the ring without pause. He slips it on his ring finger and smiles.

It looks good, he says. I'll give you fifty bucks.

I don't need any money.

Come on. You must want something.

Jude is stalking around our luggage like a panther that hasn't had dinner. I duck out of the rest room with Henry's lucky hat pulled low over my eyes. I go to the newsstand and grab a stack of magazines: *Vogue* and *Rolling Stone, Penthouse, Sports Illustrated* and *Mother Jones*. I get sugarless bubble gum and a carton of cigarettes and a box of nontoxic superabsorbent tampons.

I return to Jude bearing these gifts. She eyes my new hat but doesn't say a word. I tear open the gum and she takes two sticks, crushing them in her mouth. In a parallel universe, I might kiss her.

What's the problem?

The train is delayed. They won't say how long.

It's Christmas Eve. Be patient.

Where did you get that ridiculous hat?

Listen, fuck you. Take a pill or something. Go wash your face.

She turns and walks away, her bootheels flashing like hammers. I like the way she walks. She takes long arrogant strides, her ass and hips swinging. She holds her head high, her shoulders back like a dancer. Everyone gets out of her way, I notice. I sit down beside the green icebox, smiling. It's been a long time since I argued pointlessly with a woman and I forgot how much fun it could be.

*

I look around. There's still no sign of the Blister and I decide not to worry about him. I flip through a magazine and smoke half a cigarette before a little girl gives me a long dirty look and points at the NO SMOKING sign. I look up and see Jude near the ticket window. She's talking to a woman with short black hair. Their faces are just inches apart and they could be fighting. They could be leaning to kiss. Jude glances my way and she knows I'm watching her. She looks furious. Her face is cold and white, her hands clenched. She whispers something to the woman and they separate. The woman with black hair looks familiar. She wears high heels, white stockings. But she walks away and I never see her face. Jude comes toward me with an expression that says *don't say a fucking word*. She sits down beside me.

Jude, I say.

Don't say a fucking word.

Who was that woman?

She was no one. She was someone I used to work with.

Not a friend, then.

No, she says. Definitely not.

Funny, I say. She looked very familiar.

Henry steps out of the bathroom, his hair bleached and wet and cut like a fright wig. His eyes linger on Jude before he turns away.

Minutes crawl past us on all fours. The Valium is wearing off and I feel a rush of clarity. I want to be sweet to Jude, to make her laugh. I show her a funny picture of a man taking a bath with a pig. She barely smiles. She takes a single tampon from the box and goes to the bathroom. She comes back silent, skulking. She tells me she hates to bleed. I take her hand and kiss it.

Sorry, she says. I'll feel better when we're on the train.

Have you ever done this before?

What? she says.

Have you ever cozied up with one of your victims?

I've never wanted to.

She puts her head in my lap and I flinch, then reach to stroke her hair. I think I'm embarrassed by her sudden affection, her trust. I'm fifteen and I don't want anyone to know she's my girlfriend.

Jude falls asleep. I hold my breath for a minute, afraid to move and wake her. I take off my jacket and fold it square. I slip it under her head and go to a pay phone. I watch Jude sleep and then look away as I dial the hospital. I turn Henry's baseball cap around backward and force a sheepish grin onto my face. I am immediately put on hold. I snap my fingers and continue to grin. Thank you, I say. I listen to elevator music for three minutes. I watch the second hand on my watch. A nurse comes on and asks if I'm a family member. I'm Frank, I say. I'm Eve's older brother. I am put on hold again.

Eve's voice is thin and tough. I don't have a brother, she says.

It's me.

Phineas. Where are you?

Are you okay?

I'm fine. They kept me overnight but I'm okay.

I'm sorry.

Will you come see me?

I can't. I wish I could.

Crumb is here, she says. He's taking care of me.

I smile and wonder what manner of equipment Crumb is stealing from Eve's room.

What about Georgia?

I don't know, she says. She's missing. She never came to the hospital with me and I don't know where she is. I'm going to kill her.

She's okay, I say. She was on a lot of drugs and she probably freaked out when the cops came. She's crashing on somebody's floor.

The necklace you gave me, she says. The black locket. It's gone.

I'm sorry. I tell myself not to be sorry, not to care. But I can't help it.

There's a woman sitting on a bench across from me. It could be the woman I saw talking to Jude. Her face is buried in a magazine. She has short, muscular legs in white stockings. A short gray dress. She crosses her legs and smoothes the nylon along one thigh with her palm. The dress slips and I see the lace of a garter. My knees weaken. My wife used to wear a garter when she was feeling like a dirty girl.

Phineas, did you hear what I said?

I close my eyes and hold them shut.

What? What did you say?

It wasn't rape.

Eve, please. Listen to me. The man who did this is dead. He's dead.

No, she says. It wasn't rape.

Okay, I say. It's okay.

This might sound crazy, she says. But sometimes I think it was a woman. A very strong woman.

I open my eyes and the woman is gone. The crossed white legs and flash of garter were an illusion. I turn to look at Jude. She still sleeps, her face innocent and dreaming and I tell myself nothing sounds crazy.

What did she look like? What color was her hair?

I'm sorry, Eve says. I don't know.

What about the police? What do they think?

They think I'm in shock and I'm nineteen. They think I'm a lesbian. I love the cops.

They asked me a thousand questions about you, she says.

And Georgia is missing, I say.

It was Georgia, she says.

I don't say a word. I watch Jude sleep. I can hear Eve breathing. I tell her to lock her doors, to be careful of strangers. I tell her I can't talk anymore.

The phone buzzes in my hand. I hang up and call the hospital again. I ask for the emergency room and I am put on hold. The same void. The same churning in my belly. I watch Jude sleep and finally a sexless voice comes on the line. Emergency room. Can I help you?

I need to speak with Rose.

I'm sorry. The voice coughs, or chokes. Rose?

Rose White. She's an intern. A student.

Perhaps you would like to leave a message.

Perhaps perhaps perhaps.

Excuse me, sir?

I want to speak with her.

Hold on. And papers rattle. A metallic whine and other voices distorted, underwater. A male voice comes on the line, suspicious and cold. He asks me to identify myself.

I know who I am. Who are you?

The voice hesitates, then tells me that there is no one in the emergency room named Rose White.

I'm hearing things. The ticket clerk chews a breath mint and I hear the delicate crunch of teeth against bone. A boy with gold hair is tossing pennies at a wax paper cup and the coins ring against the floor like high heels. An old woman with pale, stretched cheeks has sewage in her lungs and every time she takes a breath, I can hear the liquid rattle in her chest. I didn't have the wrong address when I went to the little Hobbit house to meet Rose. The Blister got there before me with a crew of federal agents dressed up like exterminators and plumbers. She opened the door with a trusting smile and they swarmed inside and devoured her. They drugged her and rolled her up in a faded Turkish rug that she found at a flea market for a real bargain and stuffed her into an unmarked white van. Then they emptied her house and surgically erased all evidence of her existence. They left the FOR SALE sign in her yard and sent the real estate agent along to deal with me.

The phone is buzzing, disconnected. I say thank you and feel myself slinking. I sit down with my back against the wall and watch Jude sleep. I close my eyes and see a brightly colored beach ball, kicked and punched and abused by sunburned drunks until it is nearly ragged, deflated. Soon the ball is pulled high by the wind and allowed to drift for a while.

I feed my last quarter into the machine and dial Moon.

He grunts, hello. And I try to sound casual, uninterested. I ask him to look into the disappearance of a young woman named Rose White.

Are you kidding.

I am silent for a long time and Moon asks if I'm okay.

It's important, I say.

Moon wants to know where I'm calling from and I hang up on him.

sixteen.

The sound of metal against metal. The train doesn't move. Jude sits with her eyes closed and her gloved fingers pressed to her temples. It's been thirty minutes since they allowed us to board and nothing is happening. I sit across from her and I see a woman in a ski mask with her fist between Eve's thighs. I wonder when the bar will open. A tall glass of vodka with ice might empty my head. I was drinking the very same thing the night I met Jude.

Why did you choose me? I say.

Her eyes become green slits. What?

At the hotel. Why me and not the bald guy with the gold watch? The midget with bad teeth or the transvestite behind door number three?

Jude smiles and I realize that my feelings will be hurt if it was pure chance. She removes one glove and bites the edge of her fingers. The tip of her tongue, fleshy and pink.

Don't be offended, she says. But you were an easy target. You were weak and disoriented and I knew you were the one as soon as I saw you.

It was fate, then.

Did you think it was your smile? Your sexy blue eyes, maybe.

Maybe.

I slide down in my seat and stare at her until a bright red dot appears
between her eyes. I close my eyes and I still see the dot. I tell myself I
will put the bullet there, when the time comes. I will kill her. I will kill
her. But I'm such a liar.

I was wondering about Pooh, I say.
    What about him?
    Before you killed him. What did he say, exactly?
    Jude removes the other glove and looks at her watch.
    We should be leaving soon.

I cross the compartment to sit beside her. I slip my left hand between
her narrow thighs and stroke her with my middle finger. The black
pants are so tight. The heat from her body is intense and I remember
she's menstruating.

What did Pooh say? I'm just curious.
    Jude moves her hips against my hand. It wasn't rape, she says.
    Her breath is quick and I wonder if she's even wearing panties.
    Pooh was never there. It was a woman, I whisper.
    Oh, that's nonsense.
    She is surging against my hand. I feel sick. I think I might come
in my own pants.
    I heard a rumor, I say. A sexy bit of gossip. An angel walked into
a hospital in Colorado Springs and turned in a lost kidney. It was
used to save a little boy.
    Don't believe it, she says. Don't.
    I pull my hand away and wipe it across my jeans. Jude lets her
head sink back against the foam cushion. Her face and throat are

flushed, her hands limp as sleeping birds.

Why did you choose me. Why?

There's a knock at the door and the train begins to move.

A young black guy in a stiff blue suit. Tickets, please.

I give him the tickets and ask for directions to the lounge car.

Jude doesn't want a drink. She takes her boots off and unbuttons her blouse. Her bra is red lace and again I see blood when I look at her. And something else catches my eye; around her neck is a small, tear-shaped black locket that I've seen before. Pooh took it from Eve as a souvenir, a trophy. And Jude took it away from him. I wonder just how stupid she thinks I am. I place my hands on the sides of my head to keep it from spinning off. I'm ten years old and I'm soaking wet. I'm standing in the rain and I refuse to believe that the sun isn't shin-ing. Look around, I say. It's coming down in fucking ropes.

What are you talking about? she says.

Nothing.

I have a headache, she says.

Lucy used to have awful headaches. She would go blind. There was nothing I could do for her and I hated her for it. I go to the sink and soak a washcloth in cold water.

Jude drapes it over her eyes and says thank you.

I want to kiss you, I say.

You stink of guilt, she says.

The lounge car has curved windows, like bubbles in the roof. The sky is blank. I take a seat at the bar and ask for vodka with orange juice. I figure the vitamins will be good for me. The bartender is at least a hundred years old and he pours my drink with trembling hands.

*

Henry takes a seat on the stool next to me. I barely recognize him. His ragged white hair is slicked back with gel that looks hard to the touch. He is dressed in a charcoal gray suit, with a crisp white shirt and black tie. My wedding ring winks at me from his creased and sun-hardened left hand.

He smiles. Greetings, brother.

Henry, I say. Care for a drink?

It's too early for me. Coffee, he says.

I didn't know you were taking the train.

Didn't I mention it?

I gaze at the pale orange drink before me and I remember Jude's strange lament. *The blood of a stranger must be spilled.* The bartender places a cup and saucer on the bar and pours the coffee without spilling a drop. I watch Henry dump several packets of sugar into his cup but no cream.

No, I say. I don't think you did.

Oh, well. It is the only way to travel. Unless you're in a hurry, that is.

The stranger could be anyone. It could be me.

In the mirror behind the bar I see Jude. She lies on a narrow bed in our compartment, black silk legs bent like a grasshopper. She is hot and has taken off her shirt. One red bra strap falls from her shoulder. She lazily flips through a magazine. She unbends her legs and rests her bare feet on the green icebox that contains my kidney. Shouldn't we hurry, I say. Before the ice melts.

She smiles at me. Oh, please. Don't worry so much.

Henry is looking at me, amused. Do you always talk to yourself?

My teeth are chattering and I sip my drink. There's no kidney in that icebox. It's money or a bomb or a sock full of dirt. I should wait until she falls asleep and have a look. I do have the key. But if it is my kidney I might fuck it up by exposing it to the world. And if it's a bomb, then Jude is a liar and I will have to kill her. I don't want to kill her. I have loved two women and one of them is already dead.

Not always, I say.

Henry finishes his coffee and runs one hand through his stiff, plastic hair.

How is your new identity working out? I say.

He smiles. It's not bad, brother. There's a truckload of details to consider, though. What's my favorite color, my birthday. What do I eat for breakfast and how do I take my coffee. Where am I from and all that shit. My wife's name and what does she look like. Speaking of which. I saw that little tiger lily you're with and riddle me this, is she as mean as she looks?

I smile. She's mean, I say. I turned my back on her once and she cut me open.

Henry laughs. The best woman is like a gun.

Henry is a good actor. He could talk trash and tell lies about women and baseball and money with anybody. I want to tell him it's unnecessary but something stops me. I don't trust him yet. After a while he stands up and pulls out a silver clip fat with new money. He drops a few bills on the bar and says he will see me later. I watch him walk away and I wonder who he's running from.

Jude is exactly as I imagined. Mostly naked and reading a magazine. The green icebox beneath one bare foot. I bend and kiss her toes and listen but the icebox isn't ticking.

Your face is sweating, she says. Is it the pain?

I sit down across from her and look out the window. The train is going west, chasing the sun.

Jude, I say. The bartender told me this train is going to Los Angeles.

That's right. Then we take another train down to El Paso.

She goes back to her magazine. She licks her finger and turns the pages slowly. They crackle with alarming volume. Everywhere I look there's a sign that says NO SMOKING. I stare at the green icebox that may or may not contain a piece of me. The key is in my pants pocket. But I am no closer to opening the icebox than I was yesterday. Nothing good would come of such a betrayal. Something would only perish. My flesh, my strange feelings for Jude.

It seems like a roundabout way to get there. We could have rented a car and gotten there tonight.

What's the rush? she says. Relax. This is like a honeymoon.

You're a scream. Isn't our merchandise perishable?

Oh, that. Listen to me. That is no ordinary icebox. The kidney is vacuum-sealed and encased in a brick of dry ice. You could thaw it next summer and it would be as good as new.

Beautiful.

Your teeth are chattering, she says.

My head is floating on warm black water like a dirty life vest.

That note you left me at the hotel, I say. Why did you want to see me?

I don't know, she says. I was feeling daffy and I thought I might give you your kidney back. But then I changed my mind. The money was more tempting.

You. You are such a good liar.

I did give it back to you. Eventually.

No. I took it from you.

Irrelevant, isn't it?

I wrap my arms around my belly, suddenly cold. The pain is very bad, I say.

Jude smiles and reaches for her medical gear. I watch her prepare a hypo with the liquid Valium. She holds it to the light and I see it's a lovely gold color. Jude crosses the compartment and straddles my clenched knees. A length of rubber tube between her teeth like a rose. Give me your arm, she says.

I bare my left arm and I think of dogs. When a dog meets another dog in the park, the weaker dog rolls over and exposes his genitals, his naked belly. The stronger dog can rip open his belly and eat his genitals if he chooses. The weaker dog trusts him not to do so. Jude ties off my arm with the rubber tube and quickly finds a fat blue vein. The shot spreads through me, cold and then warm and I'm at the edge of dream and sleep. I feel myself slipping but I want to stay awake and still dream. Every sound and smell is hazy and somehow clarified and Jude's dark yellow skin is hot and porous and unstable as dry sand. I kiss and lick greedily at her breasts and fumble with the straps of her bra and my mouth is wet and I realize I'm weeping. Jude ties my wrists together with the rubber tube and pushes me back against the seat and I think oh I'm going to like this but she whispers hush, hush. She strokes my hair until I fall asleep.

seventeen.

And it's possible that I followed Rose home that night. She dropped
me off at the Hotel Peacock and I watched her drive away. I hailed a
cab and said with a crooked smile, follow that car. It was a long silent
drive, snowflakes hypnotically rushing at the headlights. Her little red
truck pulled into a curved driveway and disappeared behind snow-
covered bushes. The address was 1013 Alpine, a red and white house
with a round front door. I told the driver to stop. I gave him fifty dollars and asked him to forget he ever saw me. I walked up to her door,
weak from blood loss but alive with the rush and promise of her. Rose
opened the door and she wasn't surprised to see me. Her red hair was
pulled back into a ponytail, and her lips were wet, as if she had been
washing her face when the doorbell rang. She wore faded green and
black pajamas; the shirt was missing two buttons and her belly
showed white. She pulled the door open and I limped past her and I
smiled when I saw the cat. He was a fat bastard, gray and black with
Persian blood. He lounged in a windowsill and regarded me with dis-
dain. Rose said his name was Castro. I took a seat on the couch and it
felt very good to sink into the soft cushions; I became weightless for
a moment. Rose asked if I was hungry and I said I would love some

ice cream. She smiled and disappeared. I opened my suitcase and took out the 9mm; I touched my lips to the silent metal and asked the gods for luck and forgiveness. I slipped the gun between two pillows as Rose returned. She had a gallon of cookie dough ice cream and two spoons. We passed the ice cream back and forth and shared our spoons and watched the evening news without sound. I wanted to kiss her, to taste her mouth and it was hopeless. I wondered if she would feel my pain at all and slowly pulled the gun from the pillows.

I hear voices but I'm blind. Something soft and translucent covers my eyes and I try to remove it but my wrists are still bound. Jude is talking to someone, another woman. Jude is so cold. She measures her words like spoonfuls of salt. The other woman is asking for something. She is almost begging but not quite. There's too much hate in her voice, liquid and untouchable as mercury. The voice is familiar.

I never went to the little Hobbit house and chatted with any real estate agent about copper plumbing and afternoon light and a lovely baby's room. That was a false memory. That was something Lucy did. When she was trying to get pregnant she often went looking at houses and station wagons and patio furniture. Lucy must have told me about that little house with the gargoyle birdbath. I was never there. I was at Eve's apartment that day; I wore a black ski mask and I climbed the fire escape like a monkey. I pushed open her window and found her in bed with Georgia. They were so graceful together, so sweet. And I knew I wouldn't need my gun. I pulled Georgia from Eve's arms and pressed my knife to her throat. I gave her the duct tape and watched, impatient and hot, as Georgia fumbled with the tape. She was furious, breathing through her teeth as she taped Eve's hands and feet together. I was sick with desire. Georgia came at me spitting and slashing; she was very strong and finally I punched her in the throat. She dropped to the floor, gasping. I dragged her to the bathroom and shoved a rag in her mouth. I hoped she would suffocate because I couldn't bear to kill her. I went back to Eve's room and took off my pants. She lay silent, waiting. I cut the tape from her feet and rolled her onto her belly.

I wake again and my hands are free. The cloth covering my face is a red gauze scarf of Jude's. It smells of honey and dirt. I sit up and flex my hands. The compartment is empty. The green icebox and Jude's black bag are gone. I am terribly thirsty, as if my tongue were cut out and replaced by a chunk of rotten wood. I go to the sink and fill my belly with tepid, sterile water. I splash my face and take a look in the mirror and I see that my reflection is misproportioned, its movements unrelated to my own. If I concentrate I might appear normal. I examine my teeth, blunt and white and all present. I stroke my beard and consider shaving it but I decide it makes me look less gaunt and malnourished. My hair is growing back, blond and fine. I wet my hands and slick it back. I change into a clean shirt and go to look for Jude.

Pooh was easy to kill. I found him asleep in his truck, parked in a hump of snow outside Jude's motel room. It was five in the morning and the sky was turning a dreamy pink. Pooh lay across the front seat like a dead cow. The windows bright with long cracked fingers of ice. I climbed into the truck and checked his pulse; it was steady as a clock. I unfastened his belt and pulled his filthy jeans down around his ankles. He woke up then, snarling and grunting at me. I pulled him into the parking lot and he tried to fight but his own tangled jeans pulled him down. I kicked him in the head, the belly, until my legs were sore and my feet heavy as stones. He was unconscious. I stripped the rest of his clothes off and buried my knife in his thigh.

There is some difficulty walking. My legs are strangely distant, removed from my nervous system. The floor appears to move but doesn't. I fall to my knees and laugh at myself. Perhaps I'm thinking about it too much. I stare straight ahead and walk. I pass a smoke lounge and duck inside and the air is literally blue. I try to make out faces but there are only eyes and disembodied mouths, fingers and wristwatches and burning stubs. I smoke two cigarettes and slip away gasping.

I killed Lucy, of course. And that made everything else possible. I killed her in the boat. I waited until she was drunk and her words fell apart in her mouth. The sun was behind a cloud when I shot her, and the first bullet took her face apart. She was still alive, breathing through shredded nostrils. One eyes was dark with blood and extraordinarily calm. I put the gun just above her ear and shot her again. I was half naked and a little drunk myself. The water pulled me over the edge of the boat and I let myself sink. The gun so heavy but I couldn't let it go. I swam back to the boat and climbed in, nearly tipping it over. She already stank, and the flies were terrible. I put the gun in her hand and swam ashore; I had a knife and nothing else. I don't know when her body was found. For ten days I was incoherent. I drank rainwater that pooled among rocks. I ate dandelions and chewed on the bark of a young ash. I chased my shadow like a dog. I made another cut in my arm at each sunset; I was slowly bleeding myself to death. When the state troopers found me, my tongue was swollen to the size of my fist. I couldn't speak for days.

Children stare at me. Their mothers and fathers are discreet and look away, smiling. I bite my lip until it bleeds and I'm surely awake this time. I seem to walk for miles and then I pass through a doorway into the dining car. White tablecloths and cheap silverware and plastic flowers in blue vases. The smell of chicken and rosemary. A woman drinks iced tea with a bright twist of lemon and I have an urge to take it from her hands and pour it over my face. A man in a white jacket moves to intercept me. He holds a menu in one hand and his fingers are long and so white I think he's wearing gloves, but his fingernails are sharp and yellow as bone.

Pardon me, sir. This dining car is for first-class passengers only.

Yes, I say. Of course. What does that mean?

He sighs. Are you traveling by coach or in a private compartment?

In a compartment. A box.

I see. And the number?

I'm not hungry. I just want some of that iced tea.

He smiles and shows me a mouthful of teeth. I'm glad he finds this amusing and I'm about to say so when Jude steps forward, a white napkin in her left hand.

Hello, I say.

This is my husband, she says. He's easily confused, that's all.

The man mutters his apologies and offers me a menu. I smile with lips that feel drained of blood.

I want some of that iced tea.

Of course, sir. He bites each word.

Jude takes my hand. Come on, dear. I have already ordered for you.

She leads me like a donkey. I follow and practice my smile. It doesn't feel right and I want to ask her what she thinks. What's wrong with you? she says.

Nothing's wrong. A bit high.

You must be joking. If there had been a security guard on this car I think he would have shot you.

Why? I'm wearing a clean shirt. I have a nice smile.

You were leaning over that woman like you might rip out her throat.

The woman with the tea. I look back over my shoulder and she is pale as a ghost. Her husband is consoling her and the waiter is bringing a tray of complimentary pies.

Jude stops at our booth and I turn to see that we are not dining alone.

Now be nice, she whispers.

eighteen.

Sometimes there is nothing so horrible as a familiar face. The woman at Jude's table, however, is a mutant. She's two or three women at once. I see the woman from the train station. The same black high heels and white lace garter belt. A short wool dress the color of a cloudy day. Her hair is short as a young boy's and black. She touches a napkin to her mouth and it comes away marked with red lipstick. She looks like an elf, a woodland fairy. I see the sweet young medical student from the emergency room. Rose White. She had bright red hair and pale white skin, I'm sure. I try to summon her face but I see only ashes. The hair and clothes are exactly like my dead wife's. But she isn't Lucy. She smiles across the table.

Phineas, says Jude. This is Isabel, someone I used to know. I haven't seen her in years and then today I run into her on a train. Isn't it a small world?

I sit down across from Isabel and take a sip of water. Jude's medical bag dangles from a hook on the wall; the green icebox is nowhere to be seen. Jude is busily composing her face. I look under the table and between her legs. I look over my shoulder and under the butter dish.

Jude. Where is the icebox?

She bites my ear and whispers for me to shut up.

Isabel is preening herself. She touches up her lipstick, her bloody mouth. She frowns at her nose and snaps shut a compact mirror. I stare at her hair and wonder if it's a wig. If I try to pull it off and it's real there might be a lot of excitement and confusion. The waiter brings my iced tea on a silver dish.

Isabel grins at me. It's very nice to meet you, Phineas.

I lift my glass and I can feel Jude watching me. Her fingers dance along my thigh.

It's a pleasure, I say.

Isabel takes a roll from the bread basket and daintily smears it with butter. She tears off a small piece and it disappears between her teeth. She chews silently and swallows.

Oh, she says. I almost forgot. Congratulations.

I chew a piece of ice. For what?

Jude tells me you just got married.

That's right. We just ran off like a couple of kids.

It must be nice, she says. To be in love.

Love is a reptile, I say. Don't you think? If you cut off its tail it grows another one.

I stare at Isabel without blinking. I stare until I can see the pale roots of her natural hair and the expensive skin cream that changed her skin from milk to olive and the colored lenses that gave her yellow eyes and I wonder how she changed her breasts and ass and shortened her legs. I stare at her until her eyes are pointed and her teeth glitter like fangs and I have to close my eyes. If she said her name was Lucy and she faked her death I would believe her.

Jude pokes me and asks if I want chicken or beef.

Isabel shifts in her seat.

Chicken, I say.

Why are you staring at me? says Isabel.

Because you have an unusual face. Did anyone ever say that you look exactly like someone else?

She frowns. Of course.

Phineas, says Jude.

But you look like two or three people at once. Isn't that funny?

Phineas, says Jude.

What?

Let go of the glass, she says. Let go.

I look down and the iced tea glass in my hand is cracked. A brown stain is forming on the tablecloth as tea and melted ice drip from my wrist. I let go and the glass falls apart. Two busboys appear and whisk away the tablecloth and everything on it.

Are you bleeding? Jude says. Her voice sounds funny, as if it's about to come apart like the glass. I look at her closely and I see how red her eyes are, how colorless her lips. She looks like she wants to throw up. I lift my dripping hand so she can see there's no blood.

I'm sorry.

I notice you aren't wearing a wedding ring, says Isabel.

Jude shrugs. She opens her mouth and someone starts to laugh.

Well, brother. I thought I might find you here.

Henry is standing over us and the sun is coming through the window behind him. His face is completely obscured by shadow. His laugh is thick and lecherous. He sits down next to Isabel and offers her his hand. I'm Henry, he says. Phineas and I are associates. Which one of you is his beautiful wife?

With the slightest shudder of her thin shoulders, Jude asks Isabel and

Henry to join us in our compartment for a drink. Henry grins so wide I can see the metal in his teeth. As we leave the dining car, Isabel asks us to excuse her; there's a phone call she must make. Jude narrows her eyes and says that will be fine.

My stomach hurts and I realize that I'm starving. I never touched my chicken.

The drugs have faded and I am aware of my body again. Henry bows and offers to escort Isabel to her compartment. The train enters a tunnel and I automatically close my eyes. Everything is pink and I see shadow images. I open my eyes and see Henry leaning to whisper at Jude's ear. His hand on her shoulder as if he's pressing her down. She nods and says something, her lips barely moving. Henry winks at me and hurries to catch up with Isabel.

I grab Jude by the wrist and I feel the electricity in her. She's full of juice.

What did he say?

She pushes me into a vacant bathroom the size of a coffin. I pull her close to me and it's the first time I've held her without thinking of sex or violence.

His name isn't Henry, she says.

I know. It's his new identity.

How do you know him?

From the station. He gave me the lucky hat.

Jude rolls her eyes. Who the fuck is he?

He's no one. He's a drifter. An escaped convict.

No, she says. He's more than that.

What about Isabel? Don't tell me she was your college roommate.

She kisses me quickly. Let's go. I want to be ready for them.

A cocktail party, I say. What were you thinking?

She shakes her head. It's a game. Isabel wants to play and I'm going to let her.

I've met her before, you know.

Jude turns pale. What?

She was at the hospital. She was a medical student, a nurse. But she was different. She had red hair and pale skin and she was thinner, with kind of a flat chest. She gave me a ride. She gave me her phone number.

Jude doesn't say anything. There is a trace of embarrassment in her eyes, as if I have just described an imaginary friend and she doesn't have the heart to tell me that my friend isn't real.

Her name was Rose White, I say.

Rose White. What a delicious name.

I close my eyes and try to remember. I was in shock and I was drugged and she was fucking real. I'm sure of it. But I hesitate to tell Jude that this person has transformed into the body of my dead wife.

Don't worry about it, Jude says. It doesn't matter what you saw or thought you saw. She's here and we have to deal with her.

Why don't you tell me who she is?

Isabel is my partner, she says. We do the organ routine together, like a dance. We choose a target, someone that's on the edge. Someone that just stepped out of prison or rehab, someone still blinded by the sun and confused as a newborn. She seduces the target and I do the surgery. But we had a little fight about money, and I split. I decided to try a solo run, and I chose you. Is that what you want to hear?

You bitch, I whisper.

Jude smiles and touches my cheek. Oh, dear. Are you hearing

voices again?

The fuck.

I will tell you the truth, she says. Soon.

I follow Jude back down the narrow passageway. It is completely unfamiliar and I shake my head. I did just come this way. Jude stops in the lounge and I think yes, a drink is a good idea. I wait behind her like a shadow, obedient and uninformed. She briskly tells the bartender that she wants to buy a bottle of mescal. He says, oh I'm sorry miss. No alcohol leaves the lounge. Jude hits him with a charge of animal heat; she gives him bottomless eyes and hard nipples, a voice like bone marrow and a palmed fifty. The old man rolls over panting. He provides a sack of limes and a shaker of salt. Jude thanks him, twirling a shot glass on her finger.

I crack the seal on the bottle before we reach our compartment. I ask her again where the icebox is. She tells me not to worry and takes the bottle from me.

Take it easy, she says. I don't want you to get stupid.

I am stupid. I am the foolishness of flesh. Drinking gives me charm and texture.

She laughs and begins to straighten the tiny living area. She unfolds one bed.

The icebox, I say.

Jude points to a locked closet. It's safe, okay?

I take another drink from the bottle and decide she might be right; I don't need to get drunk. I am already blindfolded. I have no control, no focus. The icebox is all I can think of, but I can't bear to open it, to look inside. The kidney is a chunk of repressed memory, buried deep and crushed by heavy earth. I'm unraveling and I'm soft inside. I need to be sharp. I need to be cruel. Jude is undressing. Her body is terribly distracting and I am tempted to take her from behind in a sudden, staggering rush. I loosen my belt.

She gives me her cool stare. I don't think so, she says.

I watch her change into pale silver pajamas; the material is sheer and clings to her and the effect is maddening. I assume that's what she intended. She reclines on the bed.

Why did you tell them we were married? I say.

Instinct, she says. Off the top of my head.

I like the sound of it.

Please. Don't get misty on me.

This train stops in Vegas. We could be married in an hour.

She sighs and reaches for a magazine. The drugs are talking, she says.

I'm going to get some air, I say.

nineteen.

I stand in the passageway and try to meditate, to clear my head. I concentrate on the train beneath my feet. The constant motion, the plunge. The barely perceptible clicking of the tracks, rapid as a terrified pulse.

Henry and Isabel come toward me, their arms entwined. They have become fast friends, I see. Isabel has changed clothes. She wears a slinky black thing that might be called a dress. It might be a nightgown. She is certainly naked beneath it. I can feel blood swelling in my face and I open my mouth to tell Henry to get his hands off my wife. I laugh abruptly, grinning. I hold out my hand and Isabel looks at it with shiny contempt.

Henry laughs. Hello, brother. Why are you lurking here in the hall? You look as nervous as a thief. Or did the wife send you out for a gallon of milk?

Jude is inside, I say. I would like to speak with Isabel alone.

Certainly, he says. He kisses Isabel on the wrist and says, she is yours.

He disappears inside and I hear Jude tell him to sit down, to make himself at home. I take Isabel by the wrist, the same wrist kissed by Henry, and I imagine I can feel the warmth of his lips. I press her small bones between my thumb and fingers. She doesn't resist. She barely seems to notice me. I pull her along to a section of coach. There are two empty seats and I tell her to sit down.

What is your name?

How feeble your memory is. My name is Isabel.

Are you sure? I can call you Rose if you like.

I don't know what you mean. She carefully removes my hand from her arm and rubs the skin, but there is already a bluish mark in the shape of my thumb. I'm enjoying this. I can feel it in my teeth, like I have just bitten aluminum. This is silly, I say. I take long whistling breaths.

Yes, it is. And really unnecessary. If you are interested in me, just say so.

What?

You want to sleep with me.

Is that what you think?

It's obvious. And charming, of course. But at the moment I'm rather more attracted to your friend.

Henry? He's not really my friend.

Oh, really? That's your loss, I'm sure.

I look at her full, pouting lips. She doesn't talk quite like Rose; her voice is too bitter and jagged. And she doesn't really look like Lucy. I stare at the line of her jaw, searching for evidence of makeup. An artificial tan, a bronze cream. There is nothing to see. Her small ears, her silky black hair. The heavy, round breasts. A slight tummy and hard, muscular legs.

You look nothing like the girl I remember.

And which girl do you remember, she says.

The one at the hospital. She gave me a ride to my hotel. Then on the telephone. I told her my life story and she gave me the wrong address. We had a date.

I'm sorry, she says. I'm sure I don't know who you're talking about. And you seem to be a very confused person. Delusional, I suppose. I have never seen you before today.

I do love your hair.

She smiles and cocks her head like a curious bird. I stroke a soft black wisp behind her ear, then tug it gently between my thumb and finger. It feels real.

I'm glad you like it, she says.

Oh, yes. You look exactly like Lucy, my dead wife.

Isabel presses her lips together and her face becomes pale and gaunt.

I hope so, she whispers. Jude designed me to look like her, to become her.

I could kill you.

She sighs. I didn't really care for the idea, at first.

I could kill you a thousand times.

But I played along and I really think it's a smash, don't you?

She leans forward, smiling richly. Her teeth are long and curved and there is a bright trickle of sweat down her left cheek. I'm sure it would taste like ashes.

It's perfect, I say. My head suddenly feels like it has been disconnected.

I touch the thin slip of her dress. The material feels like it might melt between my fingers. Her white thigh is smooth as porcelain and I pull my hand away.

What is most precious to you? she says.

Nothing, I say. My arms and legs.

Do you have any brothers and sisters? she says.

I have a little brother. But I haven't heard from him in five or six years.

He could be dead, she says.

He's not dead.

Isabel makes a soft clucking sound, like a hen. Did you adore him? she says.

Not really. I tolerated him most of the time.

Did you protect him?

He was my brother, I say. I periodically beat the crap out of him. But if I had a candy bar or a few dollars, I gave him half.

Then you understand, she says.

No, I don't.

What was his name? she says.

Fuck you.

I have a brother, she says. He's seventeen. He's made of glass. If I could hold him in the palm of my hand or keep him safe in my pocket, I would.

Who are you?

She sighs. It doesn't matter.

But you have seen me before, haven't you?

I chose you, she says.

No, I say. Jude chose me.

Jude preys on thieves, she says. On prostitutes and drug addicts.

I'm a drug addict.

She shakes her head. You are only confused.

Did you come to steal me away from Jude?

I came to watch over you, she says.

Like an angel.

Jude is very dangerous, says Isabel. She is not what she seems.

No one is.

Even so. You would be much safer traveling with me.

Isabel takes my hand and pushes it into the soft fold of her crotch. I suck in my breath and beg Jude to forgive me. I want to kiss this stranger, to see if her mouth is like Lucy's.

My brother's name is Everson, I say. Everson Poe.

I feel sorry for you, she says.

Why?

Your brother could be dead and you feel nothing.

My brother is in Africa. He wanders.

Isabel leans close, her lips dark and bursting with blood. I kiss her hard enough to bruise and I don't feel anything but dead skin and elusive shame.

You're not real, are you? I'm dreaming again.

She shrugs and pushes past me.

Come on, she says. They are waiting for us.

Henry juggles limes with little success. His chest is brown and smooth as stone. Isabel kicks off her shoes and crouches on the floor. The thin black dress is impossibly short; she is naked to the hip. She drops one hand between her thighs to hide her crotch, to touch herself. Limes roll in every direction and I crouch and begin to gather them. I try not to look at Isabel but I can't help it. I can't take my eyes off her.

Throw me one of those limes, brother. Don't be shy.

I flip a lime at Henry.

Now where the Christ is that bottle?

Jude takes a long drink and comes to kiss me, her mouth hot with mescal. I bite her softly and suck the breath from her and I am still hungry.

I don't like your friend.

He's harmless.

Look at him. He's a shark.

It's too late, I'm afraid.

Henry lies back on the floor and dumps salt on his slick belly. He tucks a chunk of lime between his teeth, the pale flesh outward. Isabel bends to lick the salt from his belly and drinks long from the bottle, then chews the lime in his mouth. Yellow liquor and juice run down their throats.

Henry gives me a brutal smile.

I kneel beside Isabel and crush half a lime in my fist; the juice gathers in the hollow of her throat. I lick the salt between her breasts and drink, then lick and bite at her soft throat. She laughs as if it tickles, as if we are dear friends.

Does it feel good?

It's like a fish, nibbling at me.

I look at you and I see a dead woman.

What a thing to say.

Isabel wraps her strong bare thighs around me and shrugs and suddenly I am on my back. I'm a specimen, a corpse beneath her. She bends to kiss my throat and my penis swells terribly.

Jude is silent, she's invisible.

Isabel pulls up my shirt and exposes my belly, my wound. I feel a hot, wet trickle like blood or tears and I think she's cut herself, she's menstruating and I remember Lucy saying that she and her sister were forever bleeding on the same cycle. But this isn't blood, it's urine. Jude drags her away from me, a fistful of Isabel's hair in her left hand. Their faces are almost touching.

Oh, you fucking coward.

Are you a woman or a dog?

You should be careful where you sleep.

And you should never have fucked me.

Isabel pulls off her torn dress and sits naked on the other bed. She licks salt from her hand and I see her sitting across from me at the waffle house, slowly licking whipped cream from her finger.

You have beautiful hands, I say.

She holds out her hands, grinning. Her left hand bears the hourglass birthmark. I take a drink and the worm slips between my teeth. I chew it, tasting dirt.

twenty.

Sleep is black and lifeless for me. I edge to the surface and try to dream of Lucy but nothing comes. I take myself back to a bright, hot morning. The lake is shaped like a horse's head. I rent a flat-bottom boat from a toothless, shirtless man who wears striped suspenders to hold up his pants. Lucy wears a red bikini top and short cutoff army pants that barely cover her skeletal ass. She wears a baseball cap to keep her hair from blowing away. The boat has an ancient motor; it wheezes and dies again and again as we cross the lake. There is no wind. My gun is sealed in a plastic bag to keep it dry. It sits in the bottom of a Styrofoam cooler with sandwiches and fruit and cheese. I'm going to teach her to shoot. The motor dies again and I can't get it to roll over. There are no paddles and the boat begins to drift. I curse the toothless man. Lucy takes off her bikini top to get some sun on her breasts. I open a bottle of wine and drink. The boat drifts under the staring sun. I tell Lucy to be careful she doesn't burn. She doesn't answer and I think she's asleep. The boat drifts and time is elastic. The bottle is empty. I take off my shirt and use it to cover Lucy. She's turning red now and I check the pockets of my shorts. I have a knife and nothing else. No identification. I slip over the side of the boat.

Jude is curled and silent beside me, her face pressed against my ribs.

Whoa, girl. Take it easy, now.

Jude sits naked on Henry's chest, she throws his face back with her left hand and her little stinger barely touches his exposed throat. I never heard her move. She's a cat.

What are you looking for? she whispers.

My cigarette lighter. It's nickel-plated and I'd hate to lose it.

Don't lie, she says. It's insulting.

Do you mind putting that thing away? You seem a little too eager to cut me a new smile.

Isabel is snoring in the other bed and I am struck by the thought that I don't remember if Lucy snored. I always slept like a dead man, with her. That was a lifetime ago and now I sleep like a lizard; I breathe through my eyelids.

I don't like you, Henry. I don't know you and you make me very fucking nervous.

Henry breathes evenly. I do have that effect on some people.

It's a liability, she says. Who are you?

My name is John Henry King. I was born July fourth, 1961. I sell speedboats and orange is my favorite color. I like my coffee with sugar, no cream. I don't eat breakfast unless I'm on vacation. I have a wife named Josephine back in St. Louis. She's a law student.

And what about Isabel? You seem pretty friendly with her for a married man.

My wife and I are estranged. Isabel is but a daydream, an illusion.

Jude is silent and I know she doesn't believe him. But she doesn't have much choice and she really doesn't want to kill him. Dead bodies aren't so easy to hide on a train.

I'm sorry, says Henry. I'm still working on that story. I have another one where I'm running from the federal witness protection program, but it's too bloody for polite company.

Jude laughs reluctantly, then pulls her stinger away and stands up. Henry rubs his throat and watches her. She covers her breasts and says, did you get a good look?

Oh yes, ma'am.

I'm glad, she says. I hope it keeps you awake at night. Now get out, please.

As you wish.

Jude glares at Isabel, passive and drunk in the next bed. She sneers.

Take that bitch with you.

Henry gathers himself and lifts Isabel as if she's made of air. Her arms and legs dangle. She growls and grunts, still sleeping.

Jude leans over me, perhaps to kiss me.

Did you believe him?

Jude smiles. Oh, you're awake.

She sits on the edge of the little bed, turning the stinger in her hands. It seems to comfort her.

I roll over onto my side, the blankets pulled tight around me.

Of course I didn't believe him. He's too smooth, too frightening. He's like a stockbroker with a meat cleaver in his briefcase.

I like him, I say.

She bites her lip. I may be paranoid. But I'm thinking he works for Gore and maybe Gore has decided he doesn't want to pay. Maybe he wants to kill the messenger.

I smile in the dark. But you said Gore was a nice land developer, a taxpayer.

Jude hugs her knees.

Okay, she says. I might have lied to you. Luscious Gore is hardly a land developer.

That's a shame.

Jude smiles.

Tell me the truth, I say. My teeth clash together and I marvel at my own foolishness.

The stories are better than the truth, she says. He's a bored, sick millionaire. He's a rich pervert who wants to be the big bad wolf. He likes boys, he likes farm animals…ho-hum. He wants to be a terrorist, but he has no political agenda. He loves a good bombing and random assassinations. He killed two of his own children.

She is grinning like a fool.

Okay. If Luscious Gore is so high on the food chain, why does he run the double-cross?

He might double-cross me because it's raining, because he can't find his socks. It's not about the money with him, it's about sport. Henry makes things interesting.

And what about Isabel. Isn't she interesting?

She only wants to fuck with me and send you screaming back to the nuthouse.

Hold the phone. I'm not crazy.

Oh, Phineas.

I sit up with the sheets around my waist. Bits and pieces of the sun break through cracks in the heavy curtains, and Jude's face flickers in and out of the dark. She is still naked. She plays with the stinger now, running her thumb across the cruel point.

I know about your wife, she says. And I know what she looked like. Don't you think I would check you out before I asked you to come on this joyride?

And what did you find?

I found a pack of lies and misinformation. Your wife was killed last spring and you resigned from the police department in a cloud of smoke. One newspaper said it was suicide and another said it was a boating accident. She was buried in a closed casket and there was no autopsy. One newspaper hinted that the body was never even found. You surrendered your gun and then it disappeared from evidence. The district attorney wanted to crucify you but the case was dropped suddenly.

Five years with the cops, I say. And you learn how to kill an investigation. To make a fine mess of things.

So what really happened?

My wife was killed by a gun, by my gun. Her face was blown off. There was no autopsy simply because I arranged for the medical examiner to lose the body among the Jane Does. She was cremated with a dozen nameless women.

And the gun?

I helped it disappear from evidence. I carried it around for months like a dead albatross. Then I lost it the night I met you.

Purely a coincidence.

Or fate.

Her face was blown off, says Jude. Are you sure it was her body?

This isn't television. Of course I'm sure.

And who pulled the trigger?

There is silence between us.

The bright steel against her yellow skin is too much for me. The sheets have formed a ridiculous tent between my legs. I take the stinger from Jude and she leans to take me in her mouth but I stop her. I pull my knife from its sheath and softly kiss her fingers, the back of her hand. The pale underside of her wrist. I touch the dark veins with the blade, with my tongue. The bend of her elbow is soft, vulnerable. The biceps are sleek and curved and her skin smells like almonds. Is this supposed to be fun? she says.

Trust me, I say.

I press the knife's edge into her shoulder and pull it away quickly. The cut is as long as my pinkie and maybe a quarter inch deep. Her body shudders once, then relaxes. She trusts me. She wants me to hurt her, perhaps. I push her onto her stomach; she is numb and doesn't resist. The cut is bleeding profusely now. I use the knife to cut a long white strip from the sheet and tie it around her shoulder. The blood slows, but the cut will likely require stitches. I press the blade against the back of her thigh, barely below the soft flesh of her ass. She jerks and makes a small sound. The blade leaves a mark but there is no blood. I place the knife at her tailbone and trace a hair-thin cut along the pale bikini line. The skin hesitates then opens slightly and blood appears, as if she has cut herself shaving. I move the knife to the area of her right kidney and scratch a mark that is like my own cut but will not scar. I am nearly bursting now, and my left elbow is trembling under my weight. I push her legs apart and let my body fall over hers, heavy as a blanket of snow. I drop my knife on the bed where she can reach it and I am inside her.

Minutes later I am kissing her ear, her neck. I tell her I'm sorry.

I haven't earned your tenderness, she says.

Jude is asleep on her belly and the sheets are dark with blood. Her mouth is open slightly and her lips glisten with spit. I allow myself to hate her, briefly. Then I wake her with a hurried kiss, whispering her name and she answers me in a purring, drunken voice.

Tell me about Isabel, I say.

I feel good, she says. Don't spoil it.

This is important.

Jude rolls over and uses her folded arms as a pillow. The shoulder is painful, I can tell.

Isabel is Luscious Gore's daughter, she says.

I close my eyes and I see Lucy's face.

And she doesn't have any bone disease, does she?

Jude sighs and I don't think I'm in the mood for this, not really.

I'm sorry. But I don't think I've told the truth in over a year.

A year is nothing, I say. And the truth drifts, like smoke.

I'm not in the army, she says. I'm attached to a deep-cover unit called the Platypus Project. It's a bastard child of the CIA and totally unprotected.

You're a secret agent, I say.

It sounds silly, doesn't it? But yes. For the past two years I have been undercover, living as Luscious Gore's bodyguard.

And the organ snatching? That's a hobby.

The kidney is actually intended for Isabel's brother, Horatio. He's a coke addict and he slipped into a coma four weeks ago. Almost total renal failure. He needs a transplant right away, and even if he was a legitimate citizen he would go on a waiting list. But Horatio is wanted for a dozen capital crimes; he can't just walk into the emergency room and flash his Blue Shield card.

Oh, yeah. It must be inconvenient.

Jude smiles through shadows.

Anyway, she says. Isabel disappeared one night and came back at two in the morning with a bloody, mutilated kidney in a shoebox. She had gutted a male prostitute in downtown Dallas.

I love it. Then what.

Everyone was hysterical. They had to sedate her. The funny thing is that Luscious can't stand Horatio. He would gladly pull the plug and call it a day. But Isabel adores him, so he promised her a kidney. He knew I had the surgical background to do it right, and he offered me a lot of money. It would have blown my cover to refuse. I told him I would take care of it, and I went to Denver alone. Isabel followed me.

Denver, I say. Why not Albuquerque?

It was just far enough away and removed from Gore's sphere. And no one knew me. To be honest, I wish I had gone to New Orleans. It's my favorite city in the world. It's crawling with vampires and voodoo queens. No one would have noticed a missing kidney.

Now, I say. Why did you fucking choose me?

Isabel chose you, she says. She said you were a perfect tissue match, a rare find.

I'm special.

Very.

Why not just give the damn thing to Isabel?

She doesn't have the money, says Jude. And I like to watch her twist.

It's an excellent story but I don't believe her for a minute. Jude is an organ smuggler, a flesh thief. She made the crucial error of falling in love with her victim and now she's trying to dazzle me with a lot of intrigue. Isabel is her estranged partner, perhaps her lover. Her resemblance to Lucy is all in my fucking head.

Do you know anything about Greek mythology? she says.

I stare at her. You aren't going to change me into a pig, are you?

Jude laughs. I was thinking of Orpheus, the poet. His wife was killed and he was so shattered by grief that he followed her to the underworld.

Poor bastard.

Orpheus begged the gods to release his wife, but they refused.

I light a cigarette. I really don't like this story.

For years he charmed them with his pitiful music and finally the gods couldn't stand it anymore. They agreed to let Orpheus take his wife back to the living, on one condition.

The gods always have to fuck with you. It's not enough to just kill you.

But Orpheus was given such a simple task, she says. Like a walk in the park. All he had to do was lead his wife out of the underworld without looking back. And he almost made it. At the very end, he turned to look at his wife. He loved her and he didn't quite trust her. He wasn't sure she would follow him. When he looked at her, she vanished and was gone.

That's just great.

There's no smoking in here, says Jude.

It's cool. I disabled the smoke detectors.

I might love you, she says.

Yeah. And what happened to Orpheus?

Don't laugh, but he was killed at an orgy. He was torn apart by a pack of young girls.

My face is suddenly cold. I feel something like a rush of stupidity and I don't know the difference between love and sorrow.

Something bothers me, she says.

What?

You never kiss me on the mouth.

I know you will betray me in the end, I say.

She smiles. I wouldn't do that.

I stroke her foot. What is your real name?

My only name is Jude.

Jude gives me a brief lesson in undercover field medicine. I'm doubtful but she convinces me to sterilize her wound, then seal it with Krazy Glue. She shows me how to make a butterfly bandage and it feels good to take care of her. I help her get dressed and she lets me pick out her clothes. I'm tired of her cold European goddess clothes and I choose torn blue jeans that are a little too big for her and hang loose at the hips, the burgundy boots and a tiny white T-shirt that clings to her like it's wet. Her nipples are round and dark and clearly visible.

Do you want me to look like a tart? she says.

I smile. You look like you're nineteen and you're sore from too much fucking.

You look pale, she says. Is it the pain?

I realize my hands are slick with sweat. My teeth hurt from clenching them and I've been shivering for the last hour. My eyes ache and my belly is a pool of acid. I don't really want another shot but I can't say no.

twenty-one.

Jude is hungry. She tries to talk me into having breakfast but the shot has settled into my muscles and blood, my bone structure. I am happy to watch shadows race across the floor. And I'm in no mood to see Isabel and Henry. The speedboat salesman, I say. Whoever the fuck he is. I'm bored with his game.

Jude sighs. You are so innocent, aren't you.

Bring me a piece of bread, maybe some fruit.

Okay, she says. But don't wander off without me. I don't want you to get lost again.

Don't worry. I'm safe as a bug in a glass.

This makes me giggle foolishly and Jude shrugs. She takes the blood-soiled sheets to leave elsewhere and I hear a massive click as she locks the door behind her. This isn't like any Valium I ever had. My sensory perception is ridiculously heightened and I feel shifting waves of ecstasy and paranoia. I can't say I don't like it. I watch as silent rushing trees and slabs of rock and yawning open space blur behind the window. If I listen carefully I can hear unseen animals breathing and chirping, scratching and chewing. I can even hear the sun. It sounds like a jet taking off in the middle of the night. I stare at my hands for five minutes and I see endless scars and wrinkled, discolored flesh and there is a taste like chrome in my throat. An inhuman voice invades my head and I tell myself it is only the conductor, he's telling me the train will be stopping shortly in Las Vegas. I laugh out loud and clap my hands like a monkey because I want to get off the train.

But I'm not going anywhere without the little green icebox. It's still locked in the complimentary storage compartment, a little white cupboard made of brightly painted plywood. The lock is flimsy, the kind that takes a miniature key. I'm sure Jude could pick it with a paper clip, with her eyebrow tweezers. But I was never any good at that. I use my knife to pry one hinge, but the other won't give. I manage to slide my fingers into a tiny gap and with strength that surprises me simply rip the door apart.

The icebox is maddeningly weightless, as always. She told me it was packed in dry ice and I believed her. But I can't help thinking the ice has melted and my kidney is wrapped in aluminum foil like a ham sandwich; it's floating around in there with a few cans of beer and a piece of pie.

I'm suddenly nervous about metal detectors and I drop my knife and gun on the bed. I still have Jude's little stun gun. It's graphite and plastic and it looks so harmless, like a toy.

I drift along the passageway, mumbling and schizophrenic. The train is so still, so silent. The constant motion was sickening but now it's gone and I feel lost. Isabel comes toward me, her yellow eyes bright. She's wearing a short blond wig and a black and white dress that could have come from Lucy's closet. I try to remember what I did with her clothes after the funeral but all I see are haze and yellow clouds.

What's in the box, dear?

Nothing, I say. My pet rabbit.

Oh, let me see.

Don't touch it, I say. My teeth are chattering. I really want to get off the train.

She laughs. You don't really think there's a kidney in there, do you? Let me tell you a small medical truth. An organ intended for transplant cannot survive longer than twenty-four hours without oxygen.

It's packed in dry ice. Dry ice.

It could be packed in amber and it would still be worthless, she says. It would be a dead piece of meat.

Why should I believe you? My voice is so faint I could be under-water.

Don't then, she says. Let's open it.

I don't have the key.

That hardly matters. Do you have a gun, a knife?

I push past her, hugging the icebox to my belly.

The kidney is fine, I say. Jude knows what she's doing.

Isabel blows me a kiss and against a bleeding red filter I see myself drop the icebox and grab her shoulders and snap her fine neck with the raw, damp noise of bone and tissue separating. I pull the clothes from her shattered body and watch her eyes become coins. I set fire to her hair and now she smiles and says, you will see me again.

Outside and I bend to touch the untrembling earth, the dead wood of the platform. I feel the liquid, visible heat coming from the train. A man in a shiny blue uniform tells me I have thirty minutes before the train leaves. I walk into the station, my lucky hat pulled low over my eyes. I see everything with uncomfortable clarity and I try not to whisper and giggle but the incessant bells and lights of slot machines send me into a shivering panic. The crush of people waiting in lines and talking on cell phones and waving tickets drops me to my knees. I crouch before a short, burly vending machine; it's blue and white and I think of R2D2, the droll little robot that endlessly beeped and whistled in a faraway galaxy where everyone was so polite and sometimes I wished Luke had the testicles to just vaporize him. The machine before me dispenses newspapers and I glare at one through the glass. The headlines are meaningless but the date in the left corner reads December 25. The sky outside has the impossible color and texture of morning. It's been only twenty-four hours since we left Denver.

I fucking hate Christmas. It always drags on, as if it's dying. I tried to be happy when I was with Lucy. She thought every Christmas might be her last. Everything was thick with symbolism. Every little thing took on the weight of a body, of a dead person. I spent too much money on presents and helped her decorate the tree. I tolerated the music, the smell of orange peels and cinnamon. But it all struck me as a waste of time. I wasn't any happier than I ever was. In the end, I could only get drunk and make Lucy cry. She would sit on the couch, two miles away and silent. Her face dirty with tears and her legs bent beneath her.

I crawl and stagger into a frozen yogurt shop and throw myself into a plastic booth. I want to get back on the train. I need Jude to soothe me, to make everyone stop staring at me. There is a salt shaker on the table and I unscrew the lid with twitching fingers. I pour salt into my hand and eat it, choking. It calms me down a bit. I rest my cheek on the cool yellow surface of the table. I breathe in and out until my pulse is normal. I want to get back on the train but I'm not ready to go outside, not yet. A pair of white pants enters my field of vision. The thick fur coat made from some scrawny animal whose meat is probably too bitter to eat. A black leather belt with a bright silver buckle. I look down at polished black boots and then up, at the smiling face of the Blister. He still wears the bright white gloves and I wonder if they hide prosthetic hands. He holds two sugar cones of soft chocolate yogurt, and he licks one of them boyishly. He slides into the booth and hands me the other cone and I stare at it in wonder. I touch it hesitantly with my raw tongue and it tastes impossibly good.

Are you having fun yet? he says.

Did you ever notice that frozen yogurt doesn't really melt? It uncongeals, I say. As if the molecular bond is only temporary.

I see that Jude is keeping you well anesthetized, he says. For the pain, I'm sure.

He wipes chocolate from his lips. There is a bubble of silence around our table and the churning faces of the station seem far away. But there isn't enough oxygen for the two of us and the bubble will soon burst.

I don't mind the pain so much, I say. But the drugs are a nice distraction.

His tongue flicks across his teeth. I wanted to give you a little pep talk.

I glance at my wrist and I'm surprised to see my watch is actually there. The porter said thirty minutes but that could have been hours ago.

Let's make it fast, I say.

The Blister smiles and I notice how red his lips are.

Don't worry.

I'm not worried.

A knot of chocolate surfaces at the back of my throat, apparently rejected by my stomach. I place the unfinished cone in the center of the yellow tabletop. The Blister glares at it.

I'm afraid that you are losing focus, he says. That your infatuation with Jude might distract you from your purpose. There's a lot of money involved and I have to be careful.

I don't really need your money, I say.

The Blister bites forcefully into his sugar cone. I was hoping you would say that. I enjoy conflict, now and then. It allows me to apply a little leverage.

I could use a little leverage.

Did you know that you have become quite popular with the police? Your name is on everyone's lips and they are dying to meet you in Los Angeles.

What are you talking about?

Murder, of course. And a rape for good measure.

I stare at him. You raped Eve, of course.

Don't be silly, he says. That would be far too pedestrian for me, too messy.

I'm sure you hate a mess.

He chews for a moment. The point is that the police think you raped her.

Oh, well. Then I must have raped her. And killed a person, too.

You must have, he says. He grins at me. A local drug dealer named Winston Jones. He was a piece of garbage, but still. The evidence against you may as well be on a silver platter.

Oh you motherfucker.

I am told that Mr. Jones had a daughter, the Blister says. A sweet little girl who suddenly has no daddy.

My fingers are tingling and I laugh out loud.

How are your bowels? he says. Has there been any activity?

Nothing yet. But I have my fingers crossed.

You are casual, he says. For a man with a bag of poison in his abdominal cavity.

The only bag of poison is my heart.

Oh, the drama. The Blister sighs. Jude bothers me and I want you to kill her, very soon. If not, I may be forced to do it myself. And I can just as easily lay the blame on you.

The drugs are waning. I look down at the table, at the decomposing yogurt.

Then go ahead and kill her, I say. But I don't think Jude will die easily.

The table is perhaps three feet across, half a body length. I place the icebox in the center like a bouquet of flowers. The Blister stares at it, his shoulders twitching.

Give it to me, he says.

Silence.

I insist, he says.

Everyone tells me the kidney is worthless. A sad piece of meat you couldn't feed to a dog.

It is hardly worthless.

I'm curious. Are you Luscious Gore?

He laughs. One day, perhaps. I will be.

I don't like this answer. I push the icebox to one side and lean forward as if I have a secret. The Blister bends toward me, his head slightly cocked to one side. I grab him by the ears and smash his forehead with mine. I've seen this little maneuver in a dozen movies but never actually tried it. It's absurdly painful. My eyes are hot with tears and for a second I think I may have done him a favor: I've knocked myself silly. But then his mouth turns to jelly and his cheeks are the color of cigarette ash. He slumps sideways and I come out of my seat in mock horror. My friend is drunk, I say.

No one pays any attention. This is Las Vegas and the tourists drop like flies. I slide in next to the Blister and he is trying to sit up. I find his carotid artery with my thumb and crush it. I count to five, six, seven, and let go. Unconsciousness is a delicate thing and it too easily becomes death.

twenty-two.

A year ago I might have carried the Blister up a flight of stairs. But I'm so much weaker than I used to be. I'm a fucking flower, lately. I listen to him breathe beside me. I wonder if he's dreaming. I'm bored and worried that the train will leave soon. I lean over the Blister and remove one of his white gloves. His hand is ropy and gray with scar tissue, with old, poorly healed burns. His hand is like a prehistoric claw, the gross extremity of some cave-dwelling troll. It could probably use some sunlight. I pull the slick glove over my own hand. There is still a puddle of melted yogurt on the table. With one alien finger, I trace out a wobbly heart in the sweet brown goo. I stare at the top of my finger, at the dripping white leather. The Blister breathes, in and out. His face is stupid with trust. I shrug and wipe the glove clean, then slip it back onto his hand. He comes to life suddenly, eyes rolling and incoherent. He doesn't seem to know where he is. I guide him to the bathroom, smiling and apologizing to anyone that will listen. My friend is drunk, I whisper.

The Blister says he wants to lie down. He wants to go back to sleep. I say nothing. I don't want to weaken. I drag him unprotesting to the handicap stall and prop him up on the toilet, his head dangling like meat on a string. I slap his pockets, smiling when I find a set of handcuffs and still smiling as I shackle him to the guardrail. I take his gun from the shoulder holster and unload it. I open his wallet. He has a stack of hundred-dollar bills and a startling array of false identification; he's a cop and a U.S. marshal and a secret service agent and a military investigator. He has a dozen names. I pocket the money and drop his wallet into the toilet. The Blister is made of rubber. I feel the rush, the trill of reckoning and I know that I am making a mistake. I have changed the game and now everything is personal. There will be no frozen yogurt next time and I don't mind. I have been patient for so long. The Blister has a cell phone in his jacket pocket, slim as a cigarette lighter, and I slip it into my pocket. I clumsily pull his shoes and pants off. He has very hairy legs and he wears black bikini underpants. He has also wet himself. I take the panties off with care and I'm vaguely pleased to see that his penis is uncircumcised, ugly, and quite small. Now he wears only the gloves. His eyes flutter and he begins to make unhappy noises. I kiss him on the lips and whisper, wake up sweet Romeo.

The Blister's eyes are boiling. He yanks at the handcuffs and groans like a horse. I shrug as he presses his knees together to hide his crotch. He waits for me to speak and I realize I don't know what I want from him. I crouch and stare at him for a moment, wondering if I should gag him. The men's room is suddenly alive with noise. The drone of pipes and crashing footsteps, the hum of urine against tile. Someone blows his nose bloodily. Two stalls over, a giant takes a long and terrifying shit. It sounds like he's drowning someone. The Blister becomes calm. I imagine he doesn't want anyone to notice us, but I don't really care.

Let's open the icebox, I say. Shall we?

The Blister is blank now. He looks at me as if I am speaking a foreign language.

You must be a tiny bit curious.

He doesn't answer and I decide to ignore him. I dig through my pockets and come up with the key that I took from Jude's purse. That was a hundred years ago. I take a deep breath and stare at the icebox until I feel disconnected. If my kidney is inside, I will chew it up like hamburger and go home. I sniff the air and wonder what stinks, but it's only me. I smell of sulfur, of fear. I'm slick with sweat and my hands are pale as fish. I'm afraid to open the box, to gaze on the lost, bloodied piece of myself. I put the key in my mouth and it's bitter beneath my tongue.

For a long shimmering moment I point the Blister's gun at the icebox and I'm tempted to just fill it with holes. The Blister is soon laughing at me, his voice forced and artificial.

What?

There is a bomb in that box, he says. And I would dearly hate to perish with my pants down.

Do I have a stupid face? Why does everyone think they can sell me a pack of lies?

The Blister laughs like a demented wind-up toy. He's trying to give me the trembles again and it's working. I reach into the toilet and splash chemical blue water onto his thigh. And still he laughs, his voice nearly cracking and I pull out the little stun gun. I press it against his wet skin and give him a nice jolt and it doesn't seem to make a real impression so I stun him again and again and soon he begins to shriek. His face is twisting and purple and I wonder if I might have really hurt him.

I'm very sorry, I say.

His skin is the wrong color and his eyes are wandering, but he never loses consciousness.

How did you burn your hands? I say.

The Blister glances at his left hand, still gloved and shackled to the silver rail.

You will be dead before nightfall, he says. His voice is slushy.

Not likely. How did you burn your hands?

A household accident, he says. It was a stupid, childish thing.

What happened?

Did you ever hurt anyone? he says.

I blink at him. A thousand times.

No, he says. Didn't you ever hurt an animal or a child, someone that was weak?

Just for fun?

Curiosity, he says.

Oh, I say. You're ten years old and you find a frog in the woods. He's too far from the water and the sun is about to cook him. He's dragging himself through the dust and you know he's not gonna make it. You could carry him to water and save his life, or you could just sit there and poke him with a stick and watch him bleed for a while. Because it's more interesting. Is that what you mean?

Yes, he says. Because you don't feel anything.

The Blister is a strange bird. He crackles and pops with some kind of nervous rage, but he can't sustain it. He wants to be supercool and dangerous but he's too self-conscious. His face betrays him readily and his ordinary fears spill around his feet, glittering like gasoline in a puddle.

I stare at him for a long time and he barks, What?

Everyone is afraid of sympathy, I say. Everyone is cruel.

Why would I listen to you? He sneers. You were in an institution. And children are the worst, aren't they?

He crashes around, cursing me. I slip the key into the lock easily, sexually. Then crack the lid of the icebox so carefully I might be stealing a peek at a solar eclipse. I expect a rush of liquid smoke, a spill of maggots. But I bend to sniff at the crack in the lid and smell only vinyl.

Five plastic bags of heroin. I guess ten, maybe twelve ounces each. Five tight little pouches, barely two sorry kilos. I stroke one of them as if it were flesh and the plastic is smooth and cool and soft as a young girl's breast. I bite it open with my teeth and poke my tongue in through the tear. It's unpleasantly pure and I may have swallowed too much. The spine uncoils lazily and I suffer false impressions of underwater breathing and the bitter taste of melancholy. But the spiral is only temporary and I can soon form words.

Is this a fucking joke?

The Blister glares at me with such pure loathing it's almost sexy.

The street value of your kidney, he says. An unloved organ, an accessory you never really needed until you found it missing.

This is what you want?

Oh, yes.

I slit the bag open like the belly of a kitten and the Blister howls. I twirl the bag at him, then another. And soon his face and torso and wretched genitals are white. He's naked and handcuffed and in another lifetime he might be someone's lover, squealing like a baby and dipped in sugar. I drop the remaining bags into the toilet.

I'm sure they will float, I say.

The Blister is speechless. I stuff his clothing into the icebox and lock it shut.

Don't you have anything to say?

He shrugs like a sullen child and I release him from the hand-cuffs. I offer him the fur coat.

Comfort from the rain, I say.

It's been too long. I'm shivering and my legs are asleep but I feel like I might grow wings. The train will surely pull away any moment and I run through the station grinning and sweating like a maniac. I have to find Jude before the train leaves. I stop and break the glass on a fire alarm and laugh like a kid as the Klaxons start to whoop. The crowd disintegrates and I become terribly calm.

I reboard the train and hurry to the dining car. I see Jude from behind. Her thick black and blond hair like sun and shadow joined. The knots of her spine faintly reptilian through the tiny white T-shirt. Henry and Isabel sit across from her. I walk toward them, slowly. Isabel yawns lazily. Her lips are swollen and she glows with sex. Henry winks at me, twirling a chunk of sausage on his fork. Jude sucks at a piece of ice and looks at me like a stranger. I take her hand and mutter something about borrowing my wife. Isabel chews the edge of her thumb and the color stubbornly clings to her face.

What's going on? Jude says. You look insane.

I'm fine. I'm fucking great actually. I hold her hand so tightly I might crush it. I smile and say excuse me to a pair of frail old men who are maddeningly slow to get out of our way. I drag Jude behind me until she stops and pulls her hand free and I remember how strong she is.

Did you know that you have two black eyes?

What? I touch my face and I'm surprised to feel the swollen and tender bones around my eyes. The Blister's face must be a regular sunset.

Oh, well. I had a little trouble in the bathroom.

She touches my cheek and her hand hangs briefly in the air and I stare at the tip of her finger until I notice a fine white dust on her sharp blue nails. I wait for her to taste it but she doesn't even blink. She doesn't glance at the icebox. Where are we going? she says.

I don't answer and she follows me anyway. I push open the door to our compartment and tell her to get her things. We're getting off the train, I say.

Oh, no. That's what she wants. She wants me to run.

I shove my face close to hers. The adrenaline is rushing between us like visible heat.

I'm serious, Jude. Let's go.

She doesn't move. Her face is two inches away and all I see are flared nostrils, sharp teeth and cheekbones cut from stone. I wouldn't want to fight her. But she breathes with me and her face softens, she backs away. She picks up her garment bag and looks around the tiny room. The train begins to rumble.

What's happened. Who are you running from?

My own personal boogeyman. And yours.

She doesn't blink. I hope you know what you're doing, she says.

twenty-three.

I step off the train into razor sunshine as the conductor howls all aboard. The sirens have died away and two or three firemen wander irritably through the station. Jude is behind me. I walk through the thinning crowd, my eyes and ears trying to take in everything. A fat lady hunched over a nickel slot machine, her heavy right hand dipping with strange grace into a cup full of coins and in the same motion feeding a coin into the machine and pulling the handle and dipping into the cup again. A little boy eating a hot dog. His young mother has a body like a tree branch and when she bends over him the front of her dress falls open and I see her small bare breasts and narrow ribs, a flash of silver in her navel and tiny white panties. A man and woman sitting exhausted on a wooden bench. He wears no socks and there is a line of pale skin at his wrist where his watch used to be. His wife has eyes like sand; she is incapable of crying anymore and I wonder how much money they lost. The Blister is nowhere to be seen. I can't even feel his presence and I suppose he's already slithered away. Or possibly the cops have grabbed him up. A naked man with three dripping bags of heroin is not something you see every day. Jude takes my hand and squeezes it.

There is a line of taxicabs out front. I open the door to the first one and Jude climbs in. The cabbie is a skinny kid with a mustache and he hops out to put our bags into the trunk.

Where can I take you? he says.

I put my arm around him and pull him close. He is soft and smells of peanut butter. I slap one of the Blister's hundred-dollar bills into his palm.

Don't blink, I say. But that is Lisa Marie Presley in the backseat and I need to hire a private plane. Maybe you know a small, inconspicuous airport?

The kid grins. We're there in a half hour, he says.

The cab growls through slow-moving traffic. The city is naked and grim under the morning sun, clogged with too many people. Bits of paper swirl and twist in the air. Jude sits against the cracked vinyl in the backseat, her face to the window. She hasn't spoken. I rest my hand on her thigh and feel her warmth. I take the Blister's cell phone from my jacket pocket and flip it open, then take a deep breath and dial. I touch her shoulder and she looks at me. I give her the phone and tell her to ask for Detective Moon. She is put on hold and I take the phone from her. What are you doing to us? she says.

Hush. I need you to trust me.

Moon comes on the line, his voice heavy with smoke. I hesitate, nervous and shameful. As if I am fifteen and I have wrecked the car. I ran away from home and two days have passed and I'm calling my father to see how bad the damage is. Moon, I say. It's Phineas Poe.

Do you have a screw loose? he says. I'm going to hang up now.

No, I say. Talk to me, please. Tell me what you have.

I have you, he says. I have you fucking gift-wrapped. All I need to do is find you.

Don't bother tracing this.

I'm not. I don't want to look like a bigger fool than I am.

What do you have?

I have smoke and mirrors. I have a fistful of physical evidence that says you raped Eve McBride. Your fingerprints were everywhere. Your hair was in her bed, your blood between her legs. But she swears it wasn't you and I believe her.

My blood. How do you know it's mine?

Remember. The lab did everything but stool samples on you after Lucy died. And they save it all for a rainy day.

Wonderful. But it wasn't me.

Maybe. Why don't you come home and we'll talk.

No, thanks. I talked to Eve yesterday. She said it wasn't rape and maybe it was a woman.

He grunts. I'm not her husband and she doesn't have to sell me any mind games. But she's asking for some expensive therapy, if you ask me. And if it was a woman, she had a big dick. The rape kit showed massive vaginal damage.

I'm a sucker, a deaf-and-dumb asshole. I wanted to believe her, to spare her.

Do me a favor, I say. Put a car outside her apartment for a few days.

My pleasure, he says.

Thanks. And what else do you have on me.

I have a possible suicide by the name of Winston "Pooh" Jones: white male, age thirty. The funny thing is that he was also a suspect in the McBride rape. And you slept in his bed and ate his last Twinkies that same night. Pooh is then found dead in a motel room, apparently by his own hand. But it looks a lot like murder dressed up as suicide.

He used a knife to cut his fucking leg open and bleed himself to death. Meanwhile, he had a perfectly good shotgun in his truck outside, and a lot of blood on the front seat. I'm supposed to think he cut his leg open in the truck, then went up to his room and took a shower? Hair and fibers came up empty; everything was clean as a whistle. Nothing but his own blood and prints.

I'm sorry to hear that.

Of course you are. And one might think that you killed him to shut him up. But it doesn't matter because those charges are fucking gravy, they're parsley. My idiot brother could get those thrown out.

I take a breath and look at Jude. I stare at her ear until it becomes the bent and fragile leaf of a dried flower. Her reflection in the window is cut in half and I see her lips. They are moving, just barely. I wonder if she's singing, if she's counting cars. I wonder what she did with my kidney. Did she trade it for a box of heroin or did she give it up for a dying boy in Phoenix?

I also found your missing gun, he says. It was in the front seat of a black Ford Mustang.

My brain takes a spin and I see wild horses, their lips white with foam.

Whose car is it? I say.

The missing Rose White, he says. A pediatric surgeon at the same hospital where you recently did time. Dr. White was found in the trunk of her car, shot twice by your gun.

I stare at Jude's slender throat. I wonder if it will be easier to kill her than to save her.

When, I say. When was she killed?

She was pretty stiff, maybe four days old and we checked her work schedule. She never showed for her shift on the twenty-first.

The first day of winter. The day I woke up in the hospital.

Oh, yeah. Moon is eerily cheerful. The cool weather kept her fresh.

What did she look like?

She was bald, says Moon. Which was a little creepy. Her friends say she usually wore a red wig. And she was naked, but that's normal. Otherwise she was your typical dead white female.

How did she lose her hair?

What kind of question is that? She had cancer.

Did you get any prints from my gun?

Of course not. But I'm afraid your blood was found in the car.

My blood is everywhere.

Where did you find the car? I say.

1013 Alpine, he says. It was parked in the driveway of a nice little two-bedroom house for sale. The real estate agent called it in.

I stare at the back of my hand. The ink is faded to a spidery blue like the veins beneath my skin but I can still read it. *Rose 1013 Alpine 2 P.M.* I never made a date with Rose White and she never really existed. She was already dead. Isabel answered the phone that night and she gave me the bogus address. She strapped on a detachable penis and raped Eve while I was looking at the Hobbit house with a lovely room for the baby. Or maybe it was Pooh. He was looking for me, for the heroin. And he found Eve. She was a prize; she was the ring that glows in the dark, buried in a box of Cracker Jack.

It doesn't matter. Because the wound in my belly was leaking like a sieve.

I was leaving my blood behind me, in the dead woman's car and Eve's bed.

Do you have a recent photo of me? I say. You might want to show it to the real estate agent.

Phineas, says Moon. Come home and we'll work this out.

I laugh like a chump and Jude glances at me, then away. Lucy faked her death and she's having a lot of fun with me. She killed this Rose White with my gun and now she's setting me up as a killer, a rapist. She couldn't do this alone; her heart isn't hard enough and she wouldn't know how. She would need help and she would get it with melting black eyes and the voice of a dove, with the promise of velvet panties. Moon could have helped her. It would be easy for him. Moon's voice has become static and I think, satellites are crashing and my blood is everywhere. *I'm the stranger.* I drop the Blister's phone out the window and turn to watch it shatter. I feel sick and I want to hit someone, to crush a familiar face.

Lucy is alive, I say. She's killing people and Henry has my wedding ring. He stole my identity and she's going to kill him next.

It's not possible, Jude says. Your wife is dead, okay?

My stomach churns with dread and nausea. Nothing is what it seems.

twenty-four.

I lean and whisper sickly to Jude. Do you know how to fly?

She shrugs. Of course.

The cab turns down a narrow gravel road. Ahead I can see a half dozen hangars in a scattered semicircle. Two small planes sit on the runway. A car is parked beside one of them, and a man and woman move back and forth in the skeletal shadow of the plane. I tell the cabbie to park alongside their car. He leaves the engine running and jumps out to open the door for Jude. He bobs his head, clutching her hand.

It's a real pleasure, Miss Presley.

Jude frowns and I step between them. He lets go of her hand.

What's your name, kid? I say.

Bobby. My name is Robert but no one calls me that.

That's fine. Bobby, I want to thank you.

He looks nervous. What for?

For a smooth ride. For a cab that didn't smell like fried eggs. And for your professional attitude, of course. I give him another hundred. And I hope you can keep a secret. Miss Presley is a private person.

He shakes his head. Don't you worry. I'm like a priest. Nothing leaves the backseat.

Interesting analogy, says Jude.

Bobby backs away from her. No problem, he says.

He drives away and Jude turns to me, squinting. That little secret will last five minutes.

I know. But it made his day and sometimes confusion is better than nothing.

Well, she says. I assume you have a plan.

Not really. I lift the green icebox. But I'm feeling lucky.

The plane is an old twin-engine, blue and white. It has shining black propellers and I think it will be a miracle if it ever gets off the ground. The man and woman watch as we walk toward them. They appear to be in their sixties and they look friendly enough. The woman wears a yellow pantsuit and a white hat. The man wears madras shorts and a golf shirt. He holds a wrench in one hand. They might be Elvis fans but they aren't as stupid as Bobby. And I don't think they need our money.

Morning to you, the man says.

I bend over to tie my shoes and remove my gun from the ankle holster.

That's a beautiful little plane, says Jude. She drops her bag to the tarmac.

Thank you. What can I do for you?

Let us borrow it, I say.

His eyes flicker. Don't be ridiculous, young man.

I feel terrible but I bring the gun up and point it at his wife. She puts one hand to her throat. I know I'm not going to shoot her and I'm afraid the man knows it too. Jude is ten or fifteen feet away from him but she is so quick. It isn't natural. She is like a water bug, a skipping stone. I blink and she is swinging the stinger at him, a tight backhand slash like a blurred raindrop, a magician's veil. The man cries out and drops the wrench and his arm is pouring blood.

I help the lady to the car. She says her name is Marian. She hangs on to my arm and she doesn't weigh more than eighty pounds. I open the driver's side door and place her on the seat as if she might shatter. Her legs aren't nearly long enough to reach the pedals. I adjust the seat for her and she clutches at the wheel. I'm afraid she's going to faint. There's a bottle of warm water in the backseat and I make her take small swallows.

I'm very sorry, I say. I wasn't going to shoot you.

She looks at me with glazed, milky eyes.

You don't look like a nice boy, she says.

Jude brings the man over to the car. He walks unsteadily, leaning on her. She has bandaged his arm but it's already showing blood. She hands me the car keys and I lean in to start the engine. It's not a stick shift, at least. I think they might make it to the hospital.

My purse is on the plane, says Marian. It has my driver's license.

Jude offers to get it and the old woman starts to tremble at the sound of her voice.

Don't worry, I say. I'll get it.

Jude turns away from the wind and lights a cigarette. I run to the plane and bring back the purse and a leather suitcase that bears faded stickers from more countries than I can count. I give the purse to Marian and slide the suitcase into the backseat. The old man sits crumpled in the passenger seat, his face pale.

Take him straight to the hospital, I say. And be careful.

The car pulls away feebly, and I know she won't go faster than twenty miles per hour. Maybe a cop will stop her. Jude stands facing me and I ask for a drag of her cigarette. She flicks it away and walks to the plane. I look out at the desert and I remember what it's like to be alone. After a minute I follow her.

Jude is in the cockpit, her eyes dark behind sunglasses. She is looking over some charts and muttering to herself. I scan the instrument panel and feel a rush of vertigo.

This isn't like stealing a car, she says. You don't just cover the plates with mud and disappear on some back road. You go up without a registered flight plan and you get sucked into the tailwind of a passenger jet. You do a Patsy Cline and run into a fucking mountain.

I sit down in the copilot's chair. What's the problem?

There's no problem. Ma and Pa back there were headed for Taos and we will have barely enough fuel to make El Paso. We need to deviate from their flight plan a little, a lot. If we stay below the commercial flight paths and don't draw attention to ourselves we might be okay. As long as we don't stumble into a snowstorm.

She speaks without looking at me, spitting her words in a controlled monotone.

I'm glad, I say. I'm glad there's no problem.

What were you thinking? she says. If you could just be patient I would have had that old man begging us to take the plane. But you pulled your gun and you weren't going to shoot her. It was written all over your face. And you were a cop. What is the first rule in a hostage situation?

I close my eyes. Don't point your weapon at anyone unless you are willing to shoot him.

That's right. And why is that?

Because you have no power. If your bluff is called you lose.

I open my eyes and look at her. The thin white T-shirt is damp with sweat and she might as well be naked. She folds her arms across her chest and a pretty blue vein stands out in her throat.

I cut her husband because I had to do something, she says. It would have been easier and safer to kill them both and bring their bodies along. Then it looks like they went to Taos as planned and no one's the wiser. But I didn't kill him. I saved you from making a decision and you looked at me like I was the Wicked Witch.

Jude, I say.

She hits me once in the face and I know she's holding back. She could probably kill me with two fingers. Her fist is sharp as a stone. After a minute, she lets me hold her.

I don't want you to look at me that way, she says. Ever again.

The engines cough and roar to life and the propellers become ragged, blurred eyes. Jude runs the twin throttles as far as they will go and the plane trembles as if it will fall apart. I sit beside her, uneasy but strangely happy. I wish I had a mouthful of bubble gum. The plane lunges forward as she releases the brakes, and we roll down the runway in a hammering rush. I can't take my eyes off Jude. She is as calm as a cat lying half asleep, watching birds bathe themselves out of reach. Her dark lips are slightly parted and the muscles stand out along her arms. Her body is all piano wires and sinew. I hold my breath as the plane leaves the earth and Jude turns to me, her face shining.

twenty-five.

The cell is a soothing, sickening blue.

I meet Lucy when I'm still new with the cops. I'm a fool. I'm living in a rathole apartment with rented furniture. A wide-screen television and a water bed. The kind of shit that you pay nineteen bucks a week for, and as soon as you miss a payment you're looking at stained gray carpet and balls of hair and chewed fingernails and you're sleeping on the floor wrapped in a beach towel. I'm a drug dealer.

There are no windows. No sharp edges anywhere. The bed is ordinary but for the locking clamps that hold my hands and feet in place. There is a toilet in the corner. A camera is mounted above me, the lens glowing orange. I can feel the caress of foreign eyes on my flesh, like the tickle of imagined insects.

The silly thing is that I'm supposed to be an incompetent drug dealer. Someone who is dumb enough to sell to cops. I have dyed my hair black, to make me look even more pale and sick. But the dye is cheap and my hair just looks green in the light. I have been drinking too much beer and I have a new belly that peeks out from the waistband of my pants. I watch cartoons all day and wait for my telephone to ring. I am a lot like my recently dead friend Pooh.

Two men come to my room; they wear white, silent shoes. Their faces are hidden behind surgical masks, as if I am a carrier, a plague victim. I beg them to show me their faces, to speak. They give me a shot and a handful of pills to swallow. I stare at the thin red wall of my inner eyelid and listen to my skin and I can't be sure how the medication is affecting me. I can't remember how I'm supposed to feel. I can't remember my name. I have never seen my face.

Lucy lives upstairs. Her clothes are torn and don't really fit her but she's strangely beautiful. She doesn't teach ninth-grade math yet. She isn't dying yet. Her blue jeans are splattered with paint all the time and her hair is shaved to stubble. I think she wants to be an artist. I see her outside sometimes, talking to the squirrels and feeding them brightly colored cereal from her pale, stained hand. On a chilly morning I ask her what the hell she is feeding them and she doesn't flinch. Her voice is lovely, a whisper that reminds me of blown glass. I notice her ears then, sharp and pointed. She smiles quickly and says it's Cap'n Crunch. The animals love it.

I am a white male with one identifying mark, a bullet hole scar on my left leg. I stare at the cracked blue ceiling with such intensity that it drips and ripples like a ruined map of the universe. I have no shoes and my feet are pale and shrunken. I am disappearing. They feed me only liquids, and I'm rapidly losing weight. I must have done something terrible but I can remember only these blue walls. There is nothing else and my head is as empty and silent as a church.

Lucy tries to avoid me. I am a rather dirty and pathetic drug seller, after all. There is a narrow black path to my door, trodden by agitated speed freaks and slouching homeless guys and nimble hippie kids and poorly disguised cops. I watch her come and go, and I try to think of reasons I might knock on her door. I need a cup of sugar, an egg. I doubt she even has sugar. I can hear her moving above me when I mute my droning television. Her feet are small and she scurries around like a mouse.

The two men come back with a wheelchair. I am confident that I can walk but they are robotic and unsmiling. They don't seem to breathe. They lift me from the bed like I'm made of sticks, and I let them strap me into the chair. I'm a child, a ragged doll. They wheel me down a long white hall that glistens so brightly the floor and ceiling melt into one. The hall grows narrow in the distance and I try to become smaller, to pull my head into my body. I close my eyes and wait. I listen but the wheelchair makes no sound.

Lucy stops at my door one morning. She asks if I have any milk. I'm surprised and I mutter something incoherent. The truth is I do have milk. But for some reason I don't want to admit it. I stare at the floor, at Lucy's feet. She isn't wearing shoes and I briefly fall in love with her. But her legs are odd, malformed somehow, and I realize that one of them is writhing like a spider's egg sac before it bursts and I wonder if I'm taking too many of my own drugs.

Everything is oiled and waxed and padded and there is only silence.

*

Lucy's pants are not full of spiders. She has a kitten hiding in there. I tell her there are no cats allowed in the building and we both laugh. I'm a known drug dealer, but there are no cats allowed. She tells me she found the little guy in a cardboard box with his three dead brothers. Someone didn't want kittens and didn't have the energy to kill them. Again she asks if I have milk and stupidly I try to touch her face, to brush away an eyelash. She ducks away like my own shadow and I apologize.

The faint swish of an electronic door: brief and lovely, like the breath of a sparrow. I open my eyes and find myself sealed in a glass box; there's a row of holes in the glass and I can feel cool air against my face. Behind the glass are pale green walls, the color of leaves with the sun shining through them.

Two cops show up at my door and I can tell they aren't interested in buying drugs. They close the door behind them and I feel a sudden fever. On my loud, rented television Andy Griffith is telling Opie that it's really not okay to judge people by the color of their skin. The two cops tell me they know I'm working for Internal Affairs and they want to talk. I'm lucky and they merely beat the shit out of me. They don't kill me. Four hours later Lucy finds me in the stairwell. Apparently I went to get my mail and I was so tired that I sat down and fell asleep. She's horrified by my face. It's okay, I say. I can still walk. She takes me back to my apartment and cleans me up. She disconnects the telephone and tells me I'm out of business for a while. It's painful to laugh. Lucy turns off the television and tells me a story about a little boy named Edward who choked on a peach. The kitten chases himself in endless circles on my filthy carpet and I smile, watching him.

I become aware of a voice, androgynous and without emotion. The voice is like silk and shadow and I might have heard the voice for hours without realizing it. The voice has the texture of unconscious thought and I wonder if I'm dreaming, if the voice is my own. But my own thoughts, faint and muffled as a heartbeat, are distinct from the voice. I am aware of my body; it is separate from me, dead and useless.

Lucy tells me that my hair looks terrible. I don't want to dye it blond again; it would only look worse. I allow her to shave my head and now we could be brother and sister. She kisses me when I'm distracted and uneasy. I'm washing dishes and worrying about the fucking mess I've made of my job when I feel her lips on my cheek. I am easily consumed by her.

The voice tells me that my name is Phineas Poe. I am a policeman living in Denver. I recently suffered a nervous breakdown. I had been in Internal Affairs for six years. My wife is dead, apparently by suicide. Her name was Lucy and we had no children.

The kitten slips out of Lucy's window one morning and gets himself stuck in the rain gutter. I can hear him yowling up there but I ignore it. I assume he's hungry and Lucy isn't fast enough with his food. I'm trying to write out a report. My assignment is over, a failure. I haven't told Lucy that I'm a cop and I'm not sure what she will say. Then I hear a noise like someone has thrown a suitcase off the roof and Lucy never screams at all. She sits in the grass and tries not to look at her broken leg. The kitten is walking around and around her as if he can reverse time. I take Lucy to the hospital and part of me is glad her leg is broken. She won't be able to run away from me. In the waiting area

I kiss her and tell her I'm a cop. Lucy is relieved. Because you really weren't a very good drug dealer, she says. The doctor soon puts her back together again and calmly says he wants to talk to her alone. It's about her blood, he says. There's something wrong with her blood.

I open my eyes and I am in the blue room again. I study my new identity, wondering if the voice was telling the truth. My name is Phineas Poe. It might as well be.

I am shaking to pieces. But I'm only sleeping and Jude is trying to wake me. It's black outside the bubble of the cockpit and when I open my eyes, the night sky rushes at me and I'm sure that we are crashing.

Are we crashing? I say.

Jude slaps me. Wake up, please.

I'm awake. Are we crashing?

No, she says. We're somewhere over Texas.

In the glow of the controls her face is blue and stretched as a skull.

Then why did you wake me?

Because you talk in your sleep. I couldn't listen to another word.

I touch my cheek to the window. I try to remember what I was dreaming of but there's only black sky and cold skin. What did I say?

Nothing that made any sense. But it made me very uncomfortable.

I grope for the chain of thoughts that would bring the dream back to me but I can summon only the color blue. I feel a surge of nausea and I slap at the belt buckle. Jude leans over and releases me. I stagger to the back of the plane and vomit into a storage bin. My stomach holds nothing solid and what comes up is like oily water that smells of blood.

Jude calls out to me. When did you last eat anything?

I don't know.

You need to eat, okay. You look like a corpse. If you get a little protein into your system, you might stop hallucinating all the time.

I can barely stand up and I know she's right. But starvation isn't my only problem.

What's in those shots you keep giving me?

I told you, it's pharmaceutical Valium. The kind the dentist uses. It's for the pain.

Then why do I feel like a fucking junkie. I suddenly can't stop shaking and all I can think about is getting another shot. Jude gets out of her seat and comes toward me.

Are you insane? I say. We're going to crash.

Relax, she says. It's on autopilot.

She puts her arms around me and hugs me. I feel like I might break.

I never had Valium like that, I say. Never.

Do you want another shot? she says.

Fuck you. Fuck you.

Listen. You have to trust me, okay. I want to take care of you.

You should have cut out my heart.

If you don't want another shot, I won't make you. But if you don't eat, you will die.

What have you done to me? I say. What have you done?

I removed your kidney, she says. It's a simple procedure.

No, I say. You altered me somehow. You stapled my stomach into a fucking knot. And you left something inside, didn't you? Something to remember you by.

Do you hear yourself?

I'm dying, Jude.

What? she says. I can't hear you.

Never mind.

You're still alive, she says. You have one good kidney.

And if the kidney in the icebox is no good?

Then the buyer is fucked.

No. You could still offer my remaining kidney to Gore.

She doesn't smile. I never thought of that. But yes.

I hear Lucy laughing and crying in the dark and I wonder why it's so easy to pretend that my kidney is in the icebox, that I still believe.

Oh, you never thought of it.

Are you stupid? she says. If I wanted to kill you, I would have.

I'm sorry.

It's okay, she says. I saw a picnic basket in the back. I'm sure that little old lady packed a nice, wholesome dinner. I want you to sit down while I take a look. Okay?

I return to my seat, vaguely uneasy that the pilot's chair is empty. Jude comes out of the dark with turkey sandwiches, two bananas and a chocolate chip brownie. There's even a Thermos of sweet coffee. Jude sits down at the controls and examines the instruments. I take small, cautious bites of turkey. I don't feel immediately better but I don't throw up either.

We will be there soon, says Jude.

twenty-six.

Jude sets the plane down in a dead wheat field as gently as she might kiss a baby. A mile away, lights crawl along a two-lane road.

How far to El Paso? I say.

Ten miles, twenty. It doesn't matter.

I look around in the dark. The country is flat as my hand and the city lights are a tiny glow over the horizon. I have had the dry heaves for a half hour now; the turkey sandwich did not sit well and my mouth is full of acid and blood and I am inclined to think it does matter. But Jude is cool and unconcerned. I despise myself but I would love to push up my sleeve and offer her my naked arm. To close my eyes and wait for the needle. But I don't want her to know how badly I want it, and I shrug when she asks how I feel.

I watch as she unloads the gear and I realize there's more than we can carry. Jude opens her massive garment bag and produces a sleek little backpack, purple and gold with an internal frame. She transfers her purse, a few pieces of clothing and toiletries, tools and a number of small, compact items that I can't identify. She knows what she's doing, certainly. One thing catches my eye: a fat file folder with leather straps.

Jude turns to me. What can you unload? It's hot where we're going and we may do some walking.

I shake my head, hefting my duffel bag.

Give it to me, she says.

She unzips it and pokes around.

There's really nothing in there, I say. A change of clothes. Some disposable razors and a toothbrush.

She holds up a pale blond wig and I nearly swallow my tongue.

That sneaky bitch, I say.

You should be more careful, she says.

Jude.

Well, she says. This is a lot of wasted space.

Before I can say anything she transfers my meager possessions to her backpack, then tosses my empty bag onto the pile. She stands up and looks around. I pick up the green icebox and she grins at me. I'm a fool, I know. But she has a good smile.

Jude moves the discarded things several yards from the plane and makes a neat pile. She holds up Isabel's wig like a stolen scalp, then takes a book of matches from her pocket. She strikes one and there's a teardrop of blue and red at her fingertips. I blink and the hair catches fire, the flames coiling greedily around her arm. Jude drops it and patiently blows on the little fire, as if she's camping.

Let's go, she says.

I bend to touch the ground and the earth is damp. Not damp enough, perhaps.

The plane may go up, I say. The whole fucking field.

I don't care. No one is connecting that plane to me.

She wears the bulging pack and I carry the icebox in one hand, her medical bag in the other. I feel a bit like a bellboy, my arms loose in their sockets. There is no sound but the crunch of sand, the far-away cry of geese overhead. I am a few steps behind Jude, and every few minutes I turn to look back. The small fire still burns, but it appears to be contained.

What now? The road stretches black in either direction.

Nothing, she says. She begins to walk along the shoulder.

The sweep of headlights from the north and Jude tells me to get out of sight. There are no trees and little brush. A single rock the size of my head. I drop my bag and the icebox and lie facedown in the dirt. I can hear Jude cracking her knuckles, one by one. The car slows and an electric window glides down. Jude leans in to ask the driver for a ride. He says he will be happy to help and there is a sudden, fleshy noise. Then silence.

Are you coming? says Jude.

I stand up and see a long black car, the right turn signal still blinking. Jude sits on the driver's side. The car has a slick leather interior and smells new. I look over my shoulder and there is a long-legged man with no hair sleeping soundly in the backseat.

Very nice, I say. Did you give him a Vulcan nerve pinch?

Something like that, says Jude. He will wake up in El Paso, his car undamaged and his wallet intact. He will even feel refreshed, and he will have a fantastic story to tell his friends.

God as my witness but I was abducted by a hot little number, boys. She did experiments on me and tossed me back like a bad fish.

Jude doesn't laugh. Her face is blank. I think she is too tired.

She drives with one hand on the wheel. She asks me to find a radio station and I spin the dial. I find a jazz station and she says for me to leave it there. A green sign looms in the dark: EL PASO 19 MILES.

What's going to happen in El Paso? I say.

We are going to a motel called the Seventh Son, she says. Then we wait.

For what?

The explosion is like a thousand pounds of air sucked into a soda bottle, the bottle bursts and the air expands to its normal dimensions with shocking force. I look over my shoulder and see the ball of fire that was the plane. It seems to hover, as if it wants to rise and return to the clouds. Minutes later, emergency vehicles rush past. One laughable fire truck and two cop cars, their sirens screaming through us.

Jude maintains her speed at exactly the limit.

She never tells me who or what we will be waiting for.

The Seventh Son has beds that vibrate. Jude laughs and digs in her pockets for change. She feeds two quarters into the slot and the bed comes to life. She lies down with her eyes closed, her body humming.

Come on, Phineas. It feels so nice.

I drop my bag on the floor and shake my head.

If I go near that thing I will fall to pieces.

Oh, she says. I won't let it hurt you.

But I'm not in the mood. I go into the bathroom, looking for a place to hide the icebox. I shove it in a small closet and cover it with a bath towel. I pull off my clothes and stand before the mirror. Every bone in my body pushes at the surface of my white skin. I can see veins and tendons and unprotected muscle. My face is a grinning mask. I turn to examine my wound. I remove the dressing and see that the flesh is a little red, possibly infected. But the skin does seem to have closed, rejoined itself where Jude made her cut. I shudder to think of letting her open me up again, even to replace my lost kidney. I sit down on the toilet and remind myself that the precious green icebox is now stuffed with the Blister's dirty clothes. I empty my bladder like an old man, too feeble to stand.

The bed has stopped vibrating. Jude gives me another sponge bath and smears antibiotic cream over the infected skin. She leaves the wound exposed and says it needs air. She kisses me, softly at first. I am slow to respond. I put my hands on her hips, her muscular waist. She tells me to undress her. My teeth feel like they are falling out and finally I can't stand it anymore. I want to feel reborn, even if it's artificial and temporary. I want to make love to her and I need the drugs to give me strength.

I want another shot, Jude.
    Are you sure? she says.

She sits cross-legged at the end of the bed while I lay collapsed on the pillows. She appears to be at least a hundred feet away. I can't move to touch her. If I could, I would kiss her bare feet and bite her toes. I would stroke her thighs through blue jeans faded white. I would lick the exposed tummy, the long muscles in her arms, I would close my eyes and touch the dark and gold hair that falls and falls. She chews a thumbnail briefly, her eyes on me.

Haven't I warned you about getting sappy on me? she says.
    The shot, I say. Then talk and sex, okay.

Jude prepares the hypo in the bathroom. I don't want to watch, anymore. I don't need to. The thought of a needle once made me ill, now my skin tingles. I lie naked on the bed, my arms outstretched as if I am nailed there. I close my eyes and wait. Jude ties back my arm, stopping the blood. She finds the vein; I breathe through my teeth and try to think of the needle as a lover's bite.

The body is composed of water and little else. I can feel the waves inside me.

I open my eyes. I want to ask Jude the color of electricity. She is naked, crouched over me and glowing with sweat and fever. She isn't listening. Her hair is everywhere and I can't see her face. She rises and falls, impaling herself on my surprisingly erect penis. I can't feel it at all. My body, it seems, is too enamored of the drug to be bothered by ordinary sex. Jude doesn't seem to mind, she rides me like she would her own hand, and I watch her, removed and soon dreaming.

The dark swallows me. There is rough carpet beneath my naked shoulders and I'm crushed, folded into an impossible position. My knees are painlessly tucked beneath my chin. The road hums beneath me. I'm in a car, the trunk of a car. My face hurts like a raw, open wound and I snake one hand free to touch it, to feel the mass of chewed flesh and shattered bone. My face is gone and I seem to be bald as a stone. I touch my throat and I have no pulse. I hug myself and my fingers find my belly, my breasts. I'm a dead woman and I have no hair.

twenty-seven.

Sorrow is like the ocean and sometimes I wish my heart would stop.

Jude is gone. I am staring at nothing, at an unremarkable white wall. I dimly remember her whispering to me that she was going, that I wasn't to worry. I have no idea how long ago that was.

I swing my legs over the edge of the bed and my feet find the floor. I stand up and I feel fine. In a far corner of my mind, I am aware that my physical condition is misleading. I am weak from the surgery, from hunger. But when I'm drugged, I feel like a king and I can't be killed. Jude is drugging me for the pain but the true pain arrives when I am not drugged. Two minus two equals two and there is a shrinking window between the fading of the drug and the arrival of pain, when I can see and think clearly. But I will take this up with Jude later. I'm thirsty and I want a cigarette. I'm naked and shivering and I can't find my pants.

I dig through Jude's heavy backpack and vaguely remember the bound file folder. It would be worth a few minutes of my time, I think. But it isn't there, she has taken it with her. I stand half naked in the corner of the room, Jude's hairbrush in one hand and a crushed pack of cigarettes in the other.

The hairs in her brush appear dry and brittle, stripped of color like a winter sky.

I look down at the strewn contents of Jude's pack and realize that I will never put everything back so neatly, so efficiently. She will know I searched her pack, that I was looking for the folder. I tear the cellophane from the cigarettes and try to imagine the contents of the folder. There could be an extensive file on Gore, on Isabel. There could be any number of files and reports on me, the police are relentless chroniclers of their own misfortunes. And the doctors at Fort Logan must have written a telephone book on my delusions and theories, my borderline fantasies.

I remember the green room, the voice. I see two possible realities. I was a nameless mental patient, drooling and eating my fingers and killing time on the ward. I was chosen for physical reasons, nothing more. They took great pains to implant a new identity for some dark purpose.

Or I was truly Phineas Poe, fractured and suicidal ex-cop. They were merely reconstructing my identity.

I couldn't have killed Lucy. I might have thought about it, dreamed of re-creating myself in the wake of her death. But then I would find myself staring at her as she watered the plants or read a magazine, and I would tell myself she was a piece of me. I could as easily cut off a hand or foot. She would feel my eyes, then. And without looking up, she would ask me if something was the matter.

She was precious, a rare bird. Even when I was coming undone. Even when I regained consciousness on a street corner, unsure of the time or day. Unsure of where I had been. I could see myself in unrelated flashes of memory, in poor camera angles. I could see only my feet, the back of my head. I saw obscene close-ups of my face, a gray fleshy landscape with massive pink lips and scar tissue, small black hairs protruding from dead skin. I saw myself through glass, through a sheet of cracked enamel. I saw unnatural detail. I saw body parts that couldn't be mine. I heard my own voice from within, from underwater. Distorted, crashing against bone fragments.

And whenever I returned to her, I saw myself through her eyes and I was barely human. I was never the husband she remembered.

I remember waking up to find I was a dead woman with no hair. I could scream and scream until my voice is gone and I will never get that out of my head.

I find my pants in the bathroom, they are so dirty they seem to shine. I put them on anyway and sit down to drink a glass of tap water. The water is warm and slightly brown with rust. It smells of chemical treatment and it would taste much better with ice. I am wondering if it would be worth the effort to leave the room and look for an ice machine, and I find myself staring at the small closet where the green icebox was hidden. Jude took it with her and I remind myself that it's worthless now. It's worthless. And I guess she doesn't really trust me.

Jude feeds me one lie after another and I gobble them up like a baby eating mush. I suppose I know it to be mush, but I want to like it. I want her to hurt me, to betray me. And as long as I pretend to believe her, I can make excuses for not killing her. But I have no excuses now. I have nothing but a sad little drug habit and the twisting notion that I might love her.

There's a telephone beside the bed, and I'm tempted to call Moon and tell him where I am. I'm in Texas on a vibrating bed. My new girlfriend is a secret agent and she traded my kidney for a box of smack. She loves me. She loves me not and I want you to come down here with a big fucking net and take me back to Fort Logan. I need forty-eight hours of observation. I pick up the phone and dial Eve's number.

What are you doing? I say.
    Phineas, she says. Her voice is fragile, terrible.
    Are you alone?
    Why?
    I just want to talk. I want to know if anyone's listening.
    No one is here, she says. I'm lying on the couch under about ten blankets. I'm watching the news and I'm waiting for them to flash your face on the screen: have you seen this man?
    I'm invisible, I say. I'm safe.
    Are you? That cop was here yesterday, Detective Moon. He seems to be worried about you.
    Oh, yeah. He wants to arrest me.
    No, she says. I don't think so.
    What did he say?
    He said there's a lot of evidence against you. But he said it was too easy, too perfect. He doesn't think you did anything.
    And what do you think?
    Silence.

I was raped, Phineas. I was raped.

Eve, I say. You don't have to talk about it.

I'm okay, she says. I'm really okay. I have a gun under the blankets. Two days ago I was like a puppy that someone had tortured. I screamed when I heard a car door slam. And now I want to kill someone and it makes me feel good. It feels really good.

I know the feeling. It comes and goes.

Where are you? she says.

What kind of gun do you have under those blankets?

I don't know, she says. A little bitty gun, like a toy. But it's loaded.

That's fine. Is this gun an automatic?

No, she says. The chambers spin around in case you want to play Russian roulette.

Okay, Eve. It's okay.

A six-shooter, she says. In another lifetime I was Calamity Jane.

She laughs and her voice is like thin ice.

Eve, please. No one else is going to hurt you, I say. The cops are watching your apartment and the man who did this is dead.

It wasn't a man, she says. I told you it was a woman.

Eve, I say. Forgive me. But when did you last have sex with a man?

I was sixteen, she says. Three years ago. I did it with a boy who stuttered. It lasted two minutes, maybe. What are you trying to say? That I wouldn't recognize a penis?

I'm not saying anything. Tell me what happened.

Eve takes a long painful breath.

It was dark in my room, she says. I have these heavy velvet curtains that block out the sun and I was trying to sleep. Georgia was home but she couldn't talk. She was hiding in the closet and whenever I tried to touch her she growled at me, so I left her alone. I wanted to sleep. I never heard a noise, not a whisper. I always sleep on my stomach. Ever since I was a kid. And when I felt a hand on my neck I thought it might be Georgia but the hand was so strong. I tried to roll over and I saw a shadow leaning over me, slender like a woman and a black ski mask over her face. I think I still believed it was Georgia and this was one of her sex games. She liked to dress up in different clothes and pretend we were strangers. But then she started wrapping the tape around my face and I was a little scared. And the fear was exciting at first. She tied my hands and feet and cut off my T-shirt and underpants and I felt the knife against my skin. Then she started beating me and she pushed my legs apart and she shoved things inside me.

What things, I say.

Eve is crying now and I start to babble that I'm sorry, that I don't want to know.

I think there was a wooden spoon, she says. A shampoo bottle and a portable phone. And something very cold, like a gun. But maybe that was only my imagination.

My fucking god.

Now, she says. Do you think it was Georgia?

I may never know and I can't say I'm sorry anymore. I don't think I can stand the sound of my voice. I listen as she walks down the hall with the portable phone, her footsteps soft and faraway. She goes into the bathroom and I hear her pull back the shower curtain. She locks the door and I listen as she puts her finger down her throat and throws up. She does this twice, her throat racked and hoarse. She sits on the toilet and I listen to her pee. She brings the phone to her mouth and I listen to her breathe.

I'm going to go to sleep now, she says. Will you stay on the phone awhile?

twenty-eight.

Eve is asleep a thousand miles away and I lie on a rented bed, the telephone heavy on my chest.

There's a knock at the door and I tell myself it's Jude, she's forgotten her key. But she is too careful for that and I check the peephole. Distorted and grotesque through the fisheye is Isabel, and she's alone. She is smiling and confident. She wears her own hair, short and dark. She wears a new dress, silver with a metallic texture. Lucy would have looked fabulous in it. She might have a gun behind her back but I really don't care. I want to smash something. I open the door and there's nothing there. I'm only hallucinating again.

Now I wonder where Jude has gone. She does covet the air of mystery, and perhaps she has only disappeared to make me nervous. Maybe she's gone to sell the heroin and won't she be surprised when she finds the Blister's soiled clothes? Maybe she is meeting one of Gore's wraithlike henchmen, negotiating the final terms of the exchange for my remaining organ, for me. And so she had to leave me behind. I would only be cumbersome and dull. I might ask silly questions. Or else she is chatting on a cell phone with another agent back at head-quarters. But she may well be down the street at the bar of a much nicer hotel, killing time and nursing a drink. Lazily eyeing a fat, tor-pid lawyer. He is drinking bourbon on the rocks as if tomorrow will never come and she decides his kidney may be worthless, but perhaps she could move his corneas.

I want to tell her I don't care anymore, that I can forgive her. I only want to kiss her sweet lips and go to sleep. And I'm such a liar. In two days or a week, I would wake beside her sore and stinking of sex and my mouth dry as dust. I would look for flaws in her face and body, imperfections that would prove her heart was never pure. I would not love her. I would not.

I try to remember the way I felt when I first felt her eyes on me. I felt cold, as if I had touched a piece of metal or just walked into a dark movie theater.

I feel extraordinarily calm. It's time for me to run. And it's possible that Jude wants me to run. She wants me to save myself, to disappear. Perhaps she merely wants to hunt me. I roll off the bed and reach for my shoes. I fumble with the laces like a toddler and I try not to worry about the unraveling that will take place inside me when my body begins to crave the phantom drug and I find myself weeping for Jude to save me. I need to get out of here before I change my mind. Before Jude appears, warm and bending to kill me. I take almost nothing with me: knife and gun and a box of .38 ammunition. The torn and filthy clothes I am wearing and a fat wad of cash. I hesitate, then leave half of my money for Jude. I resolve to buy myself some new clothes and a hot meal.

*

Crushing white sunlight and I feel numb, shocked. I was so sure that it was night. I slouch away from the motel, feeling strangely naked without the icebox and I'm sure that everyone on the street is turning to look at me. Every passing car fills me with dread. I cross the street and hurry into an alley. The smell of rotting food drifts from the back of a restaurant and I doubt if I will be able to eat. I need to sit down, to rest. There is a discarded mattress tucked behind a garbage pail and I'm tempted to flop down on it but I'm afraid I would fall asleep and wake up in jail. But my knees are numb and soon I am sitting on a cinder block in the inelegant, squatting position of a man on a child's toilet.

My body is so cold. The sun comes and goes and the light that lingers is lifeless. Nothing has a shadow. I lift my hand to my face and there is no definition. The skin is smooth, transparent. As if I'm wearing latex gloves and the real skin glows through them.

I'm a scarecrow gloomily watching over a cornfield in winter. The goose bumps along my arm are painful to the touch. There are insects beneath my scalp, in my veins and teeth. I think I'm going to faint. I sit on the cinder block, muttering. I twist sideways and wrench the fragile, newly healed skin of my wound. The pain is an electric shock, and soon the insects subside.

Laughter. And a pack of kids swerves down the alley, their movements spidery and sudden and I think they are looking to torment the cripple. Bludgeon the drunk, the homeless man. One of them picks up my fallen baseball cap and hands it to me. I grunt and smile. They spew something in Spanish and float away.

*

Hundreds of eyes and the chirp and giggle of voices, the drone of engines. The urge to flee is a high-pitched whistle and I stare into a black cavity of space that stinks of urine and dead flowers. Of rotting oranges and leather and spray paint. I crawl into the space and find a corner. I stare into the shadows and I see several corpselike figures, coiled in burlap sacks around me. Sleeping drunks with the faces of dogs, of horses. I blink and they're not there.

I sit very still, until I am sure I won't vomit. Then I walk slowly around the building, to the front of the restaurant. There is a faded mural sprawled across the wall near the entrance, depicting a surreal bull-fight. A cartoonlike bull paws at the earth, fire spewing from his massive nostrils. The body of a dead boy lies before him. A police car with a flat tire circles the scene, a rodeo clown at the wheel. In the foreground is a matador bearing a guitar. The audience is made up of young girls, howling and tearing at their clothes. I peer through the windows of the café, shameful as a beggar. A busboy with bright red acne scars wearily mops the floor. I'm reluctant to go inside. I've been in the shadows too long, speaking to no one. I'm afraid of the faces.

I take a seat at a booth in the corner. I'm glad to see the cushions are plush red vinyl, in case I feel faint. Through a mirrored window I can see the Seventh Son. A young man comes to take my order. He is very young, perhaps sixteen. He has the beginnings of a mustache, soft as a baby dog's fur. He looks at me nervously.

What's the matter? I croak.

I'm sorry, sir. The owner says you should go.

Why?

He turns to look at a fat man with a belly like wet cement, leaning on the bar. The owner, presumably. He could break me in two with his little finger.

You don't look so good, the boy says.

I have money, I say. I want a steak and a bottle of wine.

The owner wants you to leave. Please, sir.

I throw some money on the table and stand up. The fat man comes around the bar, his movements surprisingly fluid. His eyes are impassive as pools of ink.

I'm sure you don't pay this boy enough, I say.

Get the fuck out of here, he says. You piece of trash.

On the street again, staring at my reflection in a shop window. I need new clothes, clearly. I need something. When I was with Jude, I might have passed for an eccentric junkie. A suicidal cancer patient with a beautiful wife. An extraterrestrial with a credit card. Without her I'm a leper.

I walk into a men's clothing store and drop five thousand dollars on the counter. The nearest salesperson is a thin man with wispy blond hair and bright pink skin. I'm sure he's an albino and I just can't deal with it right now. It's hard enough to try on pants under normal conditions. But in my state of mind, under the silky cold gaze of rat pink eyes, I think I might come to pieces. I might tell him about the inevitable death of the sun and how those of us that are used to living in shadows will be the new gods. But I look closely at his eyes and they are an ordinary brown. I realize he only has a sunburn.

His lip curls slightly but he shrugs when he sees the money.

I need some new clothes, I say.

The salesman hesitates, then smiles. I should say so, he says.

He isn't a bad guy, the sunburned salesman. His name is Alexander.

He's reluctant at first, but he agrees to hold on to my money. There's no one else in the store, thank god. I can't stand the artificial silence and shared humiliation that seep from the mirrors in a room full of expensive, empty clothing. Alexander takes me gently by the elbow, as if I am his blind girlfriend, his arthritic mother. He helps me pick out some gray wool pants; they are cut like military pants, with multiple pockets and fat belt loops and those small, riveted holes in the crotch that will prevent them from filling with water if I have to slog through a river. I come out of the dressing room and stand before him.

These are some nice pants, I say.

They are fantastic, he says. He turns his head sideways.

I glance at the price tag, I could get six pairs of pants at the army surplus store for that kind of cash. I sigh and realize I don't care. Money has been irrelevant to me, lately. Alexander crouches before me to tug at the hem of my pants. I wait for him to notice the gun at my ankle, and I can't decide if I will shrug and smile or kick him in the mouth like a dog. He doesn't notice it.

I need some new T-shirts, I say.

Alexander raises his left eyebrow, but says nothing. He shows me where the T-shirts are. They seem to be plain cotton T-shirts. But they are apparently designed by a French clothing guru and woven of silver thread. They cost a hundred dollars each. I choose two of them, one black and one green. Alexander coaxes me into taking a white dress shirt as well, in case I need to wear a tie. I laugh weakly at that, and he laughs with me.

What else. Does it get cold here?

At night it gets quite chilly, he says.

A jacket then. And shoes, I think.

Alexander smiles. He disappears for a moment and returns with a long, sleek jacket of heavy brown calfskin. I slip it on and the weight of it feels good. It feels like armor. I realize that my old jacket has been clinging to me like the skin of a dead rat. This jacket will give me the heart of a lion, the penis of a horse. It will cost me the price of a small Japanese car.

Alexander reaches to adjust my lapel, then trails his fingers softly, slowly down my arms.

I'll take it.

Excellent, he says.

I try on several pairs of boots, and finally settle for the simple black ones that zip up the side. I'm glad I won't need to bother with laces for a while.

Alexander looks at me awkwardly. Don't be offended, he says. But you smell like death. I really think you should have a shower before you wear these new things.

I shake my head. Nothing offends me. But I'm a little bit homeless at the moment.

There's a shower in the employee bathroom, he says. I insist.

It can't hurt, I say.

He shows me to the little bathroom and I feel like a holiday houseguest. It feels good to trust someone, if only for a few minutes. The shower is a small box with a sliding glass door. I stand under hot, pounding water and stare down at the stitches in my skin. They coil around me like the rotting skin of a snake, and I wonder if they will dissolve before my eyes. The door to the bathroom opens and I can see Alexander through the steamed glass. He has come to shoot me. Or else he wants to get in the shower with me. I don't really like either idea.

I brought you a towel, he says.

There is another customer in the shop when I come out of the bathroom. A woman, her back turned to me. She has gray hairs and a thick web of blue veins on the backs of her legs. She's no one, a stranger and still I flinch. Alexander cocks his head and puckers his mouth as if to whistle when he sees me. It's foolish, but the new clothes have changed the way I walk. They have given me a temporary sheen of confidence that will be rubbed away in a few hours. Alexander hands me a stack of bills and a leather shoulder bag. The extra shirts are inside, he says. And the money is what's left of my wad. It feels too thick and I thumb through it. A little more than three thousand in matted hundreds and twenties.

I gave you a discount, says Alexander. And I threw in a pair of silk boxers.

Thanks.

A smile creeps across my face and I reach to touch his hand. Kindness from strangers is rare and strange, it makes me weak. I want to tell him that I don't wear boxers, that I don't wear any underwear at all.

twenty-nine.

I nearly ask Alexander to have a drink with me. My tastes don't really run to thin, fair-haired men. It would just be nice to drink with someone who is normal, who isn't lying to me with every breath. I have had the odd moments, though. Some men are disturbingly pretty. The dark, heavy lips and knifelike bones and the feline muscles in their shoulders. Lucy used to drag me to one particularly damp museum in Denver. She loved a lot of postmodern shit, and I would follow her around, generally stoned and indifferent. After an hour or two I would drift away from her until I found the torso. It was a headless fragment, the broken remains of an early Roman statue. The chest and belly of a dying man, dying or twisting in pain. It was carved in marble so smooth it looked wet, and I always wanted to touch it.

I'm coming to pieces and I want to go home.

I wonder if I can pull myself together and hitchhike back to Denver. Then I can get myself a nice job at a gas station, maybe a video store. I can change my name to Freddie and I can mutter to myself and chew on my hair and tell outrageous stories to anyone who will listen. I can meet Eve for coffee and maybe a movie. I can write bad poems for her. I know she has a girlfriend but there's always hope, there's always boredom and the goofy bliss of unrequited love. But I'm far too weak. I'm feeling the first tug of chemical loss in my belly, in the palms of my hands. A stomach full of bland, heavy food will dull the need. I drag myself back to the café that banished me before, hoping the new clothes will do their thing.

The fat man still leans against the bar. His eyebrows twitch when he sees me, but that's all. I sit in the same booth, and this time a girl appears. I tell her to bring me a plate of beans and rice, a shot of tequila and a pot of coffee. The girl is perhaps fourteen and she seems to walk on her toes. She brings me a glass of fresh orange juice, on the house. She says I look very pale. Her only words to me. I drink the juice, and it sloshes around with the coffee and tequila. The beans and rice sit before me, untouched. They are barely warm when I begin to eat. I chew each bite monotonously, tirelessly. And the food stays down.

I am drinking my fourth shot of tequila, feeling slightly damp and bloated and staring out the big glass window as if it's a television and I can't be bothered to change the channel. There is nothing to see. A thousand cars pass, blurry and colorless.

Jude appears from the west, the orange sun falling behind her like a ring of fire. Her face is a shadow. She is light on her feet, as if she couldn't be happier. She carries the icebox and a dozen roses, and a tickle of guilt rises in my throat. Jude disappears around the corner to our room and I hold my breath. I count to five and she comes out of the motel at a half run, her hands empty. She looks up and down the street, and for a moment she glares right at me. I'm sure she sees me.

But I shrink back into my booth and she looks away. Finally she turns and returns to the room. I finish my drink and sit there, smoking.

Time shivers and Jude is on the street again. She has changed into fresh clothes: black jeans and a tight silver shirt that barely covers her stomach, a black trench coat that appears to be made of velvet. Heavy boots and a little black hat that clings to her head. Her backpack is slung over one shoulder. She stands on the street corner for a moment, her face gray as stone. She still holds the icebox. Either she is about to burst into tears, or she is patiently waiting for a bomb to go off. I can never be sure. A car whips past her, then a man on a motorcycle. In their wake, Jude holds out her closed fist for a heart-beat before the torn rose petals tumble away from her open hand. She walks down the street, away from me.

I drop some money on the table and walk out of the café into bruised light. Jude has vanished. I turn in widening circles. She was never there and I don't even feel myself collapse.

Lucy and I were married one year after she fell from the roof. I knew she had leukemia, that I was borrowing her. I should have taken her to France, to the moon. But we tried to shove our lives into a box. Lucy packed away her paints and brushes and let her hair grow. She became a teacher. She begged me for children. I went deeper and deeper with Internal Affairs, until I disappeared. I was underwater. I couldn't be trusted. Lucy was a meteor, burning up as she entered the atmosphere.

I spent nine weeks as a mole with Vice. I was posing as an involuntary transfer from Narcotics. I was posing as another fuck-up and it wasn't hard. My name was Stephen Crow. I had a green convertible and a little apartment two blocks from home and Lucy knew little about it. She called it my artificial life. She was teaching math to snotty kids with penetrating eyes and rapidly mutating bodies. The kids were itching to fuck each other, to kill each other. Lucy was trying to keep a straight face about death. I was supposed to get close to some rogue from Internal Affairs who was selling expensive protection to dirty cops in Vice. Of course, I never found him.

But I did get tangled up with a male prostitute. His name was T. and he had the soft, liquid brown eyes of a German shepherd. The kid was dangling on a hook between good cops and bad cops. Everybody was squeezing him and the pale brown shit was running out of his ass and mouth. The bad guys were feeding him bogus information and he was selling it to the good guys, and some of the good guys were getting killed. I casually decided to look into it, as if I were trying on a new hat. I had nothing to lose. My own assignment was dead, it was a stuffed animal. This prostitute could have been big for me. He could have been huge. I thought I could tie a string around his toe and follow him to a nest of filthy cops.

I got close to little T. without any trouble. I had some heroin I was willing to share, and all it would cost him was a little love. I shared a needle with him and we nodded for hours together in his shadowy room. He tried to feed me some of his bad information but I wasn't listening. I was staring at his long dark eyelashes, his perfect nose. He had the skin of a baby and I knew he would be dead soon. T. was arrogant and rude but not entirely stupid. He smelled the badge on me and still he gave me the most stunning blow job I ever had. He left me nearly in tears. T. sat back against the wall in a yellow splash of sunlight that fell over his bare futon and rolled a lumpy cigarette. He was pleased with himself. There was a gold fleck of tobacco on his lower lip.

He eyed my wedding ring and said, Does your wife know?

I stared at him without smiling. It was fascinating, really, that I could be so stupid, so careless. Stephen Crow was surely not married.

Does she know what? I said.

He grinned. That you like boys.

I drank flat beer from a green bottle and resisted the urge to pluck the tobacco from his lip, to twist the lip until it turned white between my fingers.

It isn't about that, I said. You could be a little girl or a dog.

T. blew smoke rings, his mouth dark and pouting.

It's about alien flesh and misplaced sympathy.

Why don't you speak English?

My wife is dying, I said. And she's so close to me that I can't touch her. I don't know you but I can see her in you. I see death in you and it's so much easier to give myself to you.

T. flicked his cigarette at a withered aloe plant.

It's a terrible feeling, I said.

But I'm not dying, he said.

I can see your dead body when I close my eyes, I said. And it makes you glow a little more brightly.

T. pulled a blue plaid shirt across his lap. I'm not dying, he said.

But you are, I said. You have fucking killed yourself. If I don't kill you, someone else will.

He threw my shoes at me and told me to get the fuck out. I marveled at how easily tenderness became cruelty and took the stairs two at a time, manic and cheerful. The kid was dead two days later. One of the good cops decided it was no fun being good all the time, and little T. was found in bed with both brown eyes gouged out and a bullet in the back of his head.

I went home to Lucy and made frantic love to her on the floor beside our bed. The sun fell in shreds. She wrapped her legs around me and told me outrageous stories about her students. Lucy told me how the kids looked at her, how she felt naked before them. She told me that she was never going to die. I couldn't tell her anything. I still had an apartment two streets away. I want to say: I saw you. Two weeks ago, when my name was Stephen Crow and I was barely awake, smoking a cigarette at my window. You walked right past me and I was a ghost behind glass. Your car must have died and you had to catch the bus. I stared at you so hard that I could see through your clothes. I could see the cancer in your blood and I was made of tin.

Lucy never asked if I had other lovers when I was undercover, when I was artificial. There's a bumpy road beneath me and I wake up choking. I blink my eyes and I'm in a fucking ambulance. I'm strapped down like a bug, my poor skull rattling. The funny thing is that no one is busy trying to save my life. I'm hooked up to no machinery. In fact, the paramedics are studiously ignoring me. The siren is off. I twist my neck around and peer at a female medic sitting in the jump seat, a clipboard in hand. She has dark skin and cropped black hair, a weirdly muscular face. She wears navy blue pants and a white shirt and polished black desert boots.

What happened? I say.

Her eyes fix on me, narrow and blue. You were asleep in the middle of the road.

I'm not dying.

She sighs. No.

Then remove these straps, please.

Relax, she says.

Take off the fucking straps and let me out.

Relax, she says. Those are for your safety.

Where are you taking me?

She squints at me. The hospital.

Oh, yeah. And who is paying for this?

The woman shrugs, then writes a few words on the clipboard. The rapid click of a mechanical pencil as she ejects a piece of broken lead. Her hand moves lazily. She could be deciding my future, or merely doodling. She could be sketching a three-dimensional box, as if she's on the phone with a dull salesman.

You are, she says. Or your next of kin.

At the hospital, I refuse to change into one of those foolish gowns. I don't want any sticky questions about weapons. I'm poked and prodded by one unsmiling male intern who assumes I came in to beg for painkillers. I have no insurance and I'm wasting his time. He asks about my scar and I tell him I recently had some work done on my bladder. He doesn't laugh. Alexander pushes through the powder blue curtain that hides one exam area from its neighbors. His cheeks are rosy as ever, his hair thin as silk. He smiles when he sees me. The intern wipes sweat from his upper lip and scowls at me. I'm not only a malnourished junkie found crumpled before oncoming traffic, but I must be queer as well. The horror. I'm tempted to roll off the table and cut his throat or at least force him to watch me give Alexander a long, sloppy kiss but really I'm too tired to do anything but flap my hand.

How is he? says Alexander.

He's dehydrated, says the intern. Among other things.

Alexander looks mildly disappointed. The intern shrugs and tells me to roll over.

Why?

I'm going to give you a shot.

No, thanks.

He stares at me, his eyes hooded. He looks like he hasn't slept in a while.

What's your name? he says.

I smile. I don't want a shot.

This is a nutritional supplement, he says.

You don't care if I take it or not, do you?

No, he says. I don't care.

Okay, then.

I slide my pants down and I'm sure my skinny ass is a sorry sight. The intern is rude and unsympathetic but he's good with a needle. I barely feel a thing. Then he tells me to relax, to wait. He disappears and I'm alone with Alexander, who sits on a stool, spinning around like a kid.

I found you, he says. I went out for coffee and I just happened to glance down the road. I saw a shadowy lump and I thought someone had run over a dog. But then I recognized your pants.

My ass is getting sore and I rub it briefly, staring at him.

I like these pants, I say.

Anyhow, he says. I checked your pulse and everything and called the ambulance.

Did you drag me out of the road?

No, he says. I didn't want to move you. In case you had a spinal injury.

I laugh at that and my mind drifts. Something else is wrong with me. The bag of smack that Jude supposedly planted in my guts, for instance.

Alexander smiles. I waved the traffic around you, like a cop. I always wanted to do that.

I hear Crumb's dry voice: *maybe there's a bomb inside you, a tumor.*

Or a litter of puppies, I say.

Excuse me? says Alexander.

Nothing.

The paramedics didn't want to take you at first, he says. They said you were drunk.

I was drunk. But that offends me.

Anyhow, I talked them into it. I told them I was a friend of yours.

A friend, I say. The word floats between us like a speck of dust.

I thought so, he says.

Silence.

Alexander plays with a discarded stethoscope. I close my eyes and listen to my gurgling belly. There's nothing in there. The intern pokes his head through the curtain.

You're finished, he says.

Alexander frowns. Are you sure?

There's nothing wrong with him.

I was wondering, I say. How much for a couple of X rays?

What? he says. You don't need X rays.

Humor me.

Well, he says. It depends on your deductible. And the radiologist's fee.

I don't have insurance. And radiologists are overpaid geeks.

He glares at me. Don't waste my time.

How much?

Two thousand dollars, maybe.

I whistle and sigh, then pull out my wallet and start counting.

This isn't a barbershop. You don't just get X rays because you feel like it.

Would you deny me medical treatment?

Alexander clears his throat. Why do you want X rays?

I lift my shirt to expose the scar. There's something inside me.

The intern laughs. Like what?

I whisper and twitch as if stricken by palsy. Rosemary's fucking baby. I don't know, okay. I don't know. That's why I want X rays.

Calm down, says Alexander.

Please, says the intern. Take your friend home and tuck him into bed.

He's not my friend, I say. He's just a salesman who was nice to me.

I see. Have you had episodes like this before?

Every day, I say.

The intern shakes his head. I will be happy to call for a psych exam.

I have a gun, I say. And I want those X rays.

This is sad, he says.

Oh, you motherfucker. I want to talk to someone else.

The intern backs away smiling and he calls for someone else. He calls security. Alexander has become green and I think he's sick to his stomach, as if he just realized he is terribly lost in the woods. I walk out with a fat rented cop who breathes through his mouth. He tells me he has sinus trouble and I want to tell him that he should keep his weaknesses private, that sometimes I'm guilty of the same random intimacy. I pay nine hundred dollars for the ambulance and the B12 shot. I call for a cab. Alexander and the cop with sinus trouble wait outside with me. Alexander scratches compulsively at his sunburn, the dead skin falling from his arm in gray flakes. I'm an asshole and I try to apologize. I nearly offer him money. He chews at the side of his mouth and doesn't look at me.

thirty.

The cab unloads me before the Seventh Son and I slink across the parking lot to my room, to our room. I imagine the roses lie half crushed on the floor, on the bed. One of the maids will find them tomorrow. She will be a single mother, overweight and uneducated. She will hate to see such pretty things wasted. She will put the roses in water and watch them die and I laugh at myself. The roses were not real.

I push open the door to our room and Isabel turns to grin at me like a car, her mouth bright with feathers. She wears the red wig, the dead stolen hair of Rose White.

Are you lonely? she says.

Terribly.

She stands on one foot, her arms uncoiled at her sides. She is pale and fleshy.

I could strangle you with that hair.

Isabel laughs. Jude told me you were easily excited, she says.

She lazily adjusts the wig, her bare arms raised above her head. She tucks a stray red wisp behind her ears. She licks her lips and sits down on the bed. I might be a madman but I think she's wearing the same silver dress as before. Perhaps I'm dreaming again. I'm only looking through a peephole. I watch her cross her legs and I have to tell myself she's not Lucy. My mouth is hot.

It didn't take you long to find us, I say.

Jude is so predictable, she says. She's like a bird, returning to nest.

How did you get in?

The manager, she says. I told him I was your wife and I wanted to surprise you.

Oh, I love a surprise.

I sink into a chair, wishing I had a glass of gin to swirl casually in my left hand.

Where is the dear girl? says Isabel.

She walks around the room, touching things. She reclines on the bed, her legs slightly apart. She's wearing the white garter belt again and this time it's cartoonish. I could bash her skull with a hammer and it would only bounce off. She would give me a wacky smile as her rubber skull popped back into place.

Jude isn't coming back, I say.

What a pity.

But I'm glad you're here. I was just thinking of you.

Nice thoughts, I hope.

Did you have any fun in Denver?

I was such a slug, she says. A fat, lazy slug.

But you did find time to kill a woman named Rose White.

And the weather was positively beastly, she says.

Did you kill her for her stethoscope? I say. And her little green scrubs?

I painted my nails and ate room service all day.

Because you can buy that shit at any drugstore.

She smiles. I love those little shrimp cocktails.

You stole her fucking hair.

She hisses at me. I invented Rose White. She never existed.

Her body was found yesterday, in the trunk of a black Mustang.

That's so strange.

Tell me one thing. Where did you get my gun?

Oh, she says. It fell into my lap. Your little wife gave it to me.

Jude, you mean.

Who else?

The tiny room spins and I smile. What do you want from me?

I want you, she says.

Fuck you.

Where is the icebox? she says.

I gave it away. I sold it to an ugly little man in Las Vegas.

She blinks rapidly and I study her. She doesn't look like Lucy at all, not really. The hair and clothes and the body are the same. But her face is a fucking mask. Her eyes look right through me. I swivel my head around woodenly. There must be something to drink in this room. The toilet flushes with a sudden boom and I turn to look at Isabel. Are we not alone, I say. The Blister walks out of the bathroom, drying his hands on a white towel. He wears the fur coat and a white silk tie and a smile like dry ice.

Oh, this gets better and better.

I believe you know my ugly little brother, says Isabel.

The Blister sits down gingerly, as if the furniture is simply too cheap and dirty.

Hello, I say. My name is Phineas Poe.

He sneers. Such wit.

What is your fucking name?

Isabel sighs. His name is Jerome Gore.

I sink into the bed. I have had such a long day.

Isabel takes off the red wig and tosses it aside. It crouches on the floor like a headless animal and my mind is coming apart, like a frayed and tangled piece of rope. The Blister laughs, or chokes. I tell myself to think of him as Jerry. My hands float before my face, disconnected and useless. Isabel runs fingers through her own sleek black hair. It is cut exactly like Lucy's was, before she lost it. She smiles and wets her lips with a flashing tongue.

Which do you prefer, she says. Sex or violence?

I try to smile. What's the difference, really.

And I slap at my pockets, desperate for a cigarette. I'm about to ask Jerry if he has any when Isabel takes two steps and she's so close to me I can smell her. She stinks of eucalyptus. She flips open an engraved silver case and slides a cigarette between my lips. Thick black smoke drifts between us and I feel better.

Just knock him on the head and be done with it, says the Blister.

Shut up, she says.

He sighs. Have your fun, then.

Isabel reaches between her breasts and unzips the silver dress to her waist. She wears a white lace bustier. Her skin is bright with warm, thick blood moving beneath the surface. She's alive, she's Lucy and I just want to touch her. I want to pull her close and tell her how sorry I am. I want to push her gently to the floor and kiss the pulse in her throat. I want to breathe her new life. I want to tell her a thousand things and close my eyes and disappear into her. But she's an illusion, a specter.

The Blister groans loudly and flicks on the television. He finds a tennis match on cable and settles back in his chair. Isabel picks up the telephone and the Blister glances at her.

Are you calling room service? he says. Because I would love a cup of tea.

Isabel yanks the plug from the wall and throws the telephone at him. It barely misses his head and he gives her a filthy look.

Turn it off, she says. Or else I'm going to make you wait outside.

Don't be such a slut, he says.

Maybe I should wait outside, I say.

No, says Isabel.

The Blister mutes the television and shrugs.

Isabel is naked now and my eyes betray me. I steal a long, hungry look at her. Her breasts are larger than Jude's, her belly softer. She has a wild black bush of pubic hair, and her thighs are creamy white and not so long and muscular. I can imagine them wrapped around my head. They are Lucy's legs.

She smiles and says, do you like me?

No. I don't like you.

Look at me, she says. Touch me. I could be your wife.

I throw a towel at her. Have some shame.

Yes, the Blister says loudly. Do us a fucking favor.

Why, she says. Why did you give the icebox to such a pig?

I shrug. He seemed to want it.

But it was empty, she says.

Oh, no. It was packed full of heroin.

Heroin, she says. Her face grows slowly, frighteningly dark.

It was excellent stuff, I say. The best.

Whose was it?

I believe it was Jerry's.

Isabel walks across the room, slowly. Her bare ass swaying as if it's Saturday night and she can't decide whether to go out or just wash her hair.

Jerome, she says. Where did the heroin come from?

The Blister stares at the silent tennis match. He takes out a giant gun exactly like the one I took from him in Vegas. He gives me a faint smile and places the gun on his thigh. Isabel laughs at him.

You spent the money on heroin, didn't you. What else did you buy?

That was a slick Lincoln town car you were driving around Denver, I say.

He looks at me. You're a mouse, he says. A bug.

And that's a nice fur coat, I say.

Isabel takes the Blister's gun from him and unloads it. She drops the bullets to the floor like shiny pebbles. She slips the gun back into his lap, snug against his crotch. The Blister's face is changing colors, humming with blood and I imagine his little penis swollen and pulsing under her thumb. He wants to fuck her, to kill her. He's terrified of her. I can almost sympathize.

My. That is a lovely fur, she says. Is it otter?

Take your hand off me, sister.

Isabel looks at me over one shoulder.

This is so embarrassing, she says. My youngest brother, Horatio, is dying. He has an immune deficiency disorder and he badly needs a kidney.

The Blister shows his teeth. Horatio has AIDS, you stupid cow. He's queer as a blue moon.

Be careful, she says.

Your brother needs a kidney, I say. He needs my kidney.

Yes, she says. I hired Jude to find a suitable donor. And she found five.

Five, I say.

Isabel shrugs and explains that Jude accessed the medical files of nine hundred inmates and medical patients. Eleven of them matched Horatio's blood and tissue type, five of them were scheduled for release. And then it was a matter of elimination. One suffered chronic hepatitis, another tuberculosis. Two of them were very unattractive, she says. They were genetically inferior.

What?

She smiles. You were the best-looking, by far.

What difference does that make?

None, she says.

I stare at her. Would you borrow a pair of shoes from an ugly girl?

What kind of shoes?

Oh, god.

She bites her lip. Ironic, isn't it?

Oh, yes. It's bad poetry.

It was really a simple transaction, she says. It was like ordering lingerie from a catalog. But my father foolishly gave Jerome a suitcase full of money and sent him to make the exchange.

I was unstoppable, says the Blister.

A disaster, she says.

I was the spy that came in from the cold and the cops were licking my bootheels.

Isabel laughs as if her head will fly off.

Jerome came home in a fury, she says. He said that Jude cheated him, that she took the kidney to another buyer. He needed his little sister's help.

Isabel touches her fingers to the Blister's lips.

Oh you wet bitch, he whispers.

Actually, I say. I think she gave the kidney to some orphan.

The Blister bites into Isabel's hand as if it were a piece of fruit. Her face turns white.

I still have my knife in the wrist sheath and I shrug and it's in my hand, cool and untrembling. My knees are like water, though. I take two endless steps through mud and black sand and push the point of the tanto into the Blister's ear. If I sneeze or flinch or tremble, the Blister has brain damage. He opens his mouth, blood on his lips. Isabel jerks her hand free and whirls away from him, screeching like a mad bird. I'm not sure if she's dancing, if she's about to attack. I glace at the Blister and he too is uneasy. Isabel whirls prettily and kicks him in the mouth with her bare heel. The Blister rolls to his knees, the big gun in his left hand. He picks up two of his loose bullets and reloads, spitting blood. I stare at him lazily. I don't even reach for my gun. The Blister backs away from us, the gun pointed at Isabel, then at me. He pulls the trigger and the hammer falls on an empty chamber with a vaguely disappointing little click. The Blister throws open the door and is gone.

Isabel is breathing hard, drunk with her own blood.

That was beautiful, she says.

It was interesting.

She licks her lips and leans close to me.

What's the matter? she says.

Are you kidding?

I would have spared you this, she says.

Yeah.

The room is shrinking. I'm stupid with hunger.

My brother is such a pill, she says.

What happened to his hands? I say.

Oh, god. I'm so tired of that story.

What happened?

Isabel is so close to me that I can feel her body vibrating. She reminds me of an electric carving knife, the blade that hums effortlessly through meat. She seems to occupy more space than I do. Isabel claps her hands together and I jump at the sound. She laughs merrily and abruptly reaches for her metallic dress, then pulls it like a sack over her head. She zips it to the throat. She asks me to find her panties. I glance around and spot a clump of white lace on the floor, barely touching Jude's hairbrush. I flick them at her and watch as she pulls them slowly up her thighs to disappear beneath her dress.

She ignores the wig and bustier. I kick them under the bed, feeling suddenly sweaty.

Are you leaving? I say.

I'm sorry, she says. I hope you didn't want to fuck me.

I see myself, bent and jerking at her unresponsive body in fierce rabbit strokes. Isabel is staring at her fingernails, perhaps thinking that what she needs is an expensive manicure. She shrugs and begins to tidy the room. She picks up the fallen telephone.

Not really, I say. I wanted to reject you.

Could you?

Fuck you. What was that, then?

That was pure theater. I call it amusing Jerome.

Why?

He deserves it.

Because of the heroin?

I take a step forward and her eyes flicker. Among other things.

Does he want your brother to die?

She takes a shallow breath and spits. He wants to be famous.

What does that mean? He wants to be on television?

He wants to be my father.

I step closer. Would your father have tried to double-cross Jude?

Isabel forces herself to shrug and she looks briefly weak. I step closer and she smiles, muscles flexing in her neck.

It's not safe here, she says.

I tell her to lock the door and she shudders. I step close enough to touch her, to hurt her. She wants me, she's pulling me in. Her eyes are downcast and she lets her body go limp. I should cut her throat or run away but my hands slip around her waist and my brain drones like television and I don't even ask myself what I'm doing and then I hear the odd jingle of the telephone as she swings it in a narrow, intimate arc that crashes into the side of my skull.

I swim through a prolonged black void to find that my arms and legs are gone. I'm sure they will come back to me when it's too late. My spine is like soup. I seem to be stretched like a corpse on my own vibrating bed. Though it's mercilessly not vibrating, currently. Isabel circles around me, her body weirdly contorted and legless. My vision must be fucked. A nice blow to the head will do that. I am so stupid, so easily foiled. It's really almost funny. If I could lift a finger I would gladly kill myself. Isabel rummages through Jude's things and cheerfully produces a set of handcuffs. She gives them a shake and they ring like new money.

What the fuck is this?

You are supposed to be asleep.

You hit me with a telephone.

I'm sorry, she says. I still need your kidney.

Oh, well. I'm afraid it's gone.

Funny, she says.

Do you know what you're doing? I say.

Hush, she says.

Jude told me that you butchered a male prostitute.

Oh, she says. That's true, actually.

She uses my own knife to cut away my fine new shirt. The room yawns around me and I wish I had gone to have a quiet drink with Alexander. Isabel shackles my hands together, gently. My face is at such an angle that I can only see the television. The silent tennis match defies gravity. Isabel washes my chest with rubbing alcohol and uses my own disposable razor to shave the hair from the right side of my torso. I wonder if the two scars will meet, if they will make a circle. I never hear the door open and I don't hear footsteps. I hear a soft, sleepy noise like air escaping. I'm aware that Isabel is twisting, falling. Then she becomes still and Jude is leaning over me and her lips are soft as shadows.

You should have run, she says. You should have run when I gave you the chance.

thirty-one.

The toe of a boot against my ribs. I wake from the gray landscape of empty dreams.

Jude, I say.

Apologies, brother. But I'm not gonna kiss you. Henry's voice.

He crouches beside me and strikes a match. His face is dirty, unshaven in the flickering glow. He smells like rain and he doesn't smile. He offers me his hand and I let him pull me to my feet. I stare blankly at my watch. One in the morning, says Henry.

I thought I had seen the last of you.

Never fear.

How did you find me?

I have a keen sense of smell, he says. I can sniff out a fuck-up from miles away.

I reach for a cigarette and say nothing. I'm still half asleep. The room is dark and I wonder if Jude knocked out the electricity. I can't see a thing but I'm sure Jude has disappeared. She is reluctant to linger, to leave a trace. Henry lights another match and I see that the bed is neatly made. There are no signs of love or struggle and Jude's things are gone.

You must be the stupidest motherfucker I ever saw, he says. Or the luckiest.

I was born under a dying star, a red dwarf.

Let's go, says Henry. I want to show you something.

He lights another match. Isabel is in the bathtub and the air is ripe with the copper smell of blood. She's curled in a ball, feline and beautiful in the unstable light.

The power comes on with a tremble. There is a long smear of black feces on the white floor, marked by a single smallish footprint that can only be Jude's. Blood seeps from Isabel's mouth and from her swollen left eye. Her lips are sewn shut. There is a sleek, unhurried cut across her breasts. Her feet bear tiny, bloodless puncture wounds. I lean over the toilet but it's full of blood. I turn and throw up calmly in the sink.

Your girlfriend, says Henry. She's a real daydream.

Oh, yeah. She'll make a nice little wife, one day.

I wipe my mouth on a towel.

This is a terrible fucking thing, says Henry.

Did you call the cops?

He grunts. Do you want to talk to the cops?

Not really.

Then shut the fuck up.

How long was I asleep?

I don't have a clue, brother. I missed the little tea party.

Jude is gone, then. I've lost her.

Henry leans against the door. He produces a cigar and pokes it between his lips.

Take it easy, little Joe. We just might catch up with her.

I sit on the edge of the bloody toilet. I notice that he has abandoned the slick, homicidal stockbroker look. He has become the drifter again, the ex-convict. He chews the cigar and grins at me.

Where is she, I say.

I have a few ideas, he says.

Let's get out of here, I say. Before the earth swallows her.

One more thing, says Henry. He pokes Isabel, who twitches like a rubber doll.

My god.

Interesting, isn't it? The body can survive a lot.

Tell me about it.

Blank blue eyes and a naked yellow sun. Two people in a boat, a man and a woman. The man is drunk or catatonic. Something is wrong with the woman and Isabel doesn't move or try to speak. There is so much blood in the bathtub that I can't believe she's alive.

She's dead. She's dead, Henry.

The dead don't move, he says.

They fucking do, I say. It's some kind of postmortem electric weirdness. I've seen it in the morgue. The dead bodies sit up and roll over and have erections and say hello all the time. It's like a party in there.

Henry smiles. I'm telling you she's alive.

You're sick.

Touch her, says Henry.

I hesitate, then jab at the body with one finger. I feel like a kid who's been dared to touch an unidentified object in the park. A decomposing squirrel, a lump of moldy clothes and garbage. Nothing happens. Isabel doesn't move. I pull out my little pocketknife and carefully cut the stitches from her lips. Fluid spills from her mouth and it's a wonder she didn't vomit and drown herself. She tries to speak but her words are like slush, malformed. The gibberish of a monkey.

What the hell is wrong with her?

Look at her left eye, says Henry.

Yeah. It's fucked.

No, he says. The eye isn't the point.

What is the point, Henry?

Jude didn't mean to blind this girl, he says. The wound is just above the eyeball.

The frontal lobe, I say.

Nice piece of work, isn't it? He chews the cigar and spits violently.

That fucking dental tool. I close my eyes and I can see Jude carefully, calmly stabbing it in beneath the ridge of bone and guiding the sleek, curved tip up and into her brain.

Henry shrugs. I thought you might want to kill her. Or shall I do it?

The boat drifts under the staring sun. I tell Lucy to be careful she doesn't burn. She doesn't answer and I think she's asleep. Time becomes elastic and the bottle is empty. I take off my shirt and use it to cover her. She's turning red now and I check the pockets of my shorts. I have a knife and nothing else. No identification. I slip over the side of the boat.

I don't want to kill her. I can't.

Someone needs to kill her.

Shut up.

Isabel sighs wetly. She's like a kid born with brain damage. She will need someone to feed her, to bathe her. I look into her mutilated eye. Do you want a doctor, I say. An ambulance?

That's enough, says Henry.

I'm going to call 911, I say.

No, says Henry.

I turn around as he pulls a gun from inside his jean jacket. Unpolished chrome 9 mm, with a black rubber grip. The barrel has been fitted with a silencer. He offers it to me like a gift and my lips are cracked, white with salt. I move in widening circles, away from the lake. I can still hear the water. She floats. Her face is gone. When the sun rises again I press the knife into my arm to make the ninth cut.

I don't want the gun.

Henry pushes me gently to one side. He bends to kiss Isabel on the cheek, then steps back. He rips the shower curtain down and wraps it around himself. Isabel screams, nodding her head madly and drumming the tub with her heels until Henry puts two quick bullets in her brain.

Henry and I sit next to each other on the bed. Henry holds his cigar and shivers, staring at the television. His face is glossy with tears. A black and white cowboy movie flickers on the screen. Isabel is a bundle of bloody rags, a dummy. She will soon be placed in a drawer in a huge, windowless room. She's not Lucy and she never was and I'm anxious to get away from her. If I turn my head slightly to the left, I can see a string of her blood stretching across the floor.

Henry sits against the wall, silent and furious. I smash the television to pieces and the room fills with smoke. I crush a cheap wooden chair with my fists and I love the rage. I wish it were mine. But it will soon disappear, like everything else. Henry rips the sheets from the bed and staggers into the bathroom to cover the body.

A half hour passes and I feel a little better. I catch a glimpse of myself in the mirror and I'm naked to the waist. Isabel cut off my shirt, I remember. I glance at my new pants and their thousand pockets. I find the leather bag that Alexander gave me and try on one of the priceless T-shirts. I slip into my new leather coat and I'm born again. Henry tells me a bad cowboy joke, about two cowboys and a hatful of water. They are taking turns guarding the hat while the other one sleeps. Soon the water seeps through the hat, and the cowboys are at each other's throat. Henry forgets the punch line, and the joke falls apart.

thirty-two.

I follow him out to his car, a long red monster with whitewall tires.

Very inconspicuous, I say.

I swear by American cars, he says. The first car I ever loved a woman in was a Cutlass Supreme. You can't maneuver properly in a little Nissan.

That's the trouble with this country, I say. Too much room for fucking.

Henry laughs and climbs in. The engine roars like a wounded elephant. I shrug and get in, happy to sit down. I want to sleep for two days. I toss my bag on the backseat and we glide out of the parking lot and onto the dark highway. The sky is still black, nearly purple. There's no moon yet, or it's in hiding.

I close my eyes and try to float.

Something is wrong with you, he says.

I can't even count the ways.

Did you ever see a crippled animal on the highway? Its back legs shattered so it has to drag itself off the road and it makes you sick to look at it.

Maybe, I say. So what?

Didn't you have the decency to stop and kill the fucking thing or did you keep driving.

Fuck you. I know what's decent.

Mercy, he says. What about mercy?

It's easy to kill someone and call it mercy.

I stare at the black, rippling road. If one is confronted with a creature that is dying, that is weak, it's easier to look away than to kill. And what did I tell the Blister in Las Vegas? That it's more interesting to torture a frog than to save it. But there is another choice that is harder than any of these.

There is silence for a mile or two. Henry offers me a cigar.

No, thanks. I think I would throw up.

You're just kicking, he says. I've seen it a thousand times.

I'm kicking. And what do you know about it?

I know Jude was shooting you up regular. Some kind of magic shit, too. You were hallucinating and paranoid and pitiful and generally falling out of your skin.

Falling out of my skin, I say. I like the sound of that.

Let me tell you right now, he says. I don't care for junkies. They got the mentality of a cockroach and they're twice as pathetic. A cockroach at least has pride. I know you didn't get hooked on purpose or anything like that. However. When I see an addict, I personally want to kick his sorry ass. Especially if he's crying like a baby, laying around in his own piss and puke. I'd be happy to put a bullet in his belly.

That's beautiful, I say. It's heartwarming, really.

The reason I mention it, he says. If you're gonna get like that, you need to warn me. Otherwise, I will stop this car and push your ass out. I will leave you in the desert to die.

Don't worry, I say. I'm right as rain. I haven't puked in an hour, at least.

I'm serious, he says. You get sick in my car and we're gonna have some words. Just kick the shit quietly, like a cowboy. Then I'll be your best friend.

My only fucking friend, more like it.

You could do worse.

Who the fuck are you?

Henry Love, he says. He turns slightly, and offers me his hand. I grasp it, weirdly grateful.

And what is your real name?

That's it. On my mother's soul and god rest her.

Henry, I say. I think it's high time we had a little chat.

Indeed.

Who do you work for?

I'm an independent contractor.

Whatever you say. But how are you involved in this game?

You and I have a mutual friend. Funny-looking bastard called Detective Moon. I spoke to him yesterday, matter of fact. And he said to say hello for him.

Moon sent you? I don't believe it.

Eucalyptus, says Henry.

What?

It's a code, goddammit.

Eucalyptus, I say.

Something about velvet panties. Moon said you would know what it means.

The cigar glows orange in his mouth.

I suppose it means I should trust you.

Moon was worried about you, brother. He said you were on the stinky end of something bad, and you were all fucked up. He said a five-year-old could hand your ass to you.

That's nice of him.

He wasn't half wrong, says Henry.

And so you came down out of the sky to save me. Are you Batman or is Moon throwing you some money?

Henry laughs. Moon doesn't have any money. He bets on everything but the weather.

Then you do know him, I say.

Maybe he made an outstanding warrant or two go away, says Henry. As a favor. And I looked into your situation, as a favor.

Warrants for what?

Just shut up and I'll tell you my life story, he says. If you're so interested.

Please, I say. I love a good story.

He drives with one hand. The other dangles out his window. I used to be a fed, he says. A long time ago, five years ago at least. I can't really believe it myself. And it wasn't much fun. A lot of pencil pushing, mostly. Like I was an insurance agent. It wasn't what I signed up for, believe me. I wanted to hunt down a serial killer or two and have a few epic gunfights with the mob, you know what I mean.

I sigh. The man from U.N.C.L.E.

Exactly, he says. That's the shit.

Television, I say. The stuff of dreams.

Henry shrugs. Whatever. It was a fucking bore. Then one fine day, I got a little too creative and maybe a little violent. I broke another agent's neck during a simulation and I was bounced out of there like a bad salesman. I drifted around for a while and figured I'd use my skills to make a little cash. I ran drugs for a while, but like I said, I developed a serious dislike for junkies. I took up bounty hunting, over in Arizona mostly. It's not half bad, it's like hunting rabbits.

I don't know. Rabbits are pretty clever.

No shit. And fast little fuckers. Humans are easier to catch. Anyway, that's how I came to encounter your pal Moon. I retrieved a boy that had jumped bail on a carjacking charge in Colorado, and Moon came to collect him. The kid was still unconscious in the back of my truck when Moon got there. And Moon didn't want to move him, see. I was a good host and broke out a bottle. Moon and me, we got drunk and stayed up half the night.

I'm curious. Why was the kid unconscious, exactly?

Henry laughs. Oh, well. I used tranquilizer darts on him. The kind the animal control uses when a mad dog gets loose in somebody's tomato garden.

That is creative. And very funny.

Then a year ago I fucked up. One of my rabbits had himself a seizure and almost perished. I had to take him to the emergency room and he was all bruised and cut up. The cops came to sort it out and I got charged with excessive force, illegal weapons, assault on a cop and contempt of court and a pile of other shit. The judge didn't much care for me and managed to hit me with the maximum for everything. I got out two months ago and found out I had bench warrants in California and Tennessee for a handful of failure charges.

I stare into the dark and wonder what color the moon will be tonight.

What kind of charges?

Failure charges, he says. Failure to pay, failure to appear, failure to comply. Moon took care of them for me and here I am. It's like a little vacation, really.

You used to be a fed, huh? That's funny. It seems like everybody wants to be a secret agent.

Who do you mean?

Jude, I say. She gave me some smoke about being in the CIA.

That's horseshit, he says. As a former agent, that offends me. Besides. I checked her out. She was in the army for a while, special forces. But she didn't last. She received a dishonorable discharge five years ago, for nonspecific fucked-up reasons. Then she became a ghost.

Or a shape-shifter, I say.

Henry grins. In those five years, there have been twelve other cases of some poor fucker just like you. They wake up in a bathtub full of ice, with staples in their guts. They all describe a different woman, but it's her. Each guy had just been released from jail or the nuthouse.

Thirteen human kidneys, I say. And you've got enough blood pudding for the queen.

Relax, brother.

I'm fucking relaxed. I'm like butter. Where did you get this information?

I still have a friend or two up at Quantico. They have some really big computers, you know.

Henry slows the car as we approach a decayed roadhouse on the left. A blinking neon sign: THE BROKEN HEART. A wide gravel lot, with a dozen cars and trucks.

Beautiful, says Henry. I would kill my granny for a beer right now.

What do you want? I say. Everybody wants something.

I told you. Moon asked me to look out for you, that's all. And it wasn't hard. I took a liking to you right away, in that bathroom. You were like a dying saint or something. The way you handed over your wedding ring for a hat.

Oh, yeah. Then why didn't you state your true purpose?

Because I wasn't sure how deep you were in with her.

You were sniffing around like a pure grifter. Looking for a crack to wiggle through.

That was an unfortunate tactic, he says. I apologize. But I wanted to see how you reacted to various stimuli. Then you got a mighty bug up your ass and hopped off the train. Which was irritating, by the way.

Stimuli, I say. Like you fucking my wife.

Your wife?

Yeah. My dead wife, Lucy. You couldn't help yourself, I guess.

Listen to yourself, brother.

Get the fuck out of the car, I say. Just get out.

Phineas.

No weapons, I say.

Henry laughs. You don't want to fight me, Phineas.

thirty-three.

The hum and buzz of music and dogs and people.

Our boots crunch in the gravel. The sky is black. Henry wobbles before me and I feel like I'm on a boat. I swing at him, my arm suddenly ten feet long. He ducks under it easily and punches me in the stomach and I am on my knees, trying to breathe. I see Lucy, naked and coiled around him. His hands gripped her soft ass like a piece of dough. I stand up, slowly. Henry watches me, his hands loose and relaxed at his sides. He has a small, sad smile on his face.

You know those fat houseflies that drift around in the winter? he says.

Like cows with wings, I say.

Exactly. You have the reflexes of a cow.

I push off the car and spin, sending a wild high kick at his head. He steps out of the way and hits me in the side of the neck, then brings his forearm up to crush my nose.

Are you finished? he says. Because this is embarrassing.

I'm finished.

Henry pulls me up. What's wrong with you? he says.

I'm so tired. And I want to hurt somebody.

Sure, he says. But I haven't done anything to you. That girl on the train was Isabel. And Moon told me your wife is dead and buried, anyhow.

I know it was Isabel on the train. But she was Lucy's shadow.

Okay, he says. It's okay. I understand.

Henry does something amazing, baffling. He hugs me. I lock my jaw to stop from weeping. He pulls away and sticks his ring finger in his mouth, tugging my wedding ring off with his teeth. He drops it in my hand and it feels warm to my skin.

Thank you, I say.

How do you feel?

I'm not bad. A little dizzy and my nose hurts.

Let's get a drink, he says. And maybe say hello to Jude.

How do you know she's here?

He winks at me. I'm psychic.

Two of the buildings are skeletal and empty, ruined by fire. The third is alive and thumping. The music growls, thick and menacing and distorted, as if it's coming from under ground. Henry and I approach the front steps. A man sits on a stool beside the door, he looks sleepy and fat with muscle. A baseball bat rests between his legs. Beside him is a shiny new shotgun. He regards me with the eyes of a polar bear at the zoo. His arms are crossed, and his hands are moving slightly, fluttering and mothlike. As if he's stroking his armpits.

Don't believe I know you boys, he says.

Not to worry, says Henry.

His elbow brushes mine and I can feel a tingle like static electricity. He's itching to hit someone, after tasting a little blood with me. I pull out a wad of cash.

What's your name, I say.

Junior, he says.

I pass him a fifty.

You a cop, he says. He examines the bill, suspiciously.

I laugh softly, and a splash of blood bubbles from my nose. He stares at it.

Henry smiles fiercely. Open the door, Junior.

Smoke. The sound of a piano and a woman singing. The only light comes from behind the bar, a long low slab of unfinished wood. There is a ragged crowd of white men and a few very young girls. The girls have black hair and skin that ranges from yellow to chocolate. They are beautiful and bright with despair. Henry drifts away and comes back with two glass jars of uncertain liquid.

This smells of death, I say.

Drink it slow.

She isn't here, I say.

Downstairs, he says. I believe the real action is in the basement.

A long, narrow room with a dirt floor and a very low ceiling. Every table is crowded with men and women hunched on plastic chairs. The women are older than the sad whores upstairs, and most of them are white. There is no music now, only the crackle and static of voices. The thick noise of impatience. At one end of the room is a shallow pit surrounded by thick chicken wire. The wire is a dull reddish color like rust. Now a murmur snakes through the crowd. A man with thick red hair and dark glasses approaches the pit. He wears a three-piece suit the color of lead. He surveys the crowd, a crooked smile on his face. Two men enter from a rear door, dressed in blue jeans and sleeveless shirts, leather gloves. One of them leads a brindle pit bull on a short chain. The dog is muzzled, silent and lunging. Another man appears leading a mottled blue dog with powerful legs and a square, wolflike head. The dog appears wild, nervous and high-strung. He wears no muzzle and doesn't make a sound.

Their vocal cords are removed, Henry says. It's creepy, isn't it?

The man with red hair begins to speak. He introduces the first dog as Spider, three years old and weighing fifty-five pounds; sired by the infamous Diablo and the winner of thirteen blood matches. The crowd howls with love and pride. The challenger is the Blue Ghost, two years old and sixty pounds. Fathered by a nameless, chicken-killing coyote. This will be his first match. The crowd whistles and jeers. The Blue Ghost is trembling now, with fear or rage. The announcer waves his arms for silence. The Ghost's mother, he says, was Bloody Mary. She was the Australian cattle dog that killed a mountain lion in the summer of '92. The crowd is pleased and soon begins to whisper and sign, placing bets.

Henry squints at me through cigarette smoke. Are you a fucking monk or something?

What do you mean?

You want to tell me what happened back there, at the Seventh Son?

Well, I say. Isabel was getting ready to gut me.

That's just pitiful, says Henry.

She was eager to take my last kidney.

How long can a young man live with no kidney at all?

Not fucking long, brother.

Henry laughs.

Jude came out of nowhere, I say. She saved my ass.

Maybe the sky is falling, he says.

Maybe she loves me, I say.

Henry turns to a burly man at the next table. A hundred on the Ghost, he says.

The man laughs. Easy money. You never seen the Spider, have you?

The men are allowed to massage and prep their dogs for a few minutes. The Blue Ghost's owner is a young kid, perhaps twenty. He whispers to his dog, stroking him and rubbing his ears. The kid is pale, biting his lip. The kid loves his dog and I feel bad for him. He should be taking his dog out to chase rabbits in the high yellow grass. The Blue Ghost is calm again. He holds his head up and stares at the Spider. The Spider's handlers poke and jab at him with a sharpened stick. They curse and snarl at him and splash chicken's blood on his face. He is soon in a frenzy, foaming through the muzzle. He gnaws at the leather, his teeth drawing blood from his own gums. His handlers smile and hold him back.

That kid owes somebody money, I say. His momma is in the hospital. They need a new roof, something. He doesn't want to fight that dog.

Henry nods. Maybe. So what?

I could help him, I say.

How are you gonna help that kid?

I could give him a couple thousand. Then he could take his dog and go home.

No, he says. The kid is proud.

I look at the kid, his face hard and glazed with tears. Henry is right, I'm sure. The kid would cut his wrists before he took money from a stranger.

The dogs are placed in the pit and the crowd surges to the edge. The kid rubs his mouth and sighs. Henry finishes his whiskey and asks if I want mine. I shake my head. The one swallow I took still churns in my belly like liquid nitrogen. I was sure it would kill me.

The dogs circle each other, slow and hypnotic, then striking in a blur of teeth and fur. The Blue Ghost is strong and unafraid. He fights well enough, using his strong legs to knock the Spider down. He opens shallow wounds on the Spider's chest and shoulders. But the Ghost lacks the proper fury. The Spider is relentless and terribly fast, moving with strange chaos and grace.

Henry is mesmerized, his mouth wet.

The Ghost is in trouble, moving clumsily and bleeding from the mouth. He has a broken rib, a puncture lung. The Spider toys with him, slashing at his legs.

The crowd is wailing like Christians in a big tent.

I look away, at the kid. He holds his face in both hands. The Spider finally takes down the Ghost, his massive jaws closed on the throat. The Ghost is a filthy, bloody lump. His neck is broken and the Spider doesn't let go until his handlers enter the pit and beat at him with rubber hoses. The kid is silent.

Henry shakes his head and drops a clump of money on the burly man's slick, wet table. He turns to me, smiling. I lean close to whisper in his ear, where the fuck is Jude.

thirty-four.

The moon is a fragment, disappearing behind clouds. Henry and I smoke cigarettes and throw stones into the dark. We make such a lovely pair. He is dangerously drunk and I'm trembling, a morphine addict. The stitches in my belly feel like they might be alive.

Is your arm made of glass? he says.

Fuck you.

Brother, he says. You throw like a pretty boy.

Enough of this shit, I say. Tell me where she is.

Keep your pants on.

What are you waiting for?

I don't know. I thought we might go find some action.

Sex or violence, I say.

He grins at me. Isabel was a hell of a girl, he says.

She was a mad hatter, I say.

Anyway, he says. There must be a decent whorehouse around here. This is Texas.

Please. I'm on my last legs.

Or we could go home.

Home?

Denver, he says.

No. There's nothing there.

Moon asked me to bring you back.

I shuffle away from him with the grace and ferocity of a diseased kid begging for spare change. I only need space to breathe. He watches me, amused. I mutter an apology and remove the gun from my ankle holster. Henry shakes his head.

Are you serious?

I probably wouldn't shoot you.

Thanks, he says.

But I'm not going back to Denver. Let's get that fucking straight.

Think of your loved ones.

What loved ones?

Don't you have a dog or a cat?

You're insane.

I'm sentimental, he says.

Do you want me to shoot you?

Listen, he says. I'm just fucking with you.

Do you know where Jude is?

Of course, he says. She's in the trunk of my car.

The dark swallows me. I'm a dead woman with no hair.

What did you say?

It's cool, he says. I grabbed her when she was coming out of the Seventh Son.

You didn't kill her.

No, he says. Oh, hell no. She fights like a goddamn tiger, though.

I finally poked her with one of those tranquilizer darts I mentioned earlier.

Oh, you dumb motherfucker. Let her out and pray she doesn't kill you.

Henry fumbles with his keys and I hold my breath. He mutters that the icebox is also in the trunk, in case I still want it. I'm afraid I might start laughing and I won't be able to stop. He bends over the trunk of his car and he's too casual. He doesn't exactly have groceries in there. The key turns with the sound of a hammer against metal and I pull him away from the car.

You want to stand clear, I say.

The trunk swings open and Jude bursts free. She breathes slowly, through her teeth.

Jude, I say.

She regards Henry with a long, piteous stare.

Jude.

I'm gonna take a walk, says Henry.

My heart uncoils in my chest. Jude relaxes, and I see that her legs are trembling. I grip her thin, hard body as if I might hurt her. She whispers to me and I bite her hair, her neck.

Henry drifts back to us and he appears sober, dangerous. I wonder if he's been faking it.

I thought you two would be snuggling like rabbits. He doesn't smile.

It's time to go, I say.

Is she coming with us?

Yes, I say.

He frowns. Let's put her back in the trunk.

Forget it.

The bitch could stab me in the neck.

I trust her, I say.

You are a fucking fool.

Didn't you take her weapons when you tranquilized her?

Yeah, he says. But I could have missed something.

Do you want me to frisk her?

Please.

Of course, she could kill you with her fingernails.

Fuck you. Just do it.

I tell her I'm sorry and she shrugs. Jude turns lazily and spreads her hands on the hood. I kick her feet apart and gently slap her down. She trembles when I touch her thigh, as if it tickles. I slide my hands over her ass and crotch, suddenly shy.

This is hopeless, I say.

Jude looks at me, her green eyes unblinking.

Do you have any weapons? I say.

No, she says.

I can barely look at Henry.

Oh, he says. I feel much better.

Jude kisses my left eye. Don't worry.

Where are we going? says Henry. And what do you want?

I stare out the dark window and wonder about that. Henry drives, muttering. He has found nothing but gospel on the radio. It reminds him of his childhood, he says. Jude sits beside him, silent. Her head is bent, waiting for the sun. The green icebox sits beside me on the backseat. I still have the little key in my pocket and soon I slip it into the lock. I open the icebox, oddly nervous. Part of me still expects to find my kidney inside. It only holds the Blister's clothes, now torn and cut to shreds. His clothes were whole when I last touched them. I smile at the back of Jude's head. I don't know what I want.

Time disappears. I recite the laws of inertia. A body placed in motion will not rest until acted up by another body. It's bullshit, I know. But I want to keep moving. I want Jude to stop me.

I lean over the seat and breathe against Jude's throat. Where is Luscious Gore?

She shrugs. I think he has a summer house around here some-where.

I'm serious.

Phineas, she says. What are you thinking?

Do you know where he is?

Of course.

The miles pass and the sun rises behind us, as if we are running from it.

I tell Henry to stop the car. He ignores me.

Humor me, I say.

He pulls to the shoulder and grunts about needing to piss any-way. There is a fine mist in the air, cool against our skin. Henry and I stand side by side, peeing noisily against rocks as the sky changes col-ors around us. Jude refuses to get out of the car. I tell her it could be hours before she has another chance, but she doesn't answer. I feel better now, having seen the sunrise. The landscape is barren and deathly quiet, stretching into the distance without pause. The silent, jagged beauty like a map of the moon.

This isn't quite over, I say.

What do you mean? says Henry.

Luscious Gore is waiting for us, I say.

No, he says. I don't really like this idea.

You don't have to come with us.

Shit, brother. I have nowhere else to be.

Then indulge me.

I get in the car and tell Jude to give him directions. She asks if I have a pen and Henry turns to give her a heavy dose of his face. Henry's face is not ugly, exactly. It's fearsome though, and deeply textured. The eyes are hard, and disturbing in their contrast. The blue one is bright as a knife blade, the brown one a hole in the earth. His beard is thick and speckled with gray. And his blunt, ragged hair is still mostly white.

Don't even think about stabbing me with a fucking pen, he says.

Jude laughs softly. You have nothing to fear.

He glances at me. You're the one who should be afraid.

I am curiously calm, and I want to tell him that Jude will take care of me, that everything will be fine. But I'm not sure I believe it. Jude pulls a crisp five-dollar bill from her pocket and quickly draws out a map across Lincoln's long, sad face. She gives the bill to Henry, like a tip.

thirty-five.

Half an hour passes and I'm bored silly. Jude says we have maybe twenty miles to go and the road bleeds away from us, an endless black rope. I play with the window, rolling it up and down. I let my hand float and drift in the rush of air. Henry chews his cigar and looks at me with one eye. The other is closed, as if seeing something else. I look away, into the distance, hoping to see a jackrabbit.

Do they test nuclear weapons out here? I say.

Go to sleep, says Henry.

I'm not tired.

Talk to your girlfriend, then.

I light two cigarettes and pass one to Jude.

This is what you wanted, I say. All along.

No, she says. It was your idea to come to Texas.

Oh, yeah. And when I'm depressed I go bowling.

But I stood you up, she says.

Why?

It was a stupid idea, she says.

I whisper, but you had two tickets to El Paso. A cozy sleeper car.

Jude shows her teeth.

The other ticket was for that idiot Pooh. He was my entertainment and muscle. And then you drifted back into my life and I was forced to improvise.

How romantic, says Henry.

It's a pile of shit, I say.

When did you stop believing me? says Jude. When did you start, for that matter?

Maybe the other ticket was for Isabel, I say.

Jude laughs. I couldn't stand Isabel.

You gave her my gun, I say. Didn't you?

Isabel is dead, she says. And she's still tying you in knots.

What did you do with my kidney?

She looks straight through me. It's in the icebox, isn't it?

What did you do with it?

I gave it to a little black bird, she says. The bird carried it for miles and miles and finally dropped it into the ocean, where a fish ate it. The fish was caught by a young boy, who took it home and gave it to his sister. The sister cleaned the fish and cooked it, and fed it to her family.

I study the shape of her face, the angle of her neck. She has effortlessly burned herself into my brain. Jerome tried to fuck her somehow. He had mysteriously blown the money on a ridiculous new car and a fur coat while his own brother lay dying. He had poor impulse control and he wanted Isabel's pet to die. Jimmy crack corn and I don't care. Black hair streaked with blond and eyes wide apart, hooded and shaped like lemons. *They are mongoloid eyes, the devil's eyes.* Jerome tried to pay her with heroin, maybe he refused to pay her at all. Jude was not amused either way. She beat him half to death and disappeared, a box of heroin in one hand and a nearly rotten kidney in the other. A scar at the edge of her mouth and fine white teeth, slightly crooked and sharp. She could have dropped the kidney down a laundry chute or found another buyer but I like to think she walked into that emergency room in Colorado Springs like an angel with snow in her hair. The stone around her neck, the horrible teardrop. It still dangles from a string of silver in a cold hollow of flesh and you had a thousand chances, I say. To cut me open a second time.

She never answers me. She doesn't need to.

The sickness comes on abruptly. It resumes, as if to remind me that I'm still alive. I have a coughing fit that nearly tears me apart. I think my intestines are unraveling. I touch my throat, my face. The skin is damp and cold as the bottom of my shoe. Jude is watching me with alien tenderness.

I'm okay, I say. I'm like a house on fire.

She sighs. You don't look well.

It's only loneliness.

Did you really miss me?

Yes. I was lost without you.

You should have run, she says.

I could use one of those shots, I say.

I'm sorry, she says. But I've misplaced my medical bag.

Henry mutters. I tossed it into a Dumpster.

She looks at him. You're dying to be my friend, aren't you?

What happened to you? he says. In the army?

Jude rolls down her window and leans out. The wind whips at her hair and I watch the dark and light streaks merge and flail apart. An almost invisible blur, like insect wings. Even when pale and shattered by withdrawals, I am still fascinated by the most meager stimuli.

Why do you ask? she says.

I like to know who I'm traveling with.

Or who you carelessly shove in the trunk of your car.

Maybe, he says.

I was in Israel, she says dreamily. During some recent foolishness that never even made the newspapers.

Oh I love this fucking country, says Henry.

I close my eyes and Jude's voice drifts. She was lost in the desert for five weeks, she says. The sand was in her bowels, her blood. But she wasn't alone. There were two boys with her. Felix was nineteen. He stuttered under pressure but he was fearless in a fight. He was a good Christian and a virgin. Cody was twenty. He was from California and he thought the world was his. He never took his eyes off her. It was so cold at night that the three of them slept together like newborn rats, huddled so close that their breath and skin mingled and became one. Felix soon went mad. He stared at the sun until his eyes were white. Jude had to tie a nylon rope to his wrist and drag him along behind her. Cody was so afraid of dying that he never shut up and he begged her to sleep with him, to have his baby. Then one day he stepped on a land mine and blew himself to bits and Jude was glad. Because she wouldn't have to listen to him anymore. She wished she had killed him herself. On the twenty-ninth day she killed Felix with a knife, because there wasn't enough water for both of them. It was like killing a dog, and her heart shrank. Jude came out of the desert, alone and slightly insane. She received a section eight discharge one month later.

That's a very good story, says Henry.

Jude stares at him, a vein turning faintly blue in her left temple.

*

Henry examines the map and slows the car, stopping at a dirt road. He stares at it bleakly, and I follow his gaze. The road is gutted with holes, ugly with rocks. The road is a mud slide, a disaster area. The road is uphill. Henry's car would be ruined and wheezing, bottomed out after twenty yards.

How long is this road? he says.

Jude grins at him. Ten miles, perhaps.

Beautiful, he says. Why didn't you say we would need a fucking all-terrain vehicle?

It slipped my mind.

It's okay, I say. We can turn around and go back to El Paso, steal a truck and come back. Or we can walk. Personally, I don't care.

Nice day, says Jude. Let's walk.

Oh, no. This is bullshit, says Henry.

What? I say.

This is the end, okay. This is as far as we go. I'm not a lovesick junkie and I'm not a fucking serial killer. I'm the only one thinking straight.

Jude squints at him, as if he is blurry around the edges.

Henry, I say.

Listen, he says. I'm not letting you go up that road with this bitch. Don't you know she will slaughter you like a goddamn chicken? I can see it in her eyes.

Poor thing, says Jude. You don't know me at all.

I hold my face in my hands, suddenly very tired.

Phineas, he says. I would rather kill you myself than let you go with her.

That's nice of you, I say.

Or I could drag your sorry ass back to Denver.

Please, says Jude. This is so dull.

Shut the fuck up, says Henry.

Jude leans close to him. Are you going to do something? Or just talk.

Henry slaps her with the back of his hand and she rocks back against the passenger door. I could kill him. He yanks the gun out of his jean jacket in an easy, fluid motion. The same gun he killed Isabel with, the gun I refused to hold. He points it at Jude's face, so close that she could put her lips around it and he may or may not be ready to shoot her. It doesn't really matter, does it? Because she takes it away from him in a flickering reflex, sudden and reptilian, and before I can make a sound she is on top of him, the gun in his eye and the shot is silenced, as if fired underwater. My hair and clothes are washed in his blood.

I fall out of the car, numb and nearly paralyzed by the rush of claustrophobia. I walk in circles, fumbling in my pockets for a cigarette. Henry's blood is in my mouth and I have to sit down.

He provoked her. He was begging for it. He shot her with an animal tranquilizer and he dumped her in the trunk of his car like a sack of fertilizer. He left her there to choke on dust for a few hours. He was rude to her. He hit her with an open hand and he all but offered her his gun.

Jude comes toward me, the sky crashing behind her and the gun in her left hand. She spreads her arms out wide and she looks pale and ghastly as a vampire.

I won't apologize, she says.

And I haven't asked you to.

I go back to the car and, like a robot, open the driver's door and shove at Henry with both hands to keep him from spilling onto the dirt road and he is so heavy, so warm, and for a moment I think I might collapse under his weight, that he will crush me like a drunken lover and now I hammer at his chest and shoulders with my fists until he falls sideways over the seat and I can slide in next to him and start the car, my foot sharing the gas pedal with his, and I drive as far up the road as I can and finally steer the giant car off the dirt and into a rocky, rainswept gully bounded by cherry trees that may just hide the car from the road and I kill the engine with a sigh, slipping from behind the wheel and without looking at Henry, I grab him by the armpits and struggle to pull him from the car but his foot is lodged somehow and my hands are soaked with sweat and blood and I am screaming, my head pounding when Jude wraps her arms around me from behind and holds me, holds me.

Minutes or hours later and I relax. She helps me pull Henry from the car and drag him through the dust to a piece of high ground. I am exhausted, destroyed. I sit beneath a deformed little tree and smoke cigarettes while she patiently, silently buries Henry under a mound of rocks that will keep the beasts from his remains, for a day or two.

thirty-six.

I walk a dozen or so yards behind her. The only sound is my own rattling breath. Jude is shrinking, disappearing ahead.

In the woods, as before. My hands are unfamiliar. Carrion birds circle overhead and I wait for them to find Lucy. She floats still, on the lake, but I can't see her for the trees. I don't think I could bear to look at her ruined face. I am bleeding to death, starving and never happier. I pull strange plants from the earth and devour the roots. Lick and suck the dew from green leaves.

When I was a child, I believed there was a sun-god. My father told me never to look directly at it, that the sun would punish you.

Two kids spot me on the ninth day. I wave to them and shout hello, my voice dusty and strange. They run from me. Soon the state police arrive, with dogs. They find me easily, and surround me. They don't expect me to fight, to strangle one of their beautiful dogs. I cry over the dog and raise my hands. One of the cops is furious, however. He screams at me and puts a single bullet in my leg. They bind my hands and feet and place me in the back of a car. One of them takes pity on me, he pours water over my cracked and blistered face. I talk to them through the iron mesh, telling them that I killed my wife. But they don't believe me. They deny that a body has been found on the lake.

My feet drag like stones over dry yellow earth. I stumble and fall and dumbly notice that I'm clutching the green icebox. I can't let go of it. Jude stops to wait for me.

I assume you have read *The Hobbit*?

Are you kidding, I say. What about it?

Gollum, she says. The wretched, stinking cave dweller.

I smile at her. My precious, I say.

They take me to the station and drop me on the floor of a tiny cell, removing the chains from my feet. No one comes to question me. A silent doctor comes to examine my leg. He smells like stale smoke. There are murmurs through the walls. They have uncovered my identity. I'm a cop from the city, from Internal Affairs. I'm a vulture, a plague dog. They come into the cell and beat me with electrical cords, they laugh and smoke cigarettes. I lose count of days and nights and on a sunny morning I am placed on a special transport bus. I am taken back to the city without ceremony or comment. Lucy's body is found several days later, and my life comes apart like a love letter in the rain.

Jude is still up ahead, farther now. She's running from me.

They first thought it was murder. Lucy was shot twice and her body mutilated. After further examination, it was decided that the first bullet was self-inflicted. She was then shot once more, and mutilated sometime later. Apparently by her husband.

The end is near. I can't go much further. Jude waits for me in a patch of shade, her hands folded like scissors in her lap.

You have been miles away, says Jude.

I'm thinking of my wife, I say.

What do you see?

I hesitate.

In your mind, says Jude. Is she alive or dead?

She's asleep.

I don't believe you, says Jude.

Why should you? I say.

A butterfly flicks past my face. I try to follow its flight but my eyes are numb. My reflexes are gone. I take a breath and listen to my body. There is pain, abstract and gray. Infinite, barely noticed. There is euphoria, like the buzzing of a disconnected telephone. Drugs would have little effect on me now.

I wish I had known her, says Jude.

The butterfly returns and I smile with unfamiliar muscles.

Why, I say.

She shrugs. We might have been friends.

I don't think so.

Jude lights a cigarette.

Other women aren't safe from you, I say.

Jude doesn't blink. She disappears. She becomes the color of stone, of dust. Her tongue flicks at the air and I tell myself not to be sorry. I extend two fingers and she gives me the cigarette.

How did Lucy die? says Jude.

I take a long rotten breath and I see everything so clearly.

She shot herself with my gun and it was one of those freakish, terrible things. The bullet should have punched through her skull and into her brain but it didn't, it skated around her head like she was made of ice and tore off her left ear and she was shocked to be alive. The pain must have been incredible and she couldn't hold the gun. She asked me to finish her and I took the gun from her too slowly and I was afraid. I hesitated and by the time I could bring myself to shoot her she was already dead. I couldn't help her.

Jude is sorry, she's so sorry. But of course she is. Her heart would have to be made of sun-bleached bone to listen to that story and shrug.

I sat in the boat with Lucy for hours. Finally I shot her once in the face and swam away.

Do you smell something dreadful? says Jude.
    I shrug. Cherry blossoms and cow manure.
    Jude looks around. It smells of death, she says.
    I walk a few feet from the road and find the body of a dead dog. He's a big puppy, a black mongrel. He was shot recently and dragged himself there. Maybe he was stealing somebody's chickens, maybe not. This is cattle country. A strange dog might be shot merely for stepping on somebody's land.
    Let's keep moving, says Jude.
    Wait a minute, I say.
    I pull out my knife and bend over the dead dog, holding my breath. His body is soft and pliable, rigor mortis a mere memory. I roll him over onto his back; his paws are limp and I scratch as his chest briefly. Blackflies crawl listlessly through his fur, but he might be sleeping. I stroke his ears and tell myself he was a good dog. He was no thief. I slip the tanto into his belly, just above his genitals.

The smell is awful.

My eyes burn and I can barely see. I wipe at them furiously, then relax.

I look down at the poor dog's spilling bowels and tell myself I'm dissecting a frog in the ninth grade. I have gym class next period, and the new girl from Virginia has an ass like a peach. Her gym shorts are too little and when she sweats they tend to get caught up in her sweet little crack. She plucks them out so daintily, so carelessly that I fall in love with her every day.

Sink my hands into the dog's open belly, startled by the heat.

Push through the organs until I find a slippery, purplish lump of tissue the size of my fist. It could be liver or kidney or bladder, I can't be sure. But it doesn't matter and I cut it loose without difficulty. It seems so small, maybe three or four ounces. I hold it in the palm of my hand like a raw chicken breast, an aborted fetus.

I wrap it carefully in a shred of my shirt and tell Jude to hand me the icebox.

She gives me a long, shivering dark look. But she brings it to me.

I unlock it and throw the Blister's clothes onto the skeletal rosebush. They hang there like a vagrant's laundry. I place the small, bloody package in the icebox and close the lid.

How long have you known? she says.

Irrelevant, I say.

But you stayed with me.

The air swirls with dust. It's strange, because there is no wind at all.

Why? she says.

I've had three or four good chances to kill you.

And you had at least one chance to run.

Oh, I tried to run. I did. I was a wreck without you.

Jude gives a false laugh and drops Henry's gun in the dust. She removes the little stinger, the dentist's tool, from the slim waistband of her panties. I stare at it and she shrugs.

I lied, she says. When you asked if I had any weapons.

Of course you did.

She drops the stinger carelessly and stares at me.

Do you think you could kill me with your bare hands?

Yes, she says.

I do have one valuable kidney, safe in my belly.

So you keep telling me.

Isn't that why you brought me here?

For once she doesn't stare at my eyes. Her gaze drifts between my teeth and throat and I think she's preparing to kill me. The tanto is in my left hand, slick with the dog's blood. I shift it to my right hand and remember the last time I cut her. She was naked and she trusted me. I couldn't bear to cut her again. I pull the .38 from my ankle holster and lift it slowly, as if it weighs ten pounds. I aim at her chest, at the cool hollow between her breasts.

Maybe, she says. Maybe I thought I could still deliver you to Gore. But it was a bad risk. Then you threw yourself in my lap and you practically begged me to come here.

And you had two fucking tickets to El Paso.

You idiot, she says. I gave you my ticket and bought another one later.

I tell myself she's full of shit. She stinks of it. The other ticket was for Isabel. They were working some kind of switch on brother Jerome and it went bad somehow. I stare at her, trying to summon the laser red dot that will make her a faceless target. Her hair is damp and hangs to her shoulders in black twists. The skin beneath her sharp green eyes is swollen. Her mouth is a pale red slash. I wonder when she last slept.

She is unflinching.

When did you change your mind? I say. Or why.

Jude smiles. Irrelevant.

Oh, you're adorable.

Do you ever wonder what I did with it? she says. Your kidney.

I would rather daydream, I say.

I like that about you. She takes a step toward me.

And the heroin, I say. Do you wonder what I did with it?

Heroin, she says. I wouldn't be caught dead moving that shit.

I shrug and gaze up at the sun. Jude takes another step.

Listen, she says. When I found that wig in your bag I was jealous.

I see a thousand red dots. Jude takes the gun away from me. I don't resist and it slips from my fingers like a shared piece of fruit.

Listen to me, she says. I don't get jealous, ever.

I don't believe you.

She glances at my gun and smiles.

The safety is on, she says.

That's funny.

You might kiss me, she says.

I give her a quick, dry kiss on the side of her mouth. The kiss of a brother. My knees buckle and I crouch down beneath the sun, waiting for it to finish me. I don't look up. Jude gathers our weapons and helps me to my feet.

What now? she says.

I would love to kill somebody. But I'm so tired.

She grins. Luscious Gore lives just around the bend.

Maybe he could buy us dinner.

Okay, she says. It's okay.

The heat is unreal. I take off my expensive leather jacket, murmur an apology to Alexander and leave it in the sun.

The road twists and doubles back, intestinal. The little green icebox holds the vital organ of an anonymous dog. Again we rest. I take off my pants and sit on the ground, my thighs white and skeletal. Jude gives me a look and I tell her I might as well get a tan.

We walk side by side, now. Jude carries the icebox.

This will be putrid before dark, she says.

There's nowhere to buy ice in the desert, I say. Diamonds are easier to come by.

She looks at me oddly. What happened to that silly hat? she says. The one Henry gave you.

It's in my pocket.

Please put it on. Before you have a stroke.

A fork in the road and we are forced to choose. Jude says she doesn't remember a fork. I sit down and hold my head in my hands. Jude walks to the top of a rise and stares into the distance.

Haven't you been here before?

Never, she says.

I thought you were a secret agent.

She laughs.

The platypus, I say. Is that a duck or a fish?

Shut up.

Flip a fucking coin.

No, she says. I believe it's to the left.

Why? We haven't seen any tracks for miles.

Only because it's so dry and stony.

Why the left, though?

I just feel it, she says.

*

Water. A dirty, crippled little stream but it's beautiful. I drink cautiously, and I remember Henry's warning that he would kill me if I should throw up in his car. I laugh and cry and roll in the dust as if I'm simple. Jude squats on her haunches, wolflike and brown from the sun. Water glows like silver on her lips.

I'm worried about you, she says.

And I'm not sure what I expect to find. An armed compound, with impenetrable walls and watchtowers manned by lazy snipers. Electric fences and spotlights and Dobermans. A teardrop-shaped swimming pool, with a dozen unemployed actresses sunning themselves.

An hour before sunset and the apparent prize lies before us. A dozen stone buildings, sprawling in a broken circle. A small chapel and a crumbling bell tower. An ancient rock well. It looks like a monastery, deserted years ago. The monks long dead. One building is larger than the others. Several cars and trucks are parked in front. There is a short runway to the south, an airplane hangar and a landing pad for a helicopter. A few dogs sleep in the shade of a flatbed truck, but there are no humans about.

There are no guards, Jude says.

It doesn't matter, I say. We aren't going to sack the place.

Do you have a plan?

No. I'm going to walk up to the front door and knock.

Look at us, she says. Bloody as two thieves.

You look beautiful.

Together we sit down in a rare circle of grass to inventory our weapons. She has Henry's gun and the little stinger. She has a book of matches and a melted chocolate bar that she gives to me. I eat it and feel dizzy.

She has nothing else. No identification, no money.

We don't need any money, she says.

It's true. I have three or four thousand dollars in my wallet, as useless as yesterday's newspaper. I have the .38 and six extra cartridges. The small silver pocketknife and the slim tanto. A dented pack of cigarettes and a lighter with no fluid. I have a ballpoint pen and a dog's kidney.

Jude says we should sleep for a few hours, and I agree.

I sink into the grass and close my eyes, wishing I were in a bathtub full of ice.

Her tongue drifts across my lips and her hand slips into my pants and squeezes my soft, sleeping penis. I open my eyes and Jude is bent over me. She takes off her shirt and I raise my mouth to her breasts but the black stone locket swings like a bitter, shrunken plum before my eyes and I reach for her throat.

I unbutton her pants and she lifts her pelvis slightly, to help me pull them down to her knees.

Her underpants are black and damp and I rip them off her.

Her teeth find my neck.

I have two fingers inside her and I whisper, is this how it was with Eve?

Her body shudders and I tell her I'm sorry I don't have a wooden spoon. Or a portable phone. But Jude is much stronger than me. She easily kicks herself free and I now sit in the dust, wearily wondering if I want to shoot her. I'm sure she would kill me first.

Phineas, she says.

Tell me the fucking truth, for once.

I was there, she says. I was looking for you. But I never touched that girl.

You destroyed her.

No, she says. The girl was sleeping when I got there, and she was sleeping when I left.

Her name is Eve, I say. And that locket was around her neck.

Then she must have taken it off before she got in the shower. Because I found it on the bathroom sink, curled up like a little spider.

thirty-seven.

It's dark when I awake. Jude is sleeping silently on the stony ground. I look at her and I know she's a scorpion, a killer. But I want to believe her and if this is my undoing then I will smile and swallow the poison of my choice. My throat is sore and I'm tempted to walk back to the dirty little creek, but it's too far. I smoke one of my few remaining cigarettes and this numbs the pain. I poke Jude with my foot and she wakes with a shrug.

We walk down to the monastery, casually, as if we have come home. Perhaps we have.

I stop at the well and haul the bucket up for a drink. The water is sweet and cool. Jude doesn't want any, and I let the bucket fall. I approach the main building, Jude behind me. When we are twenty yards away, motion-sensitive lights wash over us. A dog begins to bark. The front door swings open, and the shadow of a woman waits to greet us.

Hello, I say. My name is Phineas Poe.

The woman has the ancient, silent air of an untouchable, an indentured servant. Her face is like eroded rock. She stares at me for a long moment, then pulls the door wide.

I want to see Mr. Gore.

She coughs. Mr. Gore is having his dinner, sir.

That's okay, says Jude.

She turns without another word and leads us through a dark, stony room where two black dogs sleep among weapons and umbrellas and expensive coats. Antique swords and longbows are mounted on one wall. There are several humped coatracks and countless pairs of shoes and dusty boots. A glass case holds hunting rifles and a few handguns. The woman walks slowly, her long brown skirt rustling with the sound of fallen leaves.

Jude nudges me. What are we doing here, Phineas?

I don't know. I really don't know.

Aren't you the least bit afraid? she says.

Of what?

Aren't you afraid that I might come at you with a knife, that I might cut you open again?

Not really. I don't think Gore has any more money.

Is that the only reason?

You warned me about getting misty with you.

The old woman takes us through another doorway, into a room that is lit with perhaps a hundred candles. The walls are lined with bookshelves and the furniture is leather, cracked and dusty. In the center of the room is an empty hospital bed, the sheets turned back. The bed faces a wide-screen television.

The boy is dead, Jude says. He didn't make it.

No, I say. The sheets would be stripped.

The woman leads us to the kitchen. It is brightly lit and warm. The table is set for dinner, with fine silver and china. On one side of the table is an upholstered wingback chair that must have been dragged in from the living room. A young man is curled in the chair, apparently asleep. He is wrapped in blue and yellow blankets, faded and worn thin. His skin is extraordinarily white, his hair long and fine and seemingly colorless. The boy is dreaming and his eyes flicker rapidly behind lids so thin they can hardly block out the light. He is impossibly skinny, and I wonder if he weighs more than ninety pounds. I wonder if my kidney would have done him any good, if he might have lived even six undeserved months. At the head of the table is a heavy, bald man in an electric wheelchair. His skin is dark and cracked as leather, his eyes naked and gray as oysters. One arm is shriveled and useless, a distended flipper, an evolutionary error. The other arm is grotesquely muscled.

Who is it? he says. Who's there?

Phineas Poe, I say. And this is Jude.

Do I know you?

No. I don't think so.

Jude says softly, we know your son.

I have two sons, he says.

Jerome, I say. We know Jerome.

He wheels around and stops before me and he is obviously not feeble. I hold out my hand and smile as he crushes it. He is clearly blind, but he seems to smell me or operate by sonar. I wonder if he sleeps upside down. Gore smiles, and his teeth are shaped unlike any human teeth I have ever seen. They glitter like bits of glass and small sharp stones on the beach. If I waved my hand before his face, like a child fascinated by the blind man, I think I would lose a finger.

He is gentle with Jude's hand, which amuses me.

I'm sorry, he says. Jerome is not here. He's gone on a long business trip and I don't know when he will return. To be true, I had hoped he would be home by now.

His eyes are like sundials. They don't waver. I am uncomfortable, standing over him. He relaxes his gaze and points at the table.

Please, he says. Sit down. You must be tired.

I clear my throat. I have a small gift for you, Mr. Gore.

Jude glances at the icebox, then at me. Her eyes are bright with disgust.

How kind, says Gore. And please, call me Luscious.

He sniffs the air as I remove the dog's kidney, still wrapped in my shirt. I lay it gently on his plate, and watch as he slowly unwraps it with one hand. The kidney is surely putrid, alive with maggots, but it might as well be a box of chocolates. His expression doesn't change. I wildly remind myself that he's blind, he's blind. And he doesn't know who the hell I am.

I'm afraid I don't understand, says Gore.

And I have made a terrible mistake, I say. This was meant for Jerome.

I put the plate down on the floor, whistling softly. The two black dogs appear and quickly eat the organ of their cousin, growling at each other. The shame surges through me like a forgotten bodily fluid.

Will you please join us for supper? says Luscious.

I stand over the dogs like a mummy, fascinated by the simplicity of this transaction. I imagine the flesh of rabbits and mice that passed through the dead dog, the worms that burrowed through his corpse and into the earth. I see the blackflies that picked through his fur and wonder if the eggs they left behind have hatched. Soon the two black dogs lick the plate clean and wander away. Jude grabs at my sleeve and whispers for me to sit down. Luscious rings a silver bell, and now the old woman appears to serve us a simple meal. She places a loaf of fresh bread in the center of the table, with a brick of yellow cheese and a knife. She brings us each a steaming bowl of stew and a plate of rice and fruit.

Jude leans close to me. You're a freak.

I wonder, says Luscious. Would you mind not whispering? It makes me anxious.

Jude flushes and I don't think I've ever seen her embarrassed.

I'm so sorry, she says.

Oh, he says. It's all right.

Jude looks away, her eyes drifting over the stone walls.

I love the house, she says.

Thank you. It's fallen into disrepair, I'm afraid.

Was it ever a monastery? she says.

Yes, he says. Two hundred years ago, when this was Mexican territory. A rather eccentric order of Franciscan monks.

How were they eccentric? she says.

They took the Eucharist quite literally.

What does that mean, she says. They were cannibals?

I like to think so, he says. But the order died off abruptly, in 1809. A yellow fever epidemic, mass suicide. There were numerous stories. Most of their records were destroyed by looters.

Perfect, says Jude.

The hunger in me is stunning. I eat for several minutes without pause, and I feel the blood respond in my starved limbs. Jude picks moodily at her food.

I'm not sure how long the boy has been awake, but I feel his eyes on me like arthritic hands. I turn to look at him. His eyes are such a dark brown they seem bottomless in his white face. He has the thin, curved

lips of a young girl, and his fine cheekbones are sharp, too sharp. I
glance at Jude and she frowns, as if to say yes, he's painfully beautiful.

Strangers, he says. What a treat.

His voice is a scratched whisper, cold and curiously threatening.

Horatio, says Luscious. How do you feel, boy?

Better, he says.

Would you like a drop of wine? says Luscious.

Please introduce me to our guests.

I extend my hand. Phineas, I say. And my wife, Jude.

Jude sinks her fingernails lightly into my thigh.

Hello, she says.

They are your brother's friends, says Luscious.

Horatio smiles. Somehow, I don't think so.

What do you mean, boy?

I just have a feeling, he says.

Our clothes are bloody, of course. And our faces.

Horatio shakes his head as if he can hear my thoughts. Jerome
likes to be surrounded by people who are afraid of him, he says.

Hush, boy.

Oh, but it's true.

Jerome has countless flaws, says Luscious. But they are not for
you to number.

Fingers crawl my legs like a gang of insects and I know that Jude
is restless.

Does anyone have a cigarette? says Horatio.

I hesitate, then extract my nearly crushed box of cigarettes. There
are seven left. I place one between his lips and light a match for him.
His skin is smooth and pink in the glow and I have a sudden uncomfortable desire to see his chest, his torso. To see if it is the color of
marble, if it looks wet.

My son is ill, says Luscious.

Isn't it obvious? the boy says.

I light a cigarette to share with Jude.

What's wrong with you? she says.

Horatio smiles, a brief flicker.

I suppose my most immediate problem is that my kidneys are failing and I will soon be unable to process my own waste. He laughs. I have a problem with sewage.

Luscious sighs. You were always nasty, even as a child.

I'm sorry, he says. I just think it's funny.

How old are you? I say.

Seventeen, he says.

One of the best years.

I thought so, he says.

Of course, high school is unpleasant.

Luscious waves his good hand and Jude watches it like a diving moth.

He isn't in high school, says Luscious. He finished last year.

Good for you, says Jude.

Horatio sneers. I'm going to Stanford, in the fall.

The serving woman drifts through unseen, clearing away the dishes.

Hetty, says Luscious. We will have coffee, please. And perhaps cake.

Horatio lounges in his chair, withered and delicate in his blankets. The cigarette I gave him has shrunk to a nub, and there are ashes scattered on his chest like dirty snowflakes. He closes his eyes and Hetty leans over him to pluck the butt gently from his mouth and for a moment I think she will breathe into his mouth the way animals pass predigested foods from their mouths to the mouths of their feeble young.

thirty-eight.

When I was a small child, says Horatio. My father took the three of us to Rome. It was one of the few times we did anything as a family, a normal family.

It was soon after your mother passed, says Gore.

It was September and gray and one day we had breakfast in a little plaza near the Colosseum. There were a thousand pigeons flapping about, pecking for crumbs you know. They were fearless, and they would take bread from your hand if you sat very still.

They were vicious beasts, says Gore.

Horatio ignores him. There was a photographer there, and he offered to take our family portrait with the birds. Don't you remember, Father? The photo used to hang in the guest bathroom.

I remember, says Luscious. I remember well.

Anyway, says Horatio. My brother and sister were older than me and they had no trouble coaxing the wild pigeons to eat from their hands. And in the photo they each have birds on their outstretched fingers, the wings a mad blur. My father, too. But I was so young, so impatient that the photographer had to place a tame pigeon, a pet bird, on my left arm. And it sat there as if it were nailed there, as if it were stuffed. In the photo, my bird appears to be dead, and every time I look at it I think I am cursed.

That's ridiculous, says Luscious. It's morbid and adolescent.

Hetty returns, pushing a little table on wheels. Her arms tremble as she silently serves around coffee in small white cups. I am tempted to ask if she needs any help, but I'm sure that Luscious would frown on it. She places cream and sugar in the center of the table, then gives us each a slice of black bundt cake.

I'm curious, says Jude. If your kidneys are failing, shouldn't you be hooked up to a machine?

I like you, says Horatio.

She smiles, eerily flirting.

But yes, he says. The dreaded machine. I'm shackled to it for hours at a time. Maybe you would like to watch television with me later, if you can stand it.

I would be happy to, she says.

The machine has seen its last days, says Luscious. He takes a bite of cake and his sharp teeth flash. Jerome is arranging for the purchase of a replacement kidney, as we speak.

That's fantastic, I say.

Jude claws at my leg.

It's a waste of money, says Horatio. And I doubt he will ever come back.

Why do you say such a thing? says Luscious. Why can you not be silent? He bites his words and the veins rise in his blackened face.

Father, he says. Jerome is a plunger. He's a hyena. He will take the money you gave him and run like the wind.

Perhaps, says Luscious. If I had sent him to buy a car, yes. But this is different.

Horatio mutters. And why do you suppose Isabel has disappeared?

Damn your eyes, says Luscious. You wretched boy.

Jude had finished her cake and now begins to eat mine, which I have barely touched.

I am feeling suddenly weak, says Horatio.

Let me ring for Hetty, says Luscious. His voice becomes so gentle.

Jude grips my right hand and whispers for me to relax. She's crushing my fingers and I love her strength. But there is something sharp poking through my shirt, like a needle or tooth. I look down and she is pressing her sharp little dentist's tool into the narrow space between my second and third rib. I glance into her pretty green eyes and I recognize her, I do.

Excuse me, she says.

Luscious Gore turns his dead eyes toward her.

If I offered to give you a kidney, what would you say?

Are you joking, girl?

I cough. She has almost no sense of humor.

Hypothetical, she says.

There would be a question of compatibility, he says. My son has a rare blood type.

Jude shrugs. This is make-believe.

Then I would say thank you, if it were a gift.

And if it wasn't. If it was expensive? she says.

Then I would be the man dying of thirst in a lifeboat, he says. He blows imaginary dust from his fingers and smiles crookedly. Because I have no money left.

Horatio spits. Excellent metaphor, Dad. But wouldn't I be the one in the lifeboat?

The old man turns slightly green.

My apologies, says Jude. I was only curious.

Silence.

Jude blows into my ear and I remember to breathe. She slips the stinger into my pocket and places her slender, empty hands alongside her plate. The palms turned upward in a sweet, meaningless gesture. She is sure she can kill me with her bare hands.

I'm actually aroused, I mutter.

Don't go to sleep on me, she says softly.

Whispers, says Gore. I hear whispers.

I wonder, says Horatio. Would one of you mind helping me to my bed.

You are so trusting, says Jude.

Should we not trust you? says Gore.

I want to help you, I say. I want to be trusted. But my muscles fail me. The table is two miles wide and the sun is shrinking in a blue sky. The boat drifts and everyone is staring at me.

Jude pushes back her chair. Let me do it, she says.

Thank you. I am so tired of Hetty's cold hands. Horatio smiles, his lips thin as paper.

Jude wipes her mouth and I watch silently as she lifts Horatio from his chair as if he's made of straw. His arm swings free and it's so thin it doesn't look human. Lucy was never that skinny. Even on her worse days.

I try not to stare at Luscious Gore. I'm sure that he can sense it, that he can reverse my thoughts and send them back at me, twisted and viral. He has loomed so long at the edge of my consciousness, hideous and bloated and vaguely imagined as my own private Jabba the Hutt. I expected to hate and fear him at once. He set the machine in motion that summoned me here and he doesn't even recognize me. He doesn't know me. He released Isabel and Jerome into the world like chaotic birds of prey and they fell on me purely by accident.

I have heard stories about you, I say.

He makes a wet sound in his throat, an approximate laugh.

The truth pales, doesn't it?

He sighs and pushes aside his plate.

I must be off to bed, he says. Hetty will show you the guest quarters.

What century is this? I say.

He peers at me.

Do you offer a bed to every unwashed stranger that turns up on your doorstep?

He laughs softly. It is irregular. We don't often have visitors, here. But you are hardly a stranger.

Do you know me?

No, he says. But you are Jerome's friend. You told me so.

This staggers me.

Besides, he says. I have nothing left to steal, and death already lives in my home.

I feel slightly unhinged and I can't decide if I would rather punish this man for his faith, or prove myself worthy of it. I wish Jude would come back. Luscious rings the silver bell. He waits a moment, then rings it again.

Oh, bother.

What's the matter?

Hetty has gotten so deaf, he says. And the battery is rather low in my chair.

May I help somehow?

If you could give me a push, he says. That would be tremendous.

No problem.

The main hall is silent and shadowy, a few gas lamps flickering. I push the heavy chair along a thick burgundy carpet. Luscious is nodding, half asleep. He points to a door on the right. I stop and wait as he pushes a button and the door swings open. His room is dark and cold. Soft electric lights come on automatically as we enter. The room is minimally furnished. There is a huge bed with numerous pillows, a chest of drawers, a dressing table and mirror, a sink and toilet with handicap rails. Everything is very low to the floor. There is a lot of scattered artwork: dozens, possibly a hundred charcoal drawings of the crucifixion on yellowed paper and three abstract iron sculptures of Christ on the cross, dying alongside two anonymous thieves.

Well, then. Good night, I say.

Just a moment, he says. If you could just help me from my chair, and onto the bed. I am feeling terribly weak. It will only take a moment.

Yes. Of course, I say.

It's awkward, but I lift him from the chair in a fireman's embrace. His legs are weightless, barely there. His pants are soaking wet. I lay him down on the bed and stand up.

Your pants are wet, I say.

So they are. I suppose I lost control of my bladder, over coffee. It gets more difficult every day. We shall have to change them, won't we?

I can only nod and smile, a thin bloodless smile.

Thank you, he says.

It's nothing, I say. Really.

Luscious manages to unbutton the pants himself, but getting them off is another thing. I kneel on the bed and peel them off him like the loose skin of a banana. His legs are rather shocking. They are not legs at all, but the boneless, unformed tentacles of some sea creature. They are blue and gray and hairless. I glance away and take a small breath. His penis appears normal and is quite large.

There is a long silence.

I understand, says Luscious. That masturbation can be a man's single greatest pleasure.

My mind spins weightlessly. Oh, I say. It is a reliable source.

He lifts his head to gaze forlornly in the direction of his own awesome appendage. I can manipulate it and ejaculate with some success, he says. But I can't feel anything. I cannot even see it.

I stand over him and try to think of something, anything to say. I'm not unsympathetic.

It's lonely in this house, isn't it?

Terribly so.

The room is shrinking and I stand there nodding like a puppet.

I will just run along now, I say. If there's nothing else.

But I do need a diaper, he says. Isn't that a thing of poetry? A man like myself, of wealth and power. To sleep in a diaper.

I thought your money was gone.

He gives a dry chuckle. Quite right.

Where are the diapers? The sweat slides down my back.

They are beneath the bed, he says.

I crouch and pull out one adult diaper. With a little difficulty and coaching from Luscious, I wrestle him into the thing and fasten the sticky tape. I only pray that he doesn't ask me to powder his bottom. As I lean across him to adjust the tape he whispers in my ear.

My son is dying, he says. He's dying very badly.

I shake my head. What is a good death?

It isn't comedy, says Gore.

Haven't you read Shakespeare?

Gore smiles. *Othello* is rather funny, I suppose.

I sit reluctantly at the edge of his bed.

What happened to your family? I say.

He frowns. How do you mean?

This house, I say. It's like a crushed skull.

It's gloomy when my daughter is away.

She isn't coming back, I say.

Gore sucks at his teeth. What?

Trust me.

How do you know?

It's just a feeling.

Isabel will be back, says Gore. She adores Horatio.

There is a long, widening silence. Lucy and Isabel slither around in my head, sleeping restlessly and twined together as if their arms and legs were one. I stare at the dull black crucifix over Gore's bed and I wonder if he has any funny ideas about the nature of his own firstborn son.

What about Jerome?

My pride, he says.

But he's flawed.

He has fears, says Gore. The same as you.

I laugh softly. Jerome is not like me.

But you are friends, are you not?

Again, silence. I feel vaguely unclean.

How did Jerome burn his hands? I say.

Gore licks his lips with a long gray tongue. He breathes.

When you were a child, he says. Did you ever play with fire?

Of course.

I used to collect cars, he says. The most beautiful cars. I had five vintage Corvettes and several old Thunderbirds. A red Cadillac convertible from 1965. They were like a ring of jewels around my house, glowing in the sun. My wife was still alive, then. There were rosebushes everywhere, red and white. Three lovely children and I had more money than God. I bought cars that I never intended to drive. The boys often played in them. Jerome called the Cadillac his castle.

American cars, I say. Henry would approve.

Thirteen years ago, says Gore. Thanksgiving Day and the sun was shining. I was asleep in my chair. A football game on the television with the sound off and I woke to hear screaming. Horatio was playing in the Cadillac when it caught fire. He was three, perhaps four. Jerome saved him.

Was the boy hurt?

His hair was barely singed.

But Jerome's hands were ruined, I say.

Terrible third-degree burns, says Gore. From the tips of his fingers to his wrists.

He set the fire, I say. He had gasoline on his hands.

Perhaps, says Gore. I choose not to think so.

He wants the boy to die.

It doesn't matter what he wants. The boy is dying nonetheless.

I turn and walk away as he wriggles under the sheets like a snake. The lights dim as I leave the room, and the door closes with a whisper behind me.

thirty-nine.

I hurry down the narrow hallway and the carpet is so soft I can't hear my own footsteps and I'm sure that I will soon turn a corner and wander into a labyrinth. That I will be lost for days and when I find my way to the surface and into the sun, I will have clawed out my hair and Jude will have vanished. She will have left me.

Back through the kitchen.

Hetty has not yet cleared away the coffee and cake. I stop and pour myself a cup of the cold coffee and drink it quickly. My hands are not shaking, and I don't think I'm seeing things.

Maybe I'm through the worst of it. Maybe not.

If Jude offers to shoot me up again, I might rip my skin open looking for a vein.

The library still flickers with candlelight. The wide-screen television is on, low and murmuring. A commercial gives way to an old episode of *Star Trek,* and the color is very bad. Mr. Spock's face is green, his shirt gray. Horatio is a fetal lump on the hospital bed, white as an egg but for the black cord that extends from him and hangs limply between the bed and a humming machine.

Jude sits in a stuffed chair, a book open on her lap. It's too dark to read, however. She stares blankly at Horatio, at me. I sit on the arm of her chair and we simply hold hands. As if we are home for the holidays and after a day of spooky relatives we are finally alone.

I liked your little puppet show, I say.

Jude exhales. You weren't afraid I would gut you at the dinner table?

Not really.

Trust, she says.

A wasp crawls along your arm, I say. And you sit perfectly still, telling yourself that he won't sting you unless you flinch, unless you try to kill him. You hold your breath and hope he won't sting you and probably he doesn't want to. But that's not trust, is it. It's fear and fascination.

I want to get out of here, she says.

I'm not stopping you.

She frowns. I want you to come with me.

Not yet. My voice is cracking.

What's wrong with you? she says.

I feel sick.

You owe these people nothing, she says. Nothing.

This kid wanted to borrow life from me.

Jude laughs. You're a stranger, she says. You are no one to him.

I'm the stranger.

The fragile new scar around my torso feels so cold, as if it's blue with electricity. I clutch at the skin of my stomach and stare at the television without really seeing it. The candles stink of eucalyptus but surely that's my imagination. Jude puts her arms around me. She touches my face and I shiver from the cold. I take her ring finger between my lips and suck at it like an anxious child. She smiles and strokes the edge of my teeth.

The kid is beautiful, isn't he?

You shouldn't confuse sympathy with desire, she says.

I can't help it.

Jude doesn't smile. She wonders what will become of us. In my adolescent daydreams I see us walking back to the highway in a cool rain. Jude steals a car and we disappear into Mexico. The sky is always blue and we have sex three times a day. In a month or so we run out of money and we get bored with sex. Jude suggests a simple bank robbery. But something goes wrong and one of us is killed, probably me. Jude will mourn for two short weeks, then flee to Paris and become a very expensive assassin. I shrug and light another cigarette. There are four left, and I tell myself to leave at least two of them for the boy.

I want to leave in the morning, she says.

Okay.

Will we leave together?

I don't know. Will we?

Probably not, she says. Then laughs at my expression.

The shadows are stretching around us as the candles burn down to nothing. Jude's face is now completely in the dark and she easily sinks into it. She's happier not being seen.

This kid. He breaks your heart, doesn't he?

No, she says. But he surprises me.

He's unafraid.

She smiles. And he makes me laugh.

You never laugh.

Anyway, she says. Your kidney would have been wasted on him.

What do you mean?

He wants to die, says Jude.

Horatio is still asleep. The light that flickers around him is from the television. I wonder if he's even breathing, if he's slipping away, unnoticed.

This is a good episode, I say.

I move over to the television and it takes me about five minutes of muttering and fumbling to find the volume control. I tell Jude how Captain Kirk and the lads find this orphaned kid named Charlie on a wrecked ship and he seems like a good kid. He's nervous and shy and anxious to please and he follows everyone around like a cowardly dog but really he's a time bomb. He's tangled up in puberty and flooded with terrifying desires and he's surrounded by women in very short skirts and leather knee boots. And he also happens to have telekinetic powers that he can't control and in one scene that I can never forget he zaps an anonymous female ensign who has spurned him and she sinks cut in half and rising out of the floor.

I never watch this show, says Jude.

Don't tell me that.

She laughs. I prefer the new one.

Jesus, I say. What is it about that bald Frenchman?

His voice is sexy. And he has a strong nose, like a hawk.

The nose, I say. What do you want with his damn nostrils?

I could think of something, she says.

Horatio mutters, I'm awake. I'm awake.

I remember the boys Lucy used to bring home. They were like pets. She petted them and dressed them up and adored them. She would have eaten this kid alive.

Do you have a girlfriend, I say. A boyfriend?

Horatio stares at me.

What is your favorite sport?

Hush, says Jude.

What will you be when you grow up?

Horatio laughs suddenly, and I think he forgives me.

Jude props several pillows behind the boy's head and gently pulls him to a sitting position. I barely recognize her. She offers him a drink of water and he swallows a few drops. He begs for a cigarette and I light one for him, holding it to his lips each time he has a puff, so the ashes won't fall in his bed.

I have AIDS, he says. Two new kidneys wouldn't save me.

He shrugs and I bite my lip to stop myself from saying, yes, I know.

Jude frowns and I wonder if she would have performed the transplant, if things had gone differently. She could have easily cut herself when her hands were inside him.

It wasn't even sex, says Horatio. I was born with the virus.

I stare at him, stupidly.

My mother gave it to me. He smiles. But she didn't have the same luxury of dying from it.

Jude strokes his pale, waxy hair from his forehead.

Gore isn't your father, she says.

Oh, says Horatio. He claims to be.

Interesting, she says.

But my birth unveiled a thing or two and my mother was dead by my fourth birthday.

Don't tell me she killed herself, I say. Don't.

The cause of death was unclear, he says. He licks his teeth and for a moment I see shadows of his father in him. I wonder if he sees it. The doctors couldn't agree, he says. It was either drowning or a heart attack or a blow to the head. Or it was all three. She was found at the bottom of the swimming pool.

What was she wearing? says Jude.

Horatio looks surprised. Her pajamas.

Murder, she says.

Horatio shrugs. She was dead and my father's little empire began to fall apart. My brother was a pyromaniac. He wet the bed. He tortured animals. My sister protected me like her own child, but she was out of her mind. She was a slut.

Jude smiles dreamily. She had sex with the gardener, she says. With the stable boy. She had three abortions by the time she was sixteen and her womb was ruined.

I know, says Horatio. Childhood trauma is such a bore. It's such television.

But was it a bore when you were six?

No, he says. It was awful.

It's fucking biblical, I say. To be an infant afflicted with HIV.

I do like boys, says Horatio. I just rarely have the opportunity to get out of the house.

Have you never had sex? says Jude.

Once, he says. My sister took me into Dallas. I had a brief and not so horrible encounter with a male prostitute. He wasn't gay, of course. And he was only a year older than me. I told him that I was sick and he said it would cost twice as much, that we would use two condoms. He fucked me in the back of my father's car while Isabel drove in endless circles.

I shudder, thinking of Isabel. Dead in a bathtub, with holes in her feet.

Jude has nothing to say and I wonder if she's in the desert with Felix, the stuttering virgin. He stares at the punishing sun until she has to kill him for a mouthful of water.

My father loves me, says Horatio. I repulse him, but he does. He gave the very last of his money to my brother and packed him off to Colorado to purchase a stolen kidney. I told him to send Isabel, but he said some things are better left to men.

Jude closes one eye. As if she's glaring down a rifle sight.

What a mess, I say. What a fucking mess this is.

I'm used to it, says Horatio.

Still, she says. I think I would like to kill your brother.

He won't come back. He's on a beach somewhere, and the money is nearly gone. He's posing as a race car driver, a retired navy pilot. He's borrowing money from women and children. He's telling outrageous stories, like a monkey performing for free drinks.

Horatio is shrinking. His voice is disappearing. I can barely hear him. He is so quiet, so still. He could be a child that is holding his breath and floating facedown in dark water. He could be pretending to be dead. He could be dreaming of his former, unborn self.

I want to ask you something, he says.

Anything, I say.

I offer him the cigarette and he sucks at it, his lips touching my fingers. He's going to ask me to kill him, to put him to sleep forever. I'm weirdly calm, amazed that he would choose me rather than Jude. I'm happy and shivering and I can kill him as easily as I breathe. I will stare at him until his eyes become Lucy's and I won't hesitate, I won't weaken.

I want to kill him.

Would you kiss me? he says. I haven't been kissed in an age.

Jude laughs, nervously.

*

I flick off the television and she walks barefoot through the library, humming like a girl. I think she's looking for something to read and I'm curious to see if she will choose poetry or religion. But she merely blows out the drowning candles and I can see the night unfolding before us. The two of us will sit beside his bed without speaking until the sun creeps in and turns everything to ash. Horatio will not wake again, and he won't die.

My face is still marked with Henry's blood and I bend over this boy as if I'm taking a drink from a fountain in the park. I brush his nearly dead lips and they are dry as the back of my hand. His tongue barely touches mine and pulls away like a thief and oh Lucy if you had only asked me for this.